A CHILD ACROSS THE SKY

DOUBLEDAY
New York
London
Toronto
Sydney
Auckland

A CHILD

ACROSS THE SKY

BY JONATHAN CARROLL

PUBLISHED BY DOUBLEDAY
a division of Bantam Doubleday Dell Publishing Group, Inc.
666 Fifth Avenue, New York, New York 10103

DOUBLEDAY and the portrayal of an anchor
with a dolphin are trademarks of Doubleday,
a division of Bantam Doubleday Dell
Publishing Group, Inc.

Library of Congress Cataloging-in-Publication Data

Carroll, Jonathan, 1949–
A child across the sky / by Jonathan Carroll.—1st ed. in the U.S.A.
p.   cm.
I. Title.
PS3553. A7646C5   1990
813'.54—dc20   89-29086
CIP

ISBN 0-385-26535-2

Printed in the United States of America
August 1990

FIRST EDITION

For Beverly—My life across the sky

"They are coming to teach us good manners. . . .
But they won't succeed because we are gods."

Giuseppe Lampedusa,
The Leopard

one

*The people
one loves
should take all
their things
with them
when they die.*

GABRIEL GARCÍA MÁRQUEZ
Love in the Time of Cholera

1

A n hour before he shot himself, my best friend Philip Strayhorn
called to talk about thumbs.

"Ever noticed when you wash your hands how you don't really do
your thumbs?"

"What do you mean?"

"It's your most important finger, but because it sticks out, away from
the rest, you don't really wash it. A little dip and rub, maybe, but not
nearly enough attention for all the work it does. It's probably the finger
that gets dirtiest, too."

"That's what you called to tell me, Phil?"

"It's very symbolic. Think about it. . . . What are you reading
these days?"

"Plays. I'm still trying to find the right ones."

"I have to tell you I bumped into Lee Onax the other day. Said he'll
still give you half a million if you direct for him."

"I don't want to direct films anymore, Phil. You know how I feel."

"Sure, but five hundred thousand dollars would help your theater a
lot."

"*Five* dollars would help a lot. But if I went back and did a film now,
it'd be fun and seductive and I'd probably want to direct movies again."

"Remember in the *Aeneid* the hundred and forty thousand different kinds of pain? I wonder what number yours would be? 'I don't want to be a famous Hollywood director anymore because it'd make me confused.' Pain number 1387."

"Where are you calling from, Phil?"

"LA. We're still cutting the film."

"What's the title?"

"*Midnight Kills.*"

I grinned. "Terrific. What's the most horrible thing you do in it?"

The telephone line hissed over the three thousand miles.

"Are you still there, Phil?"

"Yeah. The most horrible thing is what I *didn't* do."

"You were making a movie, man. Bad things happen sometimes."

"Uh-huh. How are *you* doing, Weber?"

"Good. One of my main actors is really sick, but you've got to expect that when you're working here." I looked at the small Xeroxed poster tacked to the board above my desk. THE NEW YORK CANCER PLAYERS PRESENT FRIEDRICH DÜRRENMATT'S "THE VISIT." "Our opening night is in a month. We're all getting nervous."

"Theater's so different, isn't it? With movies, opening night means everything is finished: nothing you can do but sit back and watch. In the theater, though, it's all beginning. I remember that."

There was a worn-out echo in his voice that I took for exhaustion. I was wrong.

Sasha Makrianes called to tell me he was dead. She'd gone over to cook lunch and found him sitting on the patio in his favorite high-backed armchair. From behind, it looked like he'd fallen asleep while reading. A copy of Rilke's poetry was on the ground next to him, as well as an unopened can of Dr. Pepper. She called his name, then saw the book was covered with blood. Going over, she saw him slumped forward, what was left of his head spewed in a wide splintered arc over everything.

Running into the house to telephone the police, she found the body of Flea, his Shar-Pei dog, in the big brown wicker basket Phil brought from Yugoslavia.

Hearing he'd killed the dog too was almost as shocking as the news of

Phil's death. Sasha often joked through gritted teeth that he loved Flea as much as her.

The first thing that came to my mind was our thumb discussion. Was he thinking about that an hour later as he loaded the gun and put it in his mouth? Why had he chosen *that* as the topic of our last conversation?

A few years before, we'd been through an earthquake together. As the ground rumbled, Phil kept saying over and over, "This isn't a movie! This is *not* a movie!"

We'd been creating or adapting scripts so long that all part of me could think of was setting and the last words this character, Philip Strayhorn, would have chosen. I was ashamed my mind worked like that, but if Phil had known he would have laughed. In the process of spending almost twenty years trying to get our names onto the silver screen, we'd lost parts of our objectivity toward life. When someone you love dies, you should weep—not think of camera angles or last lines.

After the phone call, I went out for a walk. There was a travel agent down the street; I'd book a flight to California the next day. But a few steps out the door, I realized what I really wanted to do was visit Cullen James.

Cullen and her husband, Danny, lived up on Riverside Drive, a good hour's walk from my apartment. Pulling up my collar, I started out with the hope exercise and the tiredness it'd bring would take some of the edge off the news of Philip Strayhorn's death.

In the last few years, Cullen had become famous in a peculiar sort of way. When we first met, she was going through what could best be described as an "otherworldly experience." Every night for a number of months she dreamt of a land called Rondua where she traveled on a bizarre quest after something called the "bones of the moon." I fell in love with her then, which was very bad because she was happily married to a nice man and nursing their first child. I am not a wife stealer, but Cullen James made me crazy and I went after her as if she were the gold ring on my personal carousel. If I'd been a sailor, I'd have had her name tattooed on my arm.

In the end I didn't win her, but during that confused and passionate time I began dreaming of Rondua too. Those dreams changed my life. Those dreams and the earthquake.

When I got to the Jameses' building I was cold inside and out. The death of a loved one robs you of some kind of vital inner heat. Or perhaps it blows out the pilot light that keeps your burners lit. Whatever, it took an hour of hard walking in the blue lead cold of a New York December for me to really hold in the palm of my mind the fact my best and oldest friend was dead. He had almost no cruelty in him. After twenty years I knew Philip Strayhorn was even better than I'd ever thought. He once said there are thirty-one million seconds in a year. So few of them are worth remembering. Those that are, thrill and hurt us without end.

"Hello?"

"Cullen? It's Weber. I'm downstairs. Do you mind a visitor?"

"Oh, Christ, Weber, we just heard about Phil. Of course, come up."

There was a giant holiday wreath on their door. The Jameses loved Christmas. For them, it started in November and went on well into January. They used their daughter, Mae, as an excuse for the festivity, but it was clear they liked it more than the kid. There were always oranges stuck with cinnamon cloves in every corner of every room, Christmas cards on the windowsills, a tree out of a 1940s movie like *The Bishop's Wife* or *It's a Wonderful Life*. It was a good place. Slippers belonged there, and a friendly dog that followed you from room to room.

Cullen opened the door and smiled. There are perfect faces. I've known and slept with some, but they were meant to remain placid and untouched, not shaken or distorted by the push and pull of great emotion or a long and full night in bed. They're tuxedos—you wear them only on special occasions and then hang them up carefully in the closet afterward; a stain or wrinkle on them ruins everything. Cullen's is not a perfect face. She smiles too much, and many times it's obviously false: her safe and easy defense against a curious and persistent world. But she is beautiful and . . . whole. When I first met her she was full of love and confusion. Even then I wanted it all but knew I'd never have any. Without trying, she handcuffed herself to my heart.

When she opened the door that sad day, instead of offering a hug, Cullen took off the silver bracelet she was wearing and handed it to me. When I was trying to woo her, I'd once asked her to do that. It was the only real physical intimacy we would ever share: her warmth, my only moments of owning it. Although she'd blushed when I first told her that, since then it had become her way of saying, I'm here, friend. I'll do what I can.

"How're you doing, Weber?"

"Not so good. Where's Mae?"

"Inside with Danny. We haven't told her yet. You know how much she loved Phil."

"Such a nice man." I started to cry. "You want to know something strange as hell? The last time Phil stayed with me here, on his way back from Yugoslavia? He slept on the couch and wore my pajamas. When he left the next morning, for some strange reason I took the pajamas and put them up to my face so I could smell them. Smell *him.* I don't know why I did that, Cullen. He was there. He's gone. He was everywhere."

She put her arm around my shoulder and pulled me gently into the apartment. Almost as soon as the door closed behind us, a little black Cairn terrier that looked exactly like the dog in *The Wizard of Oz* came trotting importantly from another room. Her muzzle was completely, comically white. She'd obviously just been rooting around in something thick and foamy.

"Mama! Negnug ate all the whipped cream!" Mae James, age five, came running in, arms windmilling, tongue stuck out, big eyes delighted. "Weber!" She leapt up on me and wrapped her legs around mine.

"Hiya, Mae! I came over to say hello."

"Weber, you cannot imagine what just happened! Negnug ate all the whipped cream Mama made for the cake."

Danny walked in with his great warm smile on, something I always liked to see. He stuck out his hand and we shook hard. After a moment, he put his other hand over mine. "I'm glad you came, Weber. We were worried about you. Let's have a drink."

"But, Pop, what about the whipped cream? Aren't you going to spank Negnug? If I did that, you'd spank *me!* Now she's probably going to throw up all over the rug, like she did last time."

A small fire burned in the grate in the living room. The dog was plopped down on its side nearby. It looked pleased and exhausted. Mae walked over and, hands on hips, shook her head disgustedly at the furry traitor.

"Now our cake won't be half as good because of *you,* stinkpot."

Cullen and I sat on the couch, Danny in a paisley-covered armchair nearby.

"Mae, honey, would you do me a favor and go see if the tea is ready yet? Just tell me if the water's boiling, but don't touch anything, okay?"

"Okay, Mom."

When the child had left the room, Cullen spoke quickly. "Fool around with her a little, Weber, okay? Then she and Danny are going to the movies. You and I have to talk."

"About Phil?"

They looked at each other. Danny spoke. "About a couple of things." He reached down and pulled a box from beneath his chair. "We got a package from Phil in the mail a couple of days ago. We thought it was Christmas presents for Mae. But when we opened it, this box was inside along with two others. It's got your name on it."

I sat forward. "It's from *Phil?*"

Danny shrugged. "We didn't understand it either, except he knows we all spend Christmas together. Cullen thought maybe he wanted us to open our presents from him together."

"The water's just beginning to boil, Mama," Mae called from the kitchen. "But I didn't touch anything. Not even the potholder."

Cullen started to get up. "He was a sad man, Weber. Had absolutely *no* patience with the slowness of the world. You know that better than anyone. He did *everything* quickly and well, but that's always big trouble. Because then you're always disappointed no one else can follow suit. I loved Phil, but what happened doesn't surprise me."

"That's a pretty hard-ass thing to say, Cullen."

She was walking toward the kitchen but stopped next to me. "There are two things that don't leave you alone, Weber—love and disappointment. You can't turn either of them off like a fan or twist the direction of their *flow* a little to one side.

"I'll tell you something. Once when he was in his cups, Phil called, said one sentence, then hung up: 'Life is comprised of fuck-ups and fuck-you's.' "

"Sure, but at the same time I've never known anyone as full of life as he was. He was curious about everything."

"True, but that doesn't keep your heart full."

"What about Sasha?"

"Mom, come on. It's boiling!"

"They weren't living together anymore. Wait a minute. Let me get the tea and I'll be back." She touched my shoulder and moved on.

"Do you want to look at the package?" Danny held it out to me.

"What do you think, Dan?"

"I saw Phil last week."

"What? He was in town?"

He nodded. "Asked me to come and meet him at the Pierre but didn't want you or Cullen to know."

"Why not? Christ, what'd he say?"

"Okay, everybody! Teatime!" Cullen walked in carrying a big tray full of tea and cakes. I looked fast, then at Danny again. He shook his head, said only, "Look in the package."

"That one? The one from him?"

"Yes. We'll talk about it after you see."

"See what?"

"The videos. You want some help with that, Cul?"

There was a new log of applewood on the fire. The room had been silent for some time while Cullen and I looked into the flames. I shook my head. "He wanted to be liked and admired. He wanted to be left alone."

"Who doesn't? You know what fame is, Weber. When it comes, it's like a crazy fan who won't leave you alone. And who can be damned scary! It gets obsessed with you in all the wrong ways. You know that old line about how the woman catches her man? 'He ran after me till I caught him?' Well, that's the same thing with fame. You want it, but once you've caught it, you realize it's been waiting for you all along . . . like some kind of monster from one of Phil's films. Like Bloodstone! Philip Strayhorn wanted to be a very famous man but stay private, live his own life. Good luck with *that,* as we all know.

"Look, you guys got exactly what you wanted, what you dreamed about when you were at Harvard. Or so you've told me. But what did you two do with this fame you wanted so badly? *You* threw it over to direct dying people in obscure plays. And Phil? He shot himself. They're not new stories, Mr. Gregston."

"You're really showing your teeth today, huh?"

She sighed. "No, it's just coming up through my brain like a slow fog that sweet Phil Strayhorn is really dead. That makes two of my friends who've died violently. I hate it. Neither of them deserved that."

"Phil killed himself."

She rubbed her mouth. "Do you believe that, Weber?"

"Yes. He talked a lot about suicide."

"Shit. I believe it too. I wish I didn't. You know what I can't stop thinking about? The lovely, exact way he peeled an orange."

I opened my package from Phil before the elevator had reached the ground floor of the Jameses building. As Danny mentioned, three videotapes were inside but nothing else. I wanted a note or some kind of explanation, but there were only the three tapes, each 240 minutes long, labeled FIRST, SECOND, THIRD.

In the taxi home I continued to stare at them. What was there? I remembered telling Cullen how I'd smelled his pajamas after he visited the last time. I felt for a moment like smelling the tapes too, each one of them, in case there were some kind of trace of him there. But that was silly and strange, unnecessary: I had 720 minutes of something Phil thought important enough to show me shortly before he died. It would have to do. The answers would have to be there.

The view from one of my windows is directly into the apartment of a pretty woman who likes to walk around naked. I am convinced she drops her clothes as soon as she gets home, the way some people drop their umbrella in a stand by the door. She must have a high heating bill because summer and winter her pink skin and small pointy breasts dart and bounce through her rooms at all hours of the day. She always seems to be in a hurry. Running here and there, objects in her hands, pacing the floor while she talks on the telephone. Always busy and always bare-assed.

I have often watched her, although neither she nor her nakedness excite me. What I love is being able to live in her everyday privacy. Not as the proverbial fly on the wall, because that image evokes seeing something forbidden. No, sometimes I feel like her husband or roommate: intimate as well as comfortable enough to watch her walk into the kitchen nude, enjoying her familiar sights without having to have them.

Getting out of the taxi I looked up and saw her standing there, waiting four feet away. I had so much on my mind and was so surprised to see her close up that the first thing I said was, "Did you want this breast?"

"Excuse me?"

"Uh, this *cab*. Do you want the cab?"

"Yes, please." Her look said she thought I had a few screws loose. I got out fast and held the door for her. She had on a nice woody-smelling perfume. I almost asked her name but held back. Did I really want to know who she was? Then she would only be a Leslie or a Jill. A name, a zip code number, a Diner's Club member. Slamming the door behind her, I smiled and was happy for the first time that day. I don't know why. It made going back into my empty apartment that much easier.

After Phil saw my New York place for the first time, he laughed and said, " 'A Room in Brooklyn,' huh?" Later that day he went out and bought me a copy of *The Notebooks of Louise Bogan.* In it, he'd marked this passage:

> Edward Hopper's 'A Room in Brooklyn.' A room my heart yearns to: uncurtained, hardly furnished, with a view over roofs. A clean bed, a bookcase, a kitchen, a calm mind, one or two half-empty rooms. All my life wants to achieve, and I have not yet achieved it. I have tried too hard for the wrong things. If I would concentrate on getting the spare room, I could have it almost at once. . . . I must have it.

There are two pairs of pants in my closet, only five books allowed in the apartment at the same time. It sounds pretentious and pseudo-Zen, but living like this has been both painful and instructive for me. In my heart I am the perfect Yuppie because I like things. At one time I was a walking UN of prestigious labels and loved it. Italian leather jackets, English suits, cashmere sweaters from Hilditch and Key in Paris. Give me quality things and lots of them. If they have initials on them that's okay too—I don't mind being a walking advertisement. One of the delights of being a movie director was you were expected to wear those things because of your position as a young creative lion out there. The spoils of the battle of Hollywood: Once you'd made a film that went into the black, they encouraged you to put on your first Patek Philippe wristwatch. You took your wallet out of a Miyake pocket, and the light you turned out at night was designed either by Richard Sapper or Harry Radcliffe. Long live excess!

But after I moved to New York, I got rid of everything on purpose. Maybe because I liked it all so much, maybe because it was just simpler living in a room that was furnished only with air and white walls.

I'd come back from a year in Europe where I'd lived in the kind of pensions where you peed in the toilet down the hall and if you wanted a shower you paid extra for it. At the beginning of the trip I carried a five-hundred-dollar knapsack from Hunting World. It was promptly stolen in the Cracow train station. The rest of my year abroad was done via a Cracow fiberboard suitcase, Polish suit and shoes, and a loden coat I bought at the Vienna flea market for four dollars.

I'd read Thoreau's "Economy" and the Lives of some saints, but until the earthquake and the Europe trip, I didn't agree that life was better with less. Or that less was more. The lesson I did learn after Cracow was all those lovely expensive things in my missing bag were not indispensable and could be replaced. Too easily. How could they be so special if you could go right out and buy another, or ten, if you wanted?

So when I got back to "Morka" (as Phil called it) I got rid of a lot. Moved into a New York life with my Polish suitcase, a copy of Cullen's just-published *Bones of the Moon,* and a real desire to see if there were any other windows to look out besides the ones I'd known for the last couple of years.

But I kept two wonderful things from my "old days." I had to; it was hard to erase the movie director from inside me. Besides, I wasn't sure I wanted to. I kept a small video camera and the television video system I'd bought when loaded with residuals from my film *Sorrow and Son.*

Without taking off my coat, I turned on the TV and video machine and plugged in the first tape. Squatting in front of the set like a catcher waiting for the first pitch of the game, I rubbed my cold hands together.

The electric gray buzz and hiss cleared. Phil's face appeared. He was sitting on the couch in his living room petting Flea. The dog was lying half on him, attentively gazing into the camera. With all those impossible, hilarious wrinkles it looked like an alive hot fudge sundae.

"Hello, my man. I'm sorry about what happened. You know I love you and will miss you most of all. You were the only brother I ever had. I love you more for that than anything else. You-you-you: I'm saying that too many times.

"Danny and I met a few days ago. He'll be able to answer most questions you have. But please don't ask him anything until you've done two things: watched the rest of this tape all the way through and then called Sasha. Another thing—don't be shocked by what you see. You have some very hard stuff to do in the next few months. I hope some of what you see here will help you get through it.

"How do I know? I just do, Weber. That's part of the reason why I'm dead when you see this. Can't handle it. But I think you can. There are others who do too.

"One last thing: You won't be able to watch the second or third tapes until you've been out to California. You'll see what I mean."

The dog saw something in the camera's direction. Looking straight at me, it started to bark. Phil smiled and petted the dog back into silence. It looked at him and licked his hand.

"I love you, Weber. Don't ever forget that, no matter what."

He put up a hand and waved slowly: goodbye. The picture dimmed. A moment later everything began.

My mother died in an airplane crash when I was nine. She flew off to visit her family in Hartford, Connecticut, but never returned. The airplane ran into a flock of starlings on takeoff and, like some silly cartoon, sucked the birds into the engines. Then it stalled. Then it crashed. Seventy-seven people died. They found Mama's handbag completely untouched (there were still traces of perfume on her handkerchief) but could only identify her carmelized body via dental charts.

When they told me the news, the only thing I could think of was whether or not she had died quickly. In those days I was completely intrigued by airplane crashes, intrigued the way any preadolescent loves the macabre and dangerous from a distance. So long as it didn't bite or want to come into my living room, I would press my nose as close as I could up against its glass. But suddenly my wonderful mother was gone. The thing was loose in my life.

Unfortunately I learned enough from reading articles and gaping at pictures of catastrophes to know it could have been any of a thousand possible hideous falls to death in those last few minutes, or seconds, of life. Had her end come fast? Slow? Painfully?

They were questions that haunted me thirty years. Whenever I flew, I looked around the cabin at curtains that could burn, seats that might snap in half or send their jagged pieces through a body like medieval weapons. . . . Her body had burned and that was bad enough, but was the burning "all"? Was there more—*worse*—I didn't know? Why did I *want* to know?

I cannot say, but Phil's video answered my questions.

The first thing I heard was a muffled, phony voice speaking.

"Good afternoon, ladies and gentlemen. This is your captain, Mike Maloy. Welcome aboard flight 651 to Washington. Our flying time will be approximately one hour and fifteen minutes."

It took a moment to register that I was inside an airplane cabin, seeing it all through someone's eyes. A tracking shot. Several women wore pastel-colored Jackie Kennedy pillbox hats; men had short hair and read the *Hartford Courant* dated March 1960. "I" looked down at my lap and finally knew in a furious flash of recognition who I was—my mother. There was her red leather purse, the gray dress she wore only on special occasions. I'd sat on their bed the day she left and watched her carefully fold the dress in half and place it in her suitcase.

"When'll you be back, Ma?"

"Tuesday, dear. I'll be back before you're home from school."

The pilot went on speaking. My eyes, Mama's eyes, looked out the oval window at the runway and the little yellow trucks scuttling back and forth on the ground below. The plane revved up and began to move backward.

I saw through her eyes but had my own thoughts. Terrified and captivated, I knew exactly what was about to happen. Was this the way God saw things? Did he kick back in his leather Barcalounger upstairs and flick on the tube to someone's life in peril? The same way we sort of watch and get interested in the fate of soap opera characters?

What should I have done, stopped the film? All my life I'd wanted to know what these last minutes had been like for her. The questions around her death had been the basis of much of my young confusion, not to mention the inspiration for my first film, *The Night Is Blond*.

The man next to Mama offered her a copy of *Time* magazine. Fidel Castro was on the cover. She thanked him but said reading on a plane made her ill. He tried to make conversation, but she only smiled and busied herself with the seat belt. I remembered how nervous she became when strange men spoke to her. She was good-looking but shy; my father had won her through gentle persistence. She said she'd first fallen in love with his patience.

Her slim hands were so familiar. The gold engagement and wedding rings that slipped on and off her finger so easily whenever she washed her hands. The shiny scar above her thumb where she'd cut it deeply one day while making lunch.

The plane turned hard left, then began to taxi. A stewardess came by offering a bowl of hard candy, Mama's favorite. We often joked that she had a mouth full of sweet tooths. This last time she took two—an orange and a green. She looked out the window again at the nice weather. Some purple-gray clouds far off in the southern sky. In an hour and a half the plane was due to land in Washington. In an hour and a half firemen would still be trying to control the flames that licked up at the clear Hartford sky. She put a piece of candy in her mouth. The plane began to pick up speed. A blond stewardess hurried down the aisle toward the back of the plane, a nervous smile on her face.

The plane goes faster and faster, the view out the window begins to blur. Then that fast, stomach-lurching lift off the earth and the hard pull *up*.

A few seconds going up, up. . . .

A loud fast *thunk-thunk-thunk*. *Thunkity-thunkity*. Everything stops. Just *stops*. The whole plane feels . . . it's falling backward, crazy angle up and all. Someone screams. More screams. Explosions. I choke. The candy's gone down my throat the wrong way. I can't breathe! Choking, trying to get it out. Explosion. Dead.

The screen went dark, then lit again on Philip Strayhorn's face. "She was dead in half a second, Weber. One big blow she didn't even feel. I promise you that. I know it for sure.

"There's more on this tape you must see, but not now. You can watch your mother's part again if you want, but there's nothing new to be learned. That's how it happened.

"Call Sasha, okay?"

The tape went black again, then turned into the electronic fuzz that's so annoying at the end of any video film. I reached over and fast-forwarded it a count of one hundred, then pressed PLAY again: fuzz. Rewound it to the beginning, replayed a little of what I'd already seen: Phil in his living room with the dog. FAST FORWARD: Mama being offered candy again. More FAST FORWARD: fuzz.

I reached down for the other tapes (SECOND and THIRD) and tried them both: fuzz all the way. For no reason at all, I put the first one in again and ran it up to the end. "Call Sasha, okay?"

But this time there was more.

A little fuzz, then his face again. I jerked back like I'd been slapped.

"This tape goes on and gives you more and more, Weber, as you can see. You've obviously tried the other two now and seen they don't work. But they *will*, later, when you're ready. Like this one. The more you discover, the more the tapes will tell you. Sort of like deciphering the hieroglyphics." He smiled. "The ride starts here, Scruno. I wish I could have gone on it with you, but I tried and it ate me.

"Don't let that worry you, though. I'll still be around in here, in these tapes. I'll be able to help you in some ways. Remember Kenneth Patchen's line? 'It may be a long time till morning, but there is no law against talking in the dark.' Call Sasha, huh?"

2

Sasha Makrianes's mother was Russian and her father a Greek, one of those lucky people who invent something ridiculous like the disposable lighter and become instantly rich. Alexandra inherited not only a ton of money but the deep-set brown eyes and high cheekbones that make an attractive Russian or Greek woman intriguing, but also dark and a little scary. The words "gypsy" or "revolutionary" are in there somewhere.

Sasha and I were introduced in Vienna by friends. Although her arm was in a sling, my first impression was I couldn't imagine her ever losing, or being used. Her life must be an obedient and loving pet she led around on a silver leash without much thought. She looked spoiled but also strong and decisive. It struck me if she'd been poor she'd probably have had the same aura.

How wrong I was! A week before we met, she'd broken up with her boyfriend of two years. Her arm was in the sling because on leaving the restaurant where they'd had it out, she had stepped into the street, blind and finished, and been hit by a taxi.

"Our relationship was always thin as a spiderweb anyway: delicate and lovely, but the slightest breeze broke right through it. It got so he was like a ventriloquist with his hand up my back, moving my lips—I was so afraid of saying the wrong thing.

"Love is a bully, you know? It can't be avoided and it can't be held off at arm's length. It arrives or reappears or descends or whatever, and we might as well throw up our hands and just hope for the best, right?

"My analyst told me I ran away from my boyfriend the way a child runs when being chased by a parent—you know, laughing and yelling and looking over her shoulder the whole time, dying to be caught?"

She didn't stop talking, although after the initial boyfriend flood, most of what she said was interesting. But there is a certain pathos and desperation in the person who never lets anyone else speak.

That first evening was nearly asleep by the time we left my friends' apartment together and walked down Bennogasse to her car.

"Whenever I go to the Easterlings' house for dinner, I feel like an ugly frog swimming through an aquarium full of colorful, gorgeous fish. You know what I mean?"

I stopped walking and took her hand. "You're so *tight*. What's the matter?"

"You're Weber Gregston! You made the greatest film I ever saw: You made *Wonderful*. You think I'm an asshole, don't you?" Undoing her hand from mine, she stepped back. "I was *so* excited to meet you. I didn't want you to see this stupid arm and I didn't want to say the wrong things . . . I wanted to hear *you* talk. . . . Now I fucked up again—" She tried to say more but tears stopped her.

A beautiful woman with her arm in a sling standing on a street corner in Vienna in the middle of the night, crying, is a good picture for a movie, but not real life.

I asked her for coffee, and we went across the street to a big shabby café that was all yellow light and old cigarette smoke. I even remember the name: Café Hummel. No one hummed in the Café Hummel.

Her father was just diagnosed as having pancreatic cancer. Her boyfriend left because she bored him. She wanted to do something else with her life. We talked in the café until three, then went back to her apartment and mistakenly made love. It wasn't very good.

But something more important happened in that charged night and during our next few days together. A friendship began that immediately did us both good. Soon we liked each other so much we knew we'd found something vital and necessary.

On impulse, we dropped everything and went to Zermatt together for a long weekend because it was snowing all over Europe that winter.

There are places in the world with which one falls in love with the passion and vitality we usually save for a great love affair. We see it and know from the first this will be right and long. If we're very lucky, our being here now will add dimension and knowledge to our lives later.

When we made love there, it was without the held-breath passion of the beginning of an affair. It was gentle, unhurried and long: two great friends on a walk together through a wonderful, familiar city.

The day we left, we sat out on the balcony of our hotel room and held hands, looking up at the Matterhorn. We were tired and fulfilled, in love with a moment in our lives when we'd made the right decision and it had led us to a treasure of high ice, silence, and *Schlagobers* in our coffee.

"Escape can be expensive, but sometimes it's more necessary than breath, huh?"

"What do you mean?" The late-afternoon light had grown tired and tan.

"This whole trip has been . . . before we got on the train in Vienna, I turned around and looked at the world there. In one part of me I knew that after this trip, no matter what happened between us, things would never be the same again. Something was coming to an end for me. So . . . so I looked at Vienna as if it were somehow the last time.

"I don't do things like this, Weber. I don't go off for weekends with people unless I'm in love. We both know we're not in love. But this time has lifted me off that 'old me' earth back there. It showed me how things look from a good distance.

"It's showed me it's time I went home to America. Knowing that my friend but *not* my love, Weber Gregston, will be there soon makes it better. Thank you."

She went back a week later to be with her father while he died. We wrote often while I roamed around Europe, and she flew to California when I returned. The sexual part of our new history was over, but we were still so glad to see each other again.

I introduced her to Phil Strayhorn. At first, they scared each other.

She knew him more as a writer: had read every one of his "Midnight in Hollywood" columns in *Esquire* and loved them. When she heard he was my best friend and that I wanted her to meet him, she rented the first Midnight film. And turned it off, shouting "Enough!" after ten minutes.

"What does he look like?"

"You mean does he look like Bloodstone? No, he's sort of middle size and balding."

"But it's *so* violent, Weber! I've seen horror films before, but that was the worst. How about that part where the dogs eat the child?"

"That's from Hieronymus Bosch, 'The Garden of Earthly Delights.' Most of his worst scenes come from famous paintings or books he reads. Did I tell you Phil graduated summa with a double major in Physics and Art History? For years the only thing he wanted to do was restore paintings."

"How did he end up in horror films?"

"A month before we graduated he decided he wanted to make movies."

He thought she was too good to be true.

"Phil, please go out there and talk to her!"

"I'm making the salad." He wouldn't look at me.

"You're not making salad, you're hiding. Don't forget I was your roommate for four years."

"That's true, Weber, she's pretty, she's rich, *and* kind? Bullshit."

"She *is*. Word of honor."

"She knows I make the Midnight films? That I play Bloodstone? You told her?"

"I told her everything. You write 'em, direct 'em, act in 'em. . . . Now give me the fucking salad and go talk to her!"

They fell in love over the dog, *I* think. A black Chinese Shar-Pei named Flea. Phil called them "sharpies."

On their first formal date, he took Sasha to Beverly Center to see the new film by the Taviani brothers. While they were riding the escalator up to that monstrous beehive of a mall, a bunch of teenage girls recognized "Bloodstone" and mobbed him for autographs. He was always nice about that, but they got pushy and demanding. It reached the point where, grabbing Sasha's hand, he just ran. The kids followed until Phil pulled a few quick moves and ducked them into a pet shop.

I know the store because a hamster there costs about as much as dinner at Spago. But one of them (they later disagreed over who) saw the little black pile of wrinkles in a corner cage.

One of the oldest homilies I know is don't buy a dog from a pet store because they're inevitably sick. But Phil said he'd never seen anything like that and wasn't it great? Sasha said it looked like a piece of dehydrated fruit: drop water on it and it'd blow up to full size. Phil didn't laugh. It was the most peculiar animal he'd ever seen. He paid with a credit card and picked the creature up after the film.

It sat on the back seat of the car as regal and still as a Bugatti hood ornament—until it threw up on Sasha's suede purse. When they got back to Phil's, the puppy continued vomiting—for hours. They took it to an all-night veterinarian who said it was only nerves: getting used to a new life.

Home again, they ended up singing quietly any song they thought might calm it. Sasha said in the middle of "Yesterday" Phil came up with the name Flea.

When do people cross the line to love? Wake one morning not only with the full taste of it on the tongue, but the sureness the flavor will stay as long as we work to keep and appreciate it?

Phil said it differently. To him, you opened your mouth one astounding moment and, with the first unexpected word, realized you were suddenly able to speak and understand an entirely new language, one you'd had no previous knowledge of.

"You know when you travel in another country how you pick up some words or phrases to get by? *'Donnez-moi le pain,'* things like that. This language doesn't work that way. You either know it completely in an instant or you never know it at all. There aren't any Berlitz phrase books, and you can't pick it up on the streets. There *are* no streets where these words are used.

"But even if you know the language well, that doesn't mean you can write poems in it."

"What do you mean?"

"When I realized Sasha and I were in love, that we both spoke and understood this new language, I got excited as hell. It was our language and we could do anything we wanted with it. Pass your A.P. exam in

Italian and you think you're pretty hot stuff, right? But then read Dante or Pavese and you realize you understand Italian, which *is* great, but you can't sing to the gods with those same words the way they did."

"You mean your love wasn't enough?"

"You know me, Weber, I always want more. As soon as I knew about this new language, I wanted us to move up to the next level and communicate *without* words. ESP or something. Maybe life is only greed."

The dog puked for three days. Sasha came home once to change her clothes and give me a full report. When we talked again it was over the phone, when she called to say the dog was still sick and she was going to sleep on Phil's couch.

She did. From our time together in Vienna I knew she was willing to go to bed fast, but her relationship with Phil went differently. For a long time he didn't make any gestures in that direction and neither did she. He slept in his bedroom and she slept on the couch. They spent four straight days together talking and nursing Flea back to health. He cooked for them and never stopped asking questions about her life. Sometimes she told him the truth, sometimes she lied.

"That's when I knew I was coming close to loving him: When I started telling so many lies. I was afraid he wouldn't like me. I wanted to say all the right things."

"Did you lie to me when we met?"

"No, because I think I knew right away you and I weren't meant to love each other that way, Weber. Partly because you pitied me in the beginning. Pity is bad stuff to build your foundation with.

"Phil listened so carefully to me. I found myself talking less and less because I sensed he was really thinking about whatever I said.

"In Vienna, in that café? Your face had so much concern on it that I felt demented or handicapped. Grateful you were listening but convinced you did it because you're a nice guy, not 'cause I was an interesting person.

"Phil was intrigued."

.   .   .

She watched the first two Midnight films in silence, holding his hand the whole time. She made him turn off the set when he got up to go to the toilet.

She gave him a back massage. He made her Yugoslavian *cevapcici.* Flea felt good enough to go out on the patio and sniff around. The dog had to whine to come back in because they were kissing for the first time.

The man she'd lived with in Vienna was a rock musician who used her and her money unthinkingly but felt no compunction about treating her badly.

Phil was gallant and shy. He wasn't a good-looking man and wasn't sure his talent or intelligence was enough to hold her. He'd spent so much of his young life alone, or worrying about how to impress *any* girl, that even in his successful thirties when he was a movie star and a wealthy man, he wanted to be loved for what he was, not what he'd become. But Hollywood is not a good town to find that kind of understanding person. The actor Stephen Abbey was purported to have said, "You come to Hollywood to get famous, not laid. The greatest fuck in the world is seeing your name first on the screen. Period."

Their love grew tentatively and genuinely. They both wanted to believe, but were both smart and hurt enough to be careful of false love's Northern Lights.

One morning she called from a phone booth and said he'd asked her to move in: What should she do? That afternoon, Phil called from another phone booth and announced he'd asked her to move in. Did I think that was a good idea?

They took a trip together to Japan. When they returned they spoke with the exaggeration and intimacy of excited newlyweds. I was sure they'd get married, but they continued to live together and seemed pleased enough with that.

Sasha became involved in Phil's production company, Fast Forward, and showed herself to be a shrewd and sometimes innovative businesswoman who was largely responsible for the company's involvement in a couple of successful projects outside the Midnight series. She told me Phil had so much confidence in both her and their relationship that it naturally spilled over into other things. I told her she'd just never found the right spot to land before, but that didn't mean she wasn't capable.

She shook her head. "I know I'm capable, Weber, I've never had any reason to apply it to anything. Using your analogy, it was always easier flying around from place to place. Landing takes effort: constantly checking your dials and taking the plane off automatic pilot."

I moved to New York at the height of their happiness. My last picture of them was standing together in the driveway of Phil's house in Laurel Canyon, Flea investigating the rosebushes nearby. They had their hands behind their backs. As I was driving away, they turned around and quickly back again, both wearing those gruesome Bloodstone masks that were in the novelty stores then. They waved. Flea looked up from the bushes, saw two monsters where his friends had just been, and barked.

Later they came to New York for a visit. Over dinner, Phil sheepishly admitted they were thinking about either getting married or having a child.

"Can't you do both?"

Sasha said, "One thing at a time."

Whenever they called from California, things sounded better than ever.

Until three weeks before he killed himself, when I got this letter from Sasha.

> Weber.
>
> Phil and I aren't living together anymore. The whole thing is still tentative and not worked out, so neither of us wants to talk about it yet. You'll be the first to know when we make whatever decisions. Please tell Cullen and Danny. We'll be in touch. We promise.

I called many times to hear what was going on, but the only thing that said hello was Bloodstone's voice on their answering machine. I told it I was around if they wanted to talk or visit or whatever might help. I heard nothing more until Sasha called to tell me he was dead.

"Sasha?"

"Weber? Hi. I was expecting your call." She sounded so old and dry.

"I—uh—I had to call again, Sasha."

"I know. You got Phil's tapes?"

"You know?"

"Yes. I got one too in the mail right after we talked this morning."

"Can you tell me what was on it?"

"It was a video of Phil. Phil and Flea sitting on the couch. It's hard to . . . I—" Silence.

"Sasha?"

A long intake of breath, then: "He said he was going to show me my future.

"The next shot is of me in a hospital bed. Weber, I'm very pregnant. I thought I was there to have a child, but it's not that; I'm in the hospital because I have cancer and they're going to try and cut it out of me."

"*Are* you pregnant?"

"I can't be. Phil and I hadn't slept together in months. I just had my period, too.

"Weber, Phil came on after it was over and said everything depends on you. What was he talking about?" She began crying. "What's going on, Weber? Damn it! Where is he? My God. My God, where *is* he?"

"Wait. Sasha, sh-h-h. Wait a minute, honey. Was there anything else on the tape?"

"No. Just the tape and a Xerox copy of 'Mr. Fiddlehead.' "

"What's that?"

"A short story. It was going to be his next project."

"All right. Do me a favor: Hang up and go plug the tape back in. See if there's anything else on it."

"Okay." She didn't ask even why—hung up and called back a few minutes later. "There's nothing else. Just me pregnant in a hospital with cancer. Are you coming out?"

"Yes. I'll be there sometime tomorrow."

"I called his parents. You know what his father said? 'All right. When is the funeral?' Only that, completely calm. 'When is the funeral?' "

2
5

"Did you call his sister, Jackie?"

"The father said she can't be reached. Off studying bugs in Nigeria or something. They'll send her a telegram. I can't get over that. 'All right. When is the funeral?' " That's it. Only that. 'Hey, mister, your son's dead!' 'All right. When is the funeral?' "

An hour later I'd packed a bag and was sitting by the window thinking about everything that had happened.

When Sasha asked what was on the tapes Phil had sent me, I said only a short goodbye from him and some goof-around silliness we'd filmed with a video camera when I was last there.

After getting off the phone I put the first casette in the machine again, but there was nothing new to see. Nothing on the other two either.

I'd turned off the lights in the room because I wanted to think in the dark. After a while I realized I'd been looking across at the naked woman's unlit place without being aware of it. When both my eyes and mind came back into focus, I realized someone was sitting near the window of her dark apartment too. Was she looking over without being aware of me? I smiled. That would have made a nice scene in a movie.

The phone rang. I picked it up but kept looking at my dark neighbor.

"Weber? It's Cullen."

"Hi."

"That's all you have to say? 'Hi'? What was on the *tapes?*"

After I explained it to her in a very quiet voice, almost a whisper, there was a long silence. Then she said, "You poor man. Home movies of the apocalypse, huh? I can't imagine what it would be like to watch that. But you know something? It reminds me of what Phil said once when I asked him about a new Midnight film that was about to come out. I wanted to know if it was as gross as the others. Know what he said? 'I behaved very well in it. You'll be utterly ashamed of me.' "

The next morning the doorbell rang at seven: a postman with an express letter from California, mailed the day before. Signing for it, I looked at the red, white, and blue envelope addressed to me in Strayhorn's handwriting.

Inside was the short story Sasha had mentioned earlier, "Mr. Fiddlehead." Neatly typed. Nothing else—no note from Phil or notations on the story itself. There was no author's name anywhere, so I assumed it had been written by Phil.

MR. FIDDLEHEAD

On my fortieth birthday Lenna Rhodes invited me over for lunch. That's the tradition—when one of us has a birthday there's lunch, a nice present, and a good laughing afternoon to cover the fact we've moved one more step down the staircase.

We met years ago when we happened to marry into the same family. Six months after I said yes to Eric Rhodes, she said it to his brother Michael.

Lenna got the better end of *that* wishbone: She and Michael are still delighted with each other, while Eric and I fought about everything and nothing and then got divorced.

But to my surprise and relief, they were a great help to me during the divorce, even though there were obvious difficulties climbing over some of the thornbushes of family and blood allegiance.

They live in a big apartment up on 100th Street with long halls and not much light. But the gloom of the place is offset by their kids' toys everywhere, colorful jackets stacked on top of one another, coffee cups with WORLD'S GREATEST MOM and DARTMOUTH written on the side. Theirs is a home full of love and hurry, children's drawings on the fridge alongside reminders to buy *La Stampa*. Michael owns an elegant vintage fountain pen store, while Lenna freelances for *Newsweek*. Their apartment is like their life: high-ceilinged, thought-out, overflowing with interesting combinations and possibilities. It's always nice to go there and share it awhile.

I felt pretty good about forty years old. Finally there was some money in the bank and someone I liked talking about a trip together to Egypt in the spring. Forty was a milestone, but one that didn't mean much at the moment. I already thought of myself as being slightly middle-aged anyway, but I was healthy and had good prospects, so—So what! to the beginning of my fifth decade.

"You cut your hair!"

"Do you like it?"

"You look very French."

"Yes, but do you *like* it?"

"I think so. I have to get used to it. Come on in."

We sat in the living room and ate. Elbow, their bull terrier, rested his head on my knee and never took his eye off the table. After the meal was over, we cleared the plates and then she handed me a small red box.

"I hope you like it. I made them myself."

Inside the box were a pair of the most beautiful gold earrings I have ever seen.

"My God, Lenna, they're *exquisite!* You *made* these? I didn't know you made jewelry."

She looked happily embarrassed. "You like them? They're real gold, believe it or not."

"I believe it. They're art! You *made* them, Lenna? I can't get over it. They're really works of art: They look like something by Klimt." I took them carefully out of the box and put them on.

She clapped her hands like a girl. "Oh, Juliet, they really do look good!"

Our friendship *is* important and goes back a long way, but this was a lifetime present—one you gave a spouse or someone who saved your life.

Before I could say that (or anything else), the lights went out. Her two young sons brought in the birthday cake, forty candles strong.

A few days later I was walking down Madison Avenue, proudly wearing my new present, when, caught by something there, looked in a jewelry store window. There they were—my birthday earrings. The exact ones. Looking closer, open-mouthed, I saw the price tag: five thousand dollars! I stood and gaped for what must have been minutes. Either way, it was shocking. Had she lied about making them? Spent five thousand dollars for my birthday present? Lenna wasn't a liar and she wasn't rich. All right, so had she copied them in brass or something and just *said* they were gold to make me feel good? That wasn't her way either. What the hell was going on?

The confusion emboldened me to walk right into the store. Or rather, walk right up and press the buzzer. After a short wait, someone rang me in. The saleswoman who appeared from behind a curtain looked like a Radcliffe graduate with a degree in bluestocking. Maybe you had to to work in this place.

"May I help you?"

"Yes. I'd like to see the pair of these earrings you have in the window."

She looked at my ears as I touched them, and it was as if a curtain rose from in front of her regard. When I first entered I was only another nobody in a plaid skirt asking for a moment's sniff of their palace air. But realizing I had a familiar five grand hanging on my lobes changed everything: She would be my slave—or friend—for life, I only had to say which.

"Of course, the Dixies."

"The what?"

She smiled, as if to say I was being very funny. It quickly dawned on me that she must have thought I knew very well what "Dixies" were since I was wearing some.

She took them out of the window and put them carefully down in front of me on a black velvet card. They were beautiful; admiring them, I entirely forgot I was wearing some.

"I'm so surprised you have a pair. They only came into the store a week ago."

Thinking fast, I said, "My husband bought them for me. I like them so much I'm thinking of getting a pair for my sister. Tell me about the designer. What's his name? Dixie?"

"I don't know much, madam. Only the owner knows who Dixie is and where they come from. But whoever it is is a real genius. Apparently both Bulgari and people from the Memphis group have been in already, asking who he is and how they can get in touch with him."

"How do you know it's a man?" I put the earrings down and looked directly at her.

"Oh, I don't. It's just that the work is so masculine I assumed it. Maybe you're right; maybe it *is* a woman." She picked one up and held it to the light. "Did you notice how they don't really reflect light so much as enhance it? Golden light. You can own it any time you want. I've never seen that. I envy you."

They were real. I went to a jeweler on 47th Street to have them appraised, then to the only two other stores in the city that sold "Dixies." No one knew anything about the creator, or weren't talking if they did. Both dealers were very respectful and pleasant, but mum was the word when I asked about the jewelry's origin.

"The gentleman asked us not to give out information, madam. We must respect his wishes."

"But it *is* a man?"

A professional smile. "Yes."

"Could I contact him through you?"

"Yes, I'm sure that would be possible. May I help with anything else, madam?"

"What other pieces has he designed?"

"As far as I know, only the earrings, the fountain pen, and this key ring." He'd shown me the pen, which was nothing special. Now he brought out a small golden key ring shaped in a woman's profile: Lenna Rhodes's profile.

The doorbell tinkled when I walked into the store. Michael was with a customer and, smiling hello, gave me the sign he'd be over as soon as he was finished. He had started INK almost as soon as he got out of college, and from the beginning it was a success. Fountain pens are cranky, unforgiving things that demand full attention and patience. But they are also a handful of flash and Old World elegance: gratifying slowness that offers no reward other than the sight of shiny ink flowing wetly across a dry page. INK's customers were both rich and not so, but all of them had the same collector's fiery glint in the eye and the addict's desire for more. A couple of times a month I'd work there when Michael needed an extra hand. It taught me to be cheered by old pieces of Bakelite and gold plate, as well as another kind of passion.

"Juliet, hi! Roger Peyton was in this morning and bought that yellow Parker Duofold. The one he's been looking at for months."

"Finally. Did he pay full price?"

Michael grinned and looked away. "Rog can never afford full price. I let him do it in installments. What's up with you?"

"Did you ever hear of a Dixie pen? Looks a little like the Cartier Santos?"

"Dixie? No. It looks like the Santos?" The expression on his face said he was telling the truth.

I brought out the brochure from the jewelry store and, opening it to the pen photograph, handed it to him. His reaction was immediate.

"Why, that bastard! How much do I have to put up with this man?"

"You know him?"

Michael looked up from the photo, anger and confusion competing for first place on his face. "Do I know him? Sure, I know him. He lives in my goddamned *house,* I know him so well! Dixie, huh? Cute name. Cute man.

"Wait. I'll show you something, Juliet. Just stay there. Don't move. That shit!"

There's a mirror behind the front counter at INK. When Michael motored off to the back of the store, I looked at my reflection and said, *"Now* you did it."

He was back in no time. "Look at this. You want to see something beautiful? Look at this." He handed me something in a blue velvet case. I opened it and saw . . . the Dixie fountain pen.

"But you said you'd never heard of them."

His voice was hurt and loud. *"This* is not a Dixie fountain pen. It's a Sinbad. An original, solid-gold Sinbad made at the Benjamin Swire Fountain Pen Works in Konstanz, Germany, around 1915. There's a rumor the Italian Futurist Antonio Sant' Elia did the design, but that's never been proven. Nice, isn't it?"

It *was* nice, but he was so angry I wouldn't have dared say it wasn't. I nodded eagerly.

He took it back. "I've been selling pens twenty years, but I've only seen two of these in all that time. One was owned by Walt Disney, and I have the other. Collector's value? About seven thousand dollars. But as I said, you just don't find them."

"Won't the Dixie people get in trouble for copying it?"

"No, because I'm sure there are small differences between the original and this new one. Let me see that brochure again."

"But you have an original, Michael. It still holds its value."

"That's not the point. It's not the value that matters. I'd never sell this.

"You know the classic 'bathtub' Porsche? One of the strangest, greatest-looking cars of our time. Some smart, cynical person realized that and is now making fiberglass copies of the thing. They're very well done and full of all the latest features.

"But it's a lie car, Juliet: Sniff it and it smells only of today—little plastic things and cleverly cut corners you can't see. Not important to the car, but essential to the real object. The wonder of the thing was Porsche designed it so well and thoughtfully so long ago. That's art. But the art is in its original everything, not just the look or the convincing copy. I can guarantee you your Dixie pen has too much plastic inside where you can't see, and a gold point that probably has about a third as much gold on it as the original. Looks good, but they always miss the whole point with their cut corners.

"Look, you're going to find out sooner or later, so I think you'd better know now."

"What are you talking about?"

He brought a telephone up from beneath the counter and gestured for me to wait. He called Lenna and in a few words told her about the Dixies and my discovery of them.

He was looking at me when he asked, "Did he tell you he was doing that, Lenna?"

Whatever her long answer was, it left his expression deadpan. "Well, I'm going to bring Juliet home. I want her to meet him. . . . What? Because we've got to do something about it, Lenna! Maybe she'll have an idea of what to do. Do you think this is normal? . . . Oh, you do? That's interesting. Do you think it's normal for *me?*" A dab of saliva popped off his lip and flew across the store.

When Michael opened the door, Lenna stood right on the other side, arms crossed tight over her chest. Her soft face was squinched into a tight challenge.

"Whatever he told you probably isn't true, Juliet."

I put up both hands in surrender. "He didn't tell me anything, Lenna. I don't even want to *be* here. I just showed him a picture of a pen."

Which wasn't strictly true. I showed him a picture of a pen because I wanted to know more about Dixie and my five-thousand-dollar earrings. Yes, sometimes I am nosy. My ex-husband used to tell me I was.

Both Rhodeses were calm and sound people. I don't think I'd ever seen them really disagree on anything important or raise their voices at each other.

"Where is he?" Michael growled. "Eating again?"

"Maybe. So what? You don't like what he eats anyway."

He turned to me. "Our guest is a vegetarian. His favorite food is plum pits."

"Oh, that's *mean,* Michael. That's really mean." She turned and left the room.

"So he's in the kitchen? Good. Come on, Juliet." He took my hand and pulled me behind on his stalk of their visitor.

Before we got to him I heard music. Ragtime piano. Scott Joplin?

A man sat at the table with his back to us. He had long red hair down over the collar of his sport jacket. One freckled hand was fiddling with the dial on a radio nearby.

"Mr. Fiddlehead? I'd like you to meet Lenna's best friend, Juliet Skotchdopole."

He turned, but even before he was all the way around I knew I was sunk. What a face! Ethereally thin, with high cheekbones and deep-set green eyes that were both merry and profound. Those storybook eyes, the carrotty hair, and freckles everywhere. How could freckles suddenly be so damned sexy? They were for children and cute advertisements. I wanted to touch every one of them.

"Hello, Juliet! Skotchdopole, is it? That's a good name. I wouldn't mind havin' it myself. It's a lot better than Fiddlehead, you know." His deep voice lay in the hammock of a very strong Irish accent.

I put out a hand and we shook. Looking down, I ran my thumb once, quickly, softly, across the top of his hand. I felt hot and dizzy, as if someone I wanted had put his hand gently between my legs for the first time.

He smiled. Maybe he sensed it. There was a yellow plate of something on the table next to the radio. To stop staring so embarrassingly at him, I focused on it and realized the plate was full of plum pits.

"Do you like them? They're delicious." He picked one off the shiny orange-brown pile and, slipping the stony thing in his mouth, bit down. Something cracked loudly, like breaking a tooth, but he kept his angel's smile as he crunched away.

I looked at Michael, who only shook his head. Lenna came into the kitchen and gave Mr. Fiddlehead a big hug and kiss. He only smiled and went on eating . . . pits.

"Juliet, the first thing you have to know is I lied about your birthday present. I didn't make those earrings, Mr. Fiddlehead did. But since he's me, I wasn't *really* lying." She smiled as if she was sure I understood what she was talking about. I looked at Michael for help, but he was poking around in the refrigerator. Beautiful Mr. Fiddlehead was still eating.

"What do you mean, Lenna, he's you?"

Michael took out a carton of milk and, at the same time, a plum, which he exaggeratedly offered his wife. She made a face at him and snatched it out of his hand.

Biting it, she said, "Remember I told you I was an only child? Like a lot of lonely kids, I solved my problem the best way I could—by making up an imaginary friend."

My eyes widened. I looked at the red-headed man. He winked at me.

Lenna went on. "I made up Mr. Fiddlehead. I read and dreamed so much that one day I put it all together into my idea of the perfect friend. First, his name would be Mr. Fiddlehead because I thought that was the funniest name in the world, a name that would always make me laugh when I was sad. Then he had to come from Ireland, because that was the home of all leprechauns and fairies. In fact, I wanted a kind of life-sized human leprechaun. He'd have red hair and green eyes and, whenever I wanted, the magical ability to make gold bracelets and jewelry for me out of thin air."

"Which explains the Dixie jewelry in the stores?"

Michael nodded. "He said he got bored just hanging around, so I suggested he do something useful! Everything was fine so long as it was just the earrings and key chain." He slammed the glass down on the counter. "I didn't know about the fountain pen until today. What's with *that,* Fiddlehead?"

"Because I wanted to try me hand at it. I loved the one you showed me, so I thought I'd use that as my model. Why not? You can't improve on perfection. The only thing I did was put some more gold in it here and there."

I put my hand up like a student with a question. "But who's Dixie?"

Lenna smiled and said, "I am. That was the secret name I made up for myself when I was little. The only other person who knew it was my secret friend." She stuck her thumb in the other's direction.

"Wonderful! So now Dixie fountain pens, which are lousy ripoffs of Sinbads, will be bought by every asshole in New York who can afford to buy a Piaget watch or Hermès briefcase. It makes me sick." Michael glared at the other man and waited belligerently for a reply.

Mr. Fiddlehead's reply was to laugh like Woody Woodpecker.

Which cracked Lenna and me up.

Which sent her husband storming out of the kitchen.

"Is it true?"

They both nodded.

"I had an imaginary friend too when I was little! The Bimbergooner. But I never saw him for real."

"Maybe you didn't make him real enough. Maybe you just cooked him up when you were sad or needed someone to talk to. In Lenna's case, the more she needed me, the more real I became. She needed me a lot. One day I was just there for good."

I looked at my friend. "You mean he's been around since you were little? Living with you?"

She laughed. "No. As I grew up I needed him less. I was happier and had more friends. My life got fuller. So he was around less." She reached over and touched his shoulder.

He smiled but it was a sad one, full of memories. "I can give her huge pots of gold and do great tricks. I've even been practicing ventriloquism and can throw my voice a little. But you'd be surprised how few women love ventriloquists.

"If you two'll excuse me, I think I'll go in the other room and watch TV with the boys. It's about time for the Three Stooges. Remember how much we loved that show, Lenna? I think we saw one episode ten times. The one where they open up the hairdressing salon in Mexico."

"I remember. You loved Moe and I loved Curly."

They beamed at each other through the shared memory.

"But wait, if he's . . . what you say, how come he came back now?"

"You didn't know it, but Michael and I went through a *very* bad period a little while ago. He even moved out for two weeks and we both thought that was it: no more marriage. One night I got into bed crying like a fool and wishing to hell Mr. Fiddlehead was around again to help me. And then suddenly there he was, standing in the bathroom door smiling at me." She squeezed his shoulder again. He covered her hand with his own.

"God, Lenna, what did you do?"

"Screamed! I didn't recognize him."

"What do you mean?"

"I mean he grew up! The Mr. Fiddlehead I imagined when I was a child was exactly my age. I guess as I got older so did he. It makes sense."

"I'm going to sit down now. I have to sit down because this has been the strangest afternoon of my life."

Fiddlehead jumped up and gave me his seat. I took it. He left the room for television with the boys. I watched him go. Without thinking, I picked up Michael's half-empty glass of milk and finished it.

"Everything you told me is true?"

She put up her right hand. "I swear on our friendship."

"That beautiful man out there is an old dream of yours?"

Her head recoiled. "Ooh, do you think he's beautiful? Really? I think he's kind of funny-looking, to tell the truth. I love him as a friend, but"—she looked guiltily at the door—"I'd never want to go *out* with him or anything."

But *I* did, so we did. After the first few dates I would have hunted rats with him in the South Bronx if that's what he liked. I was, as expected, completely gone on him. The line of a man's neck can change your life. The way he digs in his pockets for change can make the heart squawk and hands grow cold. How he touches your elbow or the button that is not closed on the cuff of his shirt are demons he's loosed without ever knowing it. They own us immediately. He was a thoroughly compelling man. I wanted to rise to the occasion of his presence in my life and become something more than I'd previously thought myself capable of.

I think he began to love me too, but he didn't say things like that. Only that he was happy, or that he wanted to share things he'd held in reserve all his life.

Because he knew sooner or later he'd have to go away *(where* he never said, and I stopped asking), he seemed to have thrown all caution to the wind. But before meeting him, I'd never thrown anything away, caution included. I'd been a careful reader of timetables, made the bed tight and straight first thing every morning, and hated dishes in the sink. My life at forty was comfortably narrow and ordered. Going haywire and off the deep end wasn't in my repertoire, and normally people who did made me squint.

I realized I was in love *and* haywire the day I taught him to play racquetball. After we'd batted around an hour, we were sitting in the gallery drinking Coke. He flicked sweat from his forehead with two fingers. A hot, intimate drop fell on my wrist. I put my hand over it quickly and rubbed it into my skin. He didn't see. I knew then I'd have to learn to put whatever expectations I had aside and just live purely in his jet stream, no matter where it took me. That day I realized I'd sacrifice anything for him, and for a few hours I went around feeling like some kind of holy person, a zealot, love made flesh.

"Why does Michael let you stay there?"

He took a cigarette from my pack. He'd begun smoking a week before and loved it. Almost as much as he liked to drink, he said. The perfect Irishman. "Don't forget he was the one who left Lenna, not vice versa. When he came back he was pretty much on his knees to her. He had to be. There wasn't a lot he could say about me being there. Especially after he found out who I was and why I'd come. Do you have any plum pits around?"

"Question two: Why in God's name do you eat those things?"

"That's easy: because plums are Lenna's favorite fruit. When she was a little girl, she'd have tea parties for just us two: Scott Joplin music, imaginary tea, and real plums. She'd eat the fruit, then put the pit on my plate to eat. Makes perfect sense."

I ran my hand through his red hair, loving the way my fingers got caught in all the thick curls. "That's disgusting. It's like slavery! Why am I getting to the point where I don't like my best friend so much anymore?"

"If you like me, you should like her, Juliet. She made me."

I took his hand. *"That* part I like. Would you ever consider moving in with me?"

He kissed my fingers. "I would love to consider that, but I have to tell you I don't think I'll be around very much longer. But if you'd like, I'll stay with you until I—uh—have to go."

"What are you talking about?" I sat up.

He put his hand close to my face. "Look hard and you'll see."

It took a moment, but then I gasped: From certain angles I could see right through the hand. It had become vaguely transparent.

"Lenna's happy again. It's the old story. When she's down, she needs me and calls." He shrugged. "When she's happy again, I'm not needed, so she sends me away. Not consciously, but—look, we all know I'm her little Frankenstein monster. She can do what she *wants* with me. Even dream up that I like to eat fucking plum pits."

"It's so wrong!"

Sighing, he sat up and started pulling on his shirt. "It's wrong but it's life, sweet girl. Not much we can do about it, you know."

"Yes, we can. We can do something."

His back was to me. I remembered the first time I'd ever seen him. His back was to me then too, the long red hair falling over his collar.

When I didn't say anything more, he turned and looked at me over his shoulder, smiling.

"We can do something? What can we do?"

His eyes were gentle and loving, eyes I wanted to see for the rest of my life.

"We can make her sad. We can make her need you."

"What do you mean?"

"Just what I said, Fiddy. When she's sad she needs you. We have to decide what would make her sad a long time. Maybe something to do with Michael. Or the children."

His fingers stopped moving over the buttons. Thin, artistic fingers. Freckles.

3

Finky Linky drove me to the airport, which was nervous-making because there was always a good possibility he might drop dead at any
moment.

Finky Linky, alias Wyatt Leonard, one-time star of the funniest and
most innovative children's show on television.

> "First there was Pinky,
> then there was Winky.
> Don't forget Pee Wee—
> But the king of them all is
> *Finkyyyyyyyyyyyyyy!*"

Remember that? Remember Finky-Pinky-Rings? Or the Finky Linky
Stinky Magic Carpet that no one on the show ever wanted to ride,
despite its magic, because it smelled too much?

Wyatt made it big so fast because he was smart and crazy and willing
to do anything to make kids laugh. I have never known anyone who
loved children as much as Wyatt Leonard.

I met him a few years before he joined our Cancer Theater Group. A
friend-of-a-friend of Cullen James, he was at the peak of his success
when it was discovered he had leukemia. He accepted his fate so

calmly. Perhaps because he never really believed it would get him or else, as he said, a million children's love buoyed him over death's fearsome sea.

Six months after I began working with the group in New York, he showed up and asked if he could watch. It would be another year before we actually tried to put something on stage, because those early days were more group therapy sessions than anything else. A bitter young woman, bald from radiation treatments, pointed to her head and asked if he had a part for her on his show. He did. Remember Wig Woman with the pink dress and all those different hairdos? The first star that ever emerged from the New York Cancer Players. People associated with the show thought she was only a nut with a shaved head. Neither Wyatt nor she ever told them the truth until she died and Finky Linky did the show about death that won him an Emmy.

When the constant medical treatment and hospitalization ate into his energy and resistance, he gave up the television show and became the hardest working member of our group.

Phil was a great fan of the show and thrilled to hear I knew Wyatt, so I introduced them. A month later, Fast Forward Productions flew Finky Linky out to LA to do that bizarre bit in *Midnight Too* that had everyone laughing . . . and retching.

After I read "Mr. Fiddlehead" that morning, I called Wyatt and asked him to take over rehearsals for our play. When he found out why I was leaving town, he told me to get someone else because he was going with me.

"How come?"

"I'll tell you on the plane. What time does it go? I'll drive us out."

I've traveled with famous people before, and it's always interesting to watch how the man in the street reacts. With movie stars, you see the expected admiration and desire, but also many darker things—envy and hunger, real anger.

With Wyatt it was entirely different. When he parked his car in the long-term lot at Kennedy Airport, the attendant not only had him autograph his baseball cap but ran next door to the hot dog stand to tell the gang there. A stampede followed, all saying "Finky!" The show had been off the air for over a year, but he was still their funny hero and friend. First he had to give five people the secret handshake—touch the heart, touch the nose, blow a kiss, shake. Then autographs. One bedraggled man asked for a personal souvenir. Wyatt gave him the paperback book he had in his pocket, and the man asked him to sign it.

"But I didn't write it!"

"Yeah, but you *owned* it!"

The same thing happened in the terminal building and right onto the plane: greetings, handshakes, pure love for an old and missed pal.

After we took off, a stewardess came up and said she'd once won a wet T-shirt contest wearing a Finky Linky shirt. Wyatt looked long at her chest, smiled, and said in his Finky voice, *"That* was a lucky shirt!"

She went away smiling. I asked him why he'd come. The plane was still climbing, and before he answered we broke through the clouds into the pure blue of thousands of feet high.

"We were lovers once."

"You and *Phil?*"

He looked at me and touched my hand a moment. "He wasn't gay, Weber. Only wanted to know what it was like. Remember when I went out there to do *Midnight Too* with him? We were together a couple of days. Nothing special, just warm for me and new for him. He didn't like it very much, but I wasn't surprised."

Although I knew he was gay because we'd discussed it, Wyatt appeared straight. There'd been a bad scene in our group once when a woman fell in love with him and he didn't reciprocate. He told me sickness had replaced gender anyway in his life, that when you get cancer and they're sticking things in you or cutting them out, it's hard feeling sexy.

"Are you shocked, Weber?"

"Sure. It's interesting, too. You think you know your friends but you don't."

"Maybe I shouldn't have told you, especially now."

"No, I'm glad you did, Wyatt. One of the reasons I'm going to California is to find out why Phil shot himself. Until yesterday, I didn't think that was him either. Would you mind telling me about what happened between you two?"

"He thought I was funny, and I thought he was a genius. A mutual admiration society. We talked on the set; then we went out for something to eat after. You know the end. The strange thing was, I didn't come on to him at all. I told him I was gay and no big deal. He kept asking questions about it, so I answered them. I don't believe that deep in his heart, every hetero man is secretly gay and only waiting for the right moment to jump out and admit it to the world. Some are and some aren't. Phil wasn't gay, only curious. Curious about everything. That's why he was such an interesting man."

"If he wasn't gay, why were you together two days? Wouldn't one night have been enough?"

"Not for Phil. He wanted to know as much as he could."

To be as successful with children as Wyatt had been, you had to have the wonder and openness of a child. When I told him the story of the day before, including the experience with the magical videotapes that played back my history and fast-forwarded to Sasha's future, he only shook his head and grunted. He asked if Phil had sent anything else. I took "Mr. Fiddlehead" out of my bag and handed it to him.

"What's this?"

"A short story. Sasha said it was going to be his next project."

"I can read it?"

"Are there more things you're not telling me?"

He looked at the story in his hand. "Let me read this first." He took the famous Finky glasses out of his pocket and put them on. The tough-looking pig on the motorcycle with the wheels holding the glass? Those.

While he read, I looked out the window and thought about Phil, then about my mother. Wyatt chuckled a couple of times. Once he looked up and said, "Phil must have written this. I can hear him telling it. You're obviously Mr. Fiddlehead."

"Why? My red hair and green eyes?"

"Partly. Let me finish."

Phil dead. Phil sleeping with Wyatt. Phil writing "Mr. Fiddlehead." The plane bumped up and down and the FASTEN SEAT BELTS light came on.

"I don't understand the end."

"What's not to understand?"

"What does it mean?" He started reading from the manuscript. " 'Thin artistic fingers. Freckles. Fiddy and I were in a dazzle and knew it. He turned out the light again. Blood was rushing into my head, and I hoped I wasn't glowing in the dark. I started to hate him. I felt like blaming him for something that hadn't happened yet.' "

I took that manuscript from Wyatt and looked at it. The new sentences he'd read *were* on the page: words that hadn't been there when I'd originally read the story a few hours before.

"The story I read ended with the word 'freckles.' These last lines are new since then."

"Did Phil ever tell you about Pinsleepe?"

"Wyatt, did you hear what I said? This story's *grown* since this morning!"

"I heard. *Do* you know about Pinsleepe?"

I shook my head. The world was too much with me, and how.

A week before he died, Phil came to New York. Usually when he came it was an Indianapolis 500 of speeding around to all his favorite places and people. He didn't like the city but he loved what was in it, so his trips were manic, albeit infrequent. He liked his friends to get together: to have big rowdy dinners in restaurants where sensational or peculiar people told long stories that held the table in thrall.

The last time was different. He contacted only two people, Danny James and Wyatt Leonard. The rest of his friends and fans—the rare book dealers, a dinosaur specialist at Columbia, the vegetable chef at Benihana, *me*—knew nothing of this visit.

From what Wyatt and Danny pieced together, he stayed at the Pierre Hotel and spent most of his time traveling in and out of town, destination unknown. Both were surprised when he called and said he was there, shocked when they saw him. Danny thought he looked very ill, Wyatt that he was deranged.

"You know that crazy look people get when they're caught in a flash photograph? That was Phil's expression the whole time we were together. He was very relaxed and soft-spoken, but his eyes had the hysterical look of someone who's just seen death. Or a glimpse of ourselves in some hideous future situation. We walked around, went out to dinner, and talked for hours, but the look stayed. It scared me."

"Did you ask him what was wrong?"

"Finky Linky wants a drinky. Does Weber want a drinky too? Yes, I asked what was wrong. We were sitting in the Four Seasons eating lobster. He asked if I ever read W. H. Auden. Yes, I read Auden. Then did I know the line, 'We are lived by powers we pretend to understand'? He was taking these incredibly long, slow-motion bites, all very elegant and calm, but his eyes were those of a man about to be shot.

W. H. Auden. I said, 'That doesn't answer my question, Phil. What's the matter with you?'"

Pinsleepe was the matter.

There's an old Jewish legend that says before it's born, a child knows all the secrets of the universe. But as it's being born, an angel touches it on the mouth to make it forget. According to Wyatt Leonard, Phil believed before he died he had rediscovered those secrets, but not from within—from the Angel Pinsleepe.

"Once he started describing her and what had happened, I couldn't stop him. It was like he'd been waiting for someone to talk to about her.

"I know about 'Mr. Fiddlehead.' That's where Pinsleepe first showed up. Phil told me he'd had the idea for the story a long time ago and once in a while thought about writing it as a script. When he was in Yugoslavia filming, he began it because he was bored down there. He wrote two pages, but then there was a problem with the Yugoslav authorities or something, so he put the script down and forgot about it.

"Cut to California, a few months later. He's going through the papers he worked on in Yugoslavia and comes across five pages of a short story entitled 'Mr. Fiddlehead.' He remembered writing two pages of a *film script* with the same name. He reads these five pages and gets scared. It's the same plot he had in mind for his movie, only this is a short story, and what's there is more than what he'd written.

"He tells me all this between leisurely bites of lobster and glances from these high octane speed-freak eyes.

"Finding the short story was bad enough, but then he had his first vision. You know what it was? Flea getting killed. He saw her running out into the road and not being hit by a car but shot by some loony, joyriding in the canyon. In this vision, he knew what day it would happen, what time, even the make of the car and the face of the crazy. He also knew this was no bullshit and he'd better heed the warning. So the time it was to happen, he locked Flea in, went out of the house, and waited in the driveway. Along comes the white Toyota with the Woody Woodpecker decal on the side. The driver slowed in front of Phil's house and looked at him. Phil said the guy had such a strange expression it looked like he *knew* he'd somehow been cheated out of his dog to kill."

The visions went on and so did the short story. Phil told no one,

although Sasha began to complain about the way he was behaving. When I retraced the chronology, I realized she'd called me a couple of times then and casually mentioned how grumpy and strange he'd been since returning from Yugoslavia.

"This was *before* Matthew Portland died?"

"A long time before, Weber. Phil said Pinsleepe was coming to him every day by that time. He also said he actually was told the Portland thing would happen, but he wouldn't do anything about it."

"Tell me more about the angel."

Lunch was served. A stewardess named Andrea brought our trays and asked us to sign her autograph book. Wyatt quickly drew a picture of Finky Linky, Andrea, and me all holding hands while we flew across the sky together.

"What's this?"

"I don't know. Meat? Cake?" We poked at the same brown object on our trays.

"Maybe it's the napkin. The videos he sent you and Sasha are pretty good evidence *something* exists; whether it's an angel or not, who knows?"

"Why'd he think it was an angel?"

"Because it came to tell him to stop making the Midnight films."

The first Midnight began as a kind of desperate joke. Eight years ago, Phil Strayhorn was an inch away from bottoming out. He'd had no luck cracking the Hollywood egg and was down to doing free-lance research on anything for anyone, just to pay his bills. Because he was a plain-looking man with little acting experience, he was only another person on line at casting calls. Along the way, he'd tried working in development at a studio but was neither social nor cunning enough to be successful at it. He loved acting and loved movies, but he'd reached a point where there was no way any of it was working out for him.

Someone doing a book on the occult asked him to research Zoroastrianism. Tunneling through the subject, he discovered *The Book of Arda Viraz*, an autobiography by a Persian priest who purportedly survived death and came back to talk about what was "over there."

On the other side, among other tasks, Viraz had had to cross the

"Bridge of the Separator," where he (and all other souls) met his conscience for a reassessment of all he'd done in life.

Fascinated by the idea, Phil dug deeper and found similarities in Islamic tradition. There, the story goes that on the day of judgment one must undergo "the trial of crossing al-Sirat, a bridge that is thinner than a hair, sharper than a sword, and, in some versions, set with hooks and thorns; the righteous cross easily to the Garden, but the wicked find the bridge slippery and dark and, after expending thousands of years attempting to cross, fall into the Fire below."

I didn't see him much in those days because I was about to go to Europe to film *Babyskin* and was caught up in my own solipsism. It was probably better, though, because our relationship was strained. Since graduating from college, I'd published a collection of poetry and made a film that was well reviewed. I was on my way, and however much he loved me and cheered my success, I knew it was hard for him to watch someone else get all the A's. Especially Phil, who'd been at the head of the class all his life.

When I returned from Europe several months later, he picked me up at the airport. Pulling the car away from the LAX curb, he handed me a script.

"What's this?"

"A script I wrote. You won't like it because it's a horror movie, but please read it and tell me if it's any good. If it has any potential."

"A horror film? 'Midnight.' What's it about?"

"Meeting our conscience on a bridge."

Something *glitched* in the universe. We never find out why, but it's implied early in the film it was mankind's fault. Wars, greed, sniffing around in certain dangerous corners of science. . . . Whatever, things on a cosmic level fell apart and the ceremony of innocence met Bloodstone. Whatever happened caused part of death to cross the mortal line into life in the form of Bloodstone. He could simply be an angry little sliver of death or part of our conscience come to meet us on the Bridge of the Separator . . . *if* we were dead, but we aren't. He could even be Death itself, helplessly forced to live in our east of Eden. All that matters is Bloodstone is angry—angry to be here, angry to be in a hated foreign land. Phil always smiled and called him the xenophobe.

The degree of violence and imagination in the things Strayhorn's fiend did were both obscene and startling. Reading the script for the first time, I couldn't believe what he was doing, page after page. But Bloodstone did them repeatedly in the most inventive and ghoulish ways. I called it car-crash art—you don't want to look, but you have to.

I called Matthew Portland, a producer who was always looking for scripts full of boobs, blood, and interesting gore. He asked for the story over the phone. Instead of telling him, I read the now-famous scene of Bloodstone, the infant, and the magnifying glass.

"That's the most repellent thing I've ever heard. Who wrote it?"

The three of us went to lunch. After they shook hands for the first time, Portland said he liked the script but it needed work. We all knew it was a perfect script, but every producer says that at the first meeting. Phil smiled and quietly said Matthew's last film, *Hide and Sick,* was a steaming pile of shit. The other smiled back and said he knew that, but it'd paid the bills.

They traded insults for most of the meal and then agreed on a deal: Phil's script stayed as it was, and he would play Bloodstone. In exchange, he asked for very little money but a nice guaranteed piece of the gross.

They got a young man straight out of USC film school to direct who knew just about every horror film ever made, including such howlers as *Plan 9 from Outer Space.* But they were lucky because they'd found a genuine aficionado and fan of the genre who also knew what he was doing.

It took twenty-nine days to shoot *Midnight* in a northern California town where the entire six-hundred-person population was delighted to have a movie crew setting fire to their streets and flinging fake body pieces out their windows.

Matthew Portland and half the crew played roles. Phil played three (including Bloodstone). The director was a perfectionist who pissed everybody off but whose enthusiasm for what they were doing kept people afloat.

At a sneak preview of the film in Hibbing, Minnesota, a teenage girl had a heart attack and died. It made national news and was the best free publicity they could have wanted.

Millions were made. T-shirts and posters were licensed. Merchandisers and distributors and major studios started licking their lips and rubbing their hands together for what they saw as a possible long and happy marriage between gold and a new ghoul.

The furor grew. It was understandable. *Midnight* is a kind of masterpiece, but it is also immoral and too convincing, too real. Horror films are fun to watch because they're usually so outrageous or hyperbolic you spend half the time smiling at all that red silliness.

Midnight is different. For one, it is a very smart film. Although Phil said it was inspired by Hieronymus Bosch's work, I know a great deal of it came from his own utterly unhappy childhood. Not the horror so much as the almost tactile sadness that sits on the movie like the night demon on the sleeping woman's chest in that famous painting by Fuseli. Pauline Kael said it first when she wrote the wonderful review comparing *Midnight* to De Palma's *Carrie* and Terence Malick's *Days of Heaven*. That gave the intelligentsia permission to go to the film, much like Leonard Bernstein did in the seventies when he said he liked the Beatles.

"Do we really live in the world that Bloodstone haunts? If so, then he isn't the real monster in the story—our own mediocrity is, our silence and exile from ourselves. Forget the cunning." She also quoted the artist Robert Henri. "Low art is just telling things; as, There is the night. High art gives the feeling of night. . . . Here is an emotional landscape. It is like something thought, something remembered." In fact, "Something Thought, Something Remembered" was the title of her essay, which, with its faint reference to Proust, added even more prestige.

Years after I saw the film for the first time, I heard Spalding Gray do one of his monologues. In the middle of it, Gray said something that was also part of the essence of *Midnight:* "One of my brother's biggest fears was the basement of our house. When our parents would go away he'd turn out the lights and crawl on his belly from the bedroom down the front stairs, then down the basement stairs, and with his eyes closed he would feel the basement walls, every crack, feeling his way around the entire room until he either died or didn't die."

Somehow Phil Strayhorn had created a story that made his audience face their own basement fears with all the lights off and no weapon handy.

When Phil was a boy, his father used to tell him and his sister "bedtime stories." Not a nice man, Mr. Strayhorn probably thought of it as a good way of making up to two children he neither liked nor helped. According to his son, the stories were long and good but too often unnecessarily frightening or sad.

"He'd scare the shit out of us and make us cry. Then the bastard'd put his arm around us and say, 'It's okay, it's okay. Daddy's here! Daddy'll protect you.' He wanted both our fear and our love. That's not fair, man."

If you have seen *Midnight Too,* you're familiar with this scene. Only in the movie, Daddy is Bloodstone in disguise, and what happens to the children *isn't* okay. Phil and his parents stopped speaking after it came out. But he said too bad; they didn't like the story because the parts about them were true.

M.T. was three times as successful at the box office (and video counter) as its predecessor. As a result, Phil and Matthew Portland formed Fast Forward Productions and started looking around for other properties to develop.

One of the funnier results of the first film was the surprising popularity of Matthew Portland, actor. He received so much fan mail for his portrayal of Paul Eddoes, town mayor and professional dumbo, that he and his new partner decided to keep Paul around for the second and third parts of the series. Matthew was thrilled.

That third part was *Midnight Always Comes,* but by the time they got to the end of filming, Phil was calling it "Midnight Never Leaves." He was tired of Bloodstone, tired of gore, tired of signing autographs because he was a beloved mass murderer.

"I don't want to go off-off Broadway to do *King Lear,* Weber, but it would be nice to act in something other than a bloodbath for once."

I was shooting *Wonderful* then and asked if he'd like to play the small role of the transvestite, Lily Reynard. He quickly said yes and was damned good in it.

Not long afterward, the earthquake came and Phil saved my life. If he hadn't pulled me out of the restaurant as soon as the tremors began, I'm sure I would have been crushed with the others when the roof fell in with one big, horrifying *whump!*

Tired and empty and still shaken by the sound of that roof, I left for Europe as soon as I finished *Wonderful.* I wanted out of California and was already half sure I wanted out of my life there. Europe was the green light at the end of my dock. I was convinced being there would at least give me some perspective.

I didn't hear much from Phil in my year overseas, except for a few postcards saying vague things like he was looking into possibilities.

When I came back he showed me *The Circus on Fire*. A fifteen-minute video he'd been commissioned to make by the rock group Vitamin D, the film is a beauty, a small Joseph Cornell box of wonder and deceit. You can watch it five times in a row and hope for a sixth. In many ways it's the best thing he ever did, but the thugs in the group thought it was too heavy and said no. They'd expected Bloodstone to make them a video like *Midnight*. What they got instead was some weird thing with almost no music and puppets speaking ancient maps.

Without a word he put it in a drawer and went back to work on *Midnight Kills*. When I asked how he felt about that, he said working on the video had given him a superb idea for a new film. After playing Bloodstone again, he'd have enough money to finance the whole project himself. What was this new idea? He wouldn't say. That was a good sign.

About this time two very different things happened to him. The first was meeting Sasha, the second were the killings in Florida.

Many newspapers tried to call them "The Bloodstone Murders," but luckily the nickname didn't stick. A seventeen-year-old lunatic in Sarasota saw *Midnight* too many times. Then, while babysitting one night, he killed his little brother and sister the same way Bloodstone got two people in the film.

4

The dead glow. I still don't know why, but they do. There is much love, warmth, and companionship here . . . all the good things, plus we have—or rather we are—this soft light. It is not so different, but you can't help smiling in the beginning when you look and see you have a lot in common with fireflies.

Those children Weber spoke of are here. They are quiet and sweet, and I try hard to be their friend.

I must, because it is my fault they're here. I didn't believe that when I was alive, but now I understand. That is part of the process. You are taught to understand.

There is a life review, of course, but it was so much more interesting than I had ever imagined. For one thing, they show you how and where your life really happened. Things you didn't experience or weren't ever aware of, but which dyed the fabric of your life its final color.

I was shown the night my parents slept together and conceived me (my father came so quickly, Mother patted his back and fell immediately asleep).

Unknown pieces of the real pain, surprise, and love that lived inside the walls of our growing-up house, our younger hearts: my parents', my sister's, mine.

I have seen it all now: Jeffrey Vincent murdering his little brother and sister, Sasha finding my body on the patio, even the death of Weber's mother.

I was permitted to show him that, although they say they've rarely done that before: allowed someone to see any part of their complete truth while still alive. It is an essential part of the job of living to alone find what we can of these ruins within and translate their hieroglyphics. The archaeology of the heart is the only important study.

For instance, there is a photograph of me (among others) on Weber's dresser in New York. I am in his comfortable old leather chair, hands in lap, one leg crossed over the other. My face is its usual expressionless thin spade with hair on top. On the floor next to the chair are four of those Bloodstone masks that were once popular. I'd brought them to Weber that day as a joke.

I am sitting there looking very self-satisfied in my Anderson & Shepard sport jacket, a silk ascot wrapped in a pompously correct knot around my throat. On the floor are those identical silver faces, strewn at random.

Weber has looked at that picture often, carefully or nostalgically, happily. . . . We have so many ways of looking at a photograph that means something to us. But although he has looked, he has never seen what's important there. Not that it's easy.

Why do we photograph, why do we look, why do we remember so little but forget so much? It isn't coincidence. The ancient Romans discovered what to do: haruspication. Studying the entrails of dead animals, the order and form of anything in the world, they hoped to decipher clues to the future within that order.

They were right. If Weber were to look at that photograph correctly, he would see so much of what will happen to him. Not because it is a picture of me, but because of the way the masks sit on the floor, the tight knot in the silk, the half-light across the side of my face. When he took the picture, he kept saying, "Turn your head. Move your hands. Look a little away. I have to get the masks in too. . . . That's it!"

Why was that it and not something else? Because in some part of him, my friend knew he was about to capture a splinter of his future on film. Unfortunately, his other parts didn't know how to see it, so he only framed the splinter and put it on the shelf with others.

This is true about everything. The cigarette he is about to smoke: how he holds it, the number of puffs he will take. So many answers floating *lazily in the air above our lives, like the gray smoke at the end of Weber's face.*

———————

"Did Phil ever tell you about the dog and the time death came into his room?"

"Wyatt, what happened to Pinsleepe the angel? I thought you were going to tell me about that."

He pursed his lips and nodded. "I am, but we've got another three hours to go.

"That's what I like about *The Decameron* and *Canterbury Tales*—everyone sat around telling sensational stories, since there was nothing else to do while the plague was raging outside or there were another hundred miles to ride till Canterbury.

"First let me tell you about the dog and death. It has something to do with Phil and Pinsleepe anyway.

"When he was a boy, Phil's family had a dog named Henrietta. They let her run free on the streets, so she had puppies pretty regularly. She slept in a corner of Phil's room, and when it was time to have the babies, she went over to her bed and just let them come.

"One time she had a litter with one real sick runt in it. Phil said you could tell from the first it was going to die, but Henrietta was crazy for the pup and treated it best of the bunch. Which is queer, because animals usually ignore or even kill a runt.

"But Henrietta loved it and made sure it got enough to eat and had lots of licks. . . . For a while it looked like the puppy was going to surprise everyone and actually pull through, but then it got worse somehow and started dying.

"While doing his homework one night, Phil looked up because he heard Henrietta start growling. She wasn't a growler, and when he looked around he saw there wasn't anything to growl *at*. But she wouldn't stop. *Grrrr!* On and on. Besides that, she kept looking toward one window in the room. Phil checked there too but didn't see a thing. Her tail was wagging like mad, she was snarling: all the signs of a dogfight about to start. But there was nothing there!

"Suddenly she jumped up and just stood there, back legs shaking, teeth showing, tail whipping back and forth. She was still looking toward the same corner of the room, but then her head started moving slowly, as if watching something cross the floor and come toward her.

She'd been lying next to the puppies, giving them dinner, but now all of them were staggering around on three-day-old legs, searching blindly for Mom. Except for the runt. It was so weak it couldn't move.

"Phil said he felt something in the air: not some cold wind or creepy hand on his neck, just something *else*. It might even have been pleasant; he didn't remember. But whatever it was sure made its nearness known to both boy and mother dog.

"For a couple of seconds Henrietta went stiff and silent. Frozen. Then she began whimpering and looking at the puppies. They were wiggling and whining, all except the sick one. It was dead. Very obviously dead."

"Death came in the room?"

He nodded. "That's what Phil thought. He said the mother watched it cross the room right over to the puppy, which was dead a moment later. How else would you explain it?"

"It's a scene out of *Midnight.*"

"Exactly what I said. I asked how come he'd never used it. He thought it was too beautiful to use there. I think he planned to put it in 'Fiddlehead,' though."

"What does it have to do with Pinsleepe?"

"Pinsleepe was the Angel of Death."

Strayhorn was rich, famous, and under forty. He'd survived an earthquake and been called an eminent artist by one of the most influential critics in America. He wrote a column about whatever suited him for a celebrated men's magazine.

Other people's lives come in two sizes, life size and dream size. Phil had the latter. What's more, he remained a good and sensitive man till the end of his life, which is not typical Hollywood.

I haven't said enough about Phil's humanity, and that's altogether necessary before I describe his involvement with Pinsleepe.

We lived together four years at Harvard, and there were enough late-night bullshit sessions for me to get a clear perspective of his dismal and touching childhood.

His parents cared but not enough. They substituted authority for concern, and strong adult handshakes when hugs should have been given. It's an old story and boring too, if it weren't for Phil's reaction. When they offered to shake his hand, he jumped in their laps and tried to make them laugh. They were such dour people that he considered their smiles and rare laughter to be the only true signs of their love: his real success with them. That might be why he and Finky Linky liked each other so much. It wasn't "make 'em laugh" or "all the world loves a clown" but more—if you grin, I can breathe; if you laugh, I have enough food in me to go another couple of days.

Mr. Strayhorn had a fountain pen store and for a hobby raised poodles. He'd gone to Harvard but graduated with only a diploma and the silly haughtiness that often accompanies a first-rate education to get him through the rest of his life. But after a couple of years or a first job, the world doesn't care where you went to college, as long as you succeed. The old man couldn't, so he retired from the real world on a pension of arrogance and dismissal that kept him minimally alive until he contracted cancer in his early sixties and became even more difficult.

His wife was no better. A small-town girl who never got over being grateful to her husband for marrying her, Betty Strayhorn believed what he said, no matter how outrageous—"Your father went to Harvard, remember"—but when he was wrong she kept her mouth shut. Her favorite phrase was "for the peace of the family." There was peace in the Strayhorn family, but only because Father knew best about everything and you got smacked if you ever tried for the last word.

Phil did everything "right," his sister Jackie everything wrong. He studied while she got into trouble. He made their parents laughing and proud; she made them scared and furious. He told his father he got all A's, she told the old man to fuck himself. The two kids fought together like rabid dogs but protected the other's flanks whenever the parents swooped down for a kill.

Jackie is unmistakably the model for Janine, the heroine of all the Midnight films. They even look alike. Although he was never clear about how he did it, over the years Phil helped her climb over all this self-destructive rebellion and straighten her life out. She became interested in science in her teens and went on to become a biologist. She gave full credit to her brother and none to their parents.

"He taught me one thing I've never forgotten, Weber. Once when I'd really fucked up again with the parents, we were talking about it. I said I was going to kill myself because life was so useless and unfair. He didn't get mad or shake me. Just said, 'Remember this, sister. The world doesn't need anything from you, but you need to give the world something. That's why you're alive. Kill yourself now, and you're proving the majority right—you're no different from the billion other skulls under the ground. Give it something, no matter how short- or long-lasting, and you've won."

Phil went on trying to keep his family together and smiling until the day he graduated summa cum laude from college. His father shook his hand and gave him a Sinbad fountain pen from his own collection.

When Phil told them later that summer he was going to California to try to become an actor, his father called him a ridiculous ass and walked out of the room. Mrs. Strayhorn told her pride and joy to go and apologize to Dad. Phil packed his bag and left. They didn't speak again for two years.

When we got to Los Angeles, we rented an apartment together on Mansfield Avenue in Hancock Park and started trying to become famous. It didn't work. Both of us ended up getting nowhere with our careers and consequently waited tables at different chic restaurants in Beverly Hills.

In the middle of this confused and disappointing time, I published a collection of poetry. Unknown to me, Phil went around to bookstores from Venice Beach to Hollywood Boulevard, pushing it on any store that had a poetry section. In true movie fashion, a person who worked in development for an independent production company heard me give a reading at one of these stores. Coming up afterward, she said she liked my "dialogue poems" and asked if I'd ever thought of trying to write a film. That's how I got started. It wouldn't have happened if Phil Strayhorn hadn't gone on the road and convinced the skeptics my book was worth ordering.

I was lucky. I rewrote three scripts and then did an original. Phil heard every line of every one of them and was a clear and helpful critic. My original, "Cold Dresses," was handed around for a full year before someone said yes. They gave me a lot of money for it, but the film was never made. This new financial security did allow me to slow down and rethink things, which was exactly what I needed. The result was the skeleton of my own first film, *The Night Is Blond*.

Why am I talking about myself when this is Phil's story? Because he was trying as hard as I to break through, but without success. We'd always pooled our money, but he refused to take any from my rewrites when it came in. He said it was mine. No matter what I said, he shook his head. I could take him out to dinner but nothing else. When I bought him a good pair of Leitz binoculars for his birthday, tears came to his eyes.

There are some people in the world who aren't saints but almost unconsciously put themselves second to those they love. They don't do it as a sacrifice or for credit, but simply because they love. What is all the more heartbreaking is their surprise when some of that love or consideration is returned. I don't think they feel unworthy of others' concern; only astonished that another would think of giving it back to them. Most beneficent people are startled (as well as touched) by others' generosity toward them.

His bad luck went on and on. Those of us who cared for him tried to help however we could, but the long months were Phil's "slap-in-the-face days": his image. He said he woke in the morning already cowering from a hand he *knew* was going to come out of somewhere and start batting him back and forth across the floor of his life. He could duck sometimes, but this hand invariably seemed to find him. Maybe there were even two at work.

He was dating a woman who liked him in her bed whenever possible. That kept him calm and funnily goldfish eyed, but she also did a zigzag array of heavy-voltage drugs. Phil was too low in spirit not to be tempted by her tabs of "Purple Haze" acid and her experiments with free-basing cocaine. One afternoon they smoked a few joints of psilocybin-soaked grass from Colombia. His hallucinations were so strong he walked out of her house backwards and went three blocks down the street that way.

Then, thank God, he met the pig.

Her name was Connie, and she was a Vietnamese hanging stomach pig. Imagine a wild boar without tusks, a back that drops in a hairy swaying U from shoulders to hipbones, a stomach that licks the ground, an appetite that craves M&M candies, a very clever mind, and you have Connie.

Phil was one of those people who's never put off by anything, so when this creature appeared in our backyard one evening after we'd grilled outdoors, he only bent over and asked if it had come for dessert.

I asked what the fuck it was, and he said a Vietnamese hanging stomach pig. I didn't ask how he knew that, because Strayhorn knew something about everything. He was the only person I've ever known who'd read through entire encyclopedias for fun, turned down a full graduate fellowship to Cal Tech in physics to be an actor, and kept books like Ludwig Wittgenstein's *Tractatus Logico-philosophicus* by his bed for a light read before going to sleep.

The pig wore an ornate leather dog collar with its name, "Connie," and a telephone number scratched on the side. I went into the house to call the number while Phil fed it Raisinets.

Fifteen minutes later a merry-looking old man appeared on our patio. He was short and compact, with the florid look of someone who spends time outside. A face as round as his body, talc-white hair in an army crew cut, quick bright eyes. He looked like a man who owned his own truck or worked in a plant where big guys used their hands and sweated out a quart a day.

"There you are, Connie! Hello, boys, I'm Venasque."

Phil's recovery had begun.

Venasque lived down the block in his own house with the pig and an old bull terrier named Big Top. They walked around the neighborhood three times a day, although neither of us had ever seen them before. Since they hit it off from the first, Phil began to join their parade whenever he could.

The only thing the old man clearly did for Phil in the months to come was teach him to swim. But obviously more was going on that I knew nothing about. The closer they became, the less was said. Yet it was plain from the first that the chemistry between them was very good.

Sometimes it is the smallest thing that saves us: the weather growing cold, a child's gesture, cups of excellent coffee. When I would ask what they did that day, Phil would smile and say vaguely, "swam," "talked," or "played with the animals."

Venasque was from France but hadn't been back there in thirty years. A Jew who'd fled the Nazis, he settled in California during the war because it reminded him of his home outside Avignon. He'd been married but his wife was dead. Years before, they'd owned a successful luncheonette across the street from one of the film studios. No matter when you went over to visit, he always asked, as soon as you came in, if you'd like a sandwich. They were hard to resist.

Phil and he spent more and more time together. At first I was perplexed, then a wee bit jealous. I asked what he saw in the old guy, but Phil said only "He knows things"—the greatest Strayhorn accolade of all.

Whatever Venasque knew, it made my friend happier and more at peace with himself. He stopped seeing the drug queen, quit work at the restaurant, and began doing professional research. For a time he had a small part in a dreadful sitcom that kept him busy and paid his many bills. Like me, he loved things and bought them whether he had money or not (he joked the words above the American Express or Master Charge offices should read "All Hope Abandoned Ye Who Enter Here"). Somewhere in our shared past we'd agreed that good therapy in the middle of a depression was to go out and buy something extravagant. So what if you didn't have any money—a new briefcase or first edition would cheer you up a little.

I got involved with an actress and made the mistake of moving in with her. What with that, my own career, and Venasque, Phil and I saw much less of each other for over two years.

He lived alone in our apartment a few months and then, to my surprise, moved in with the old man. It sounded like a fairy-tale household—the old man, the scholar, the dog, and the pig.

Time talks behind our back. To our face it's friendly and logical, never hesitating to give more of itself. But when we're not looking, it steals our lives and says bad things about us to the parts of us it's stolen.

Youth? You could have had a much more successful time of it if *he'd* worked harder. Friendship? No matter how much time I gave him, he never wanted to give you enough. Twenties? You could have been a contender if he'd only used me the right way. We hear these words from different sources, most particularly our inner voices, which gossip incessantly, only too happy to tell what they've heard from enemies.

Strayhorn and I wanted to be in the movies; we wanted to live interesting lives. Perhaps that's the difference between our generation of post–World War Two babies and others: Right or wrong, we came to expect as part of our birthright to have at least a fighting chance at creating a personal environment that makes it possible to wake in the morning eager and curious about what the day will hold.

But time was beginning to whisper. I made *The Night Is Blond* in 16 millimeter. No one had made a 16-millimeter film in so long that just the number made for smiles and raised eyebrows. It was black-and-white, perverse but tender. In my favorite comment, Phil said it was as hot and strange-tasting as horseradish. People argued about it as they walked out of the theater. You can still see it sometimes at places like the Thalia in New York, where it's usually on a double bill with films like *Elephant Man* or *Stranger Than Paradise*.

Before I left for Europe to make *Babyskin*, Phil and I kept a vow we'd made to each other the day we arrived in Hollywood: Whenever one of us really broke through to success, we'd go out together and get tattoos. We knew the tattoo parlor wouldn't have what we wanted, so we took an illustration we'd agreed on years before: a big black crow. Our skin birds. We had them injected high up on our shoulders to make it look like they were making the long curved flight up our backs.

When I returned from Europe five months later, Phil picked me up at the airport with the script of *Midnight* in his hand.

The morning accompanied Wyatt and me across country. The sun shone only early white light, and even thunderclouds over Colorado looked new and clean. We would land in Los Angeles at noon. Finky Linky still hadn't told me about Pinsleepe.

Getting up to go to the bathroom, I suddenly felt a terrible scratching, pulling pain in my back. It was so bad I yelped and grabbed myself there. Wyatt and the people nearby stared at me, but it was too difficult to say anything then. I was under attack; some huge mouth was trying to suck the skin off my back or something; I'd never felt anything like it before.

Walking fast down the aisle, I looked at the lights over the bathroom doors and gratefully saw one of them was vacant. Slipping into the phone-booth-size stall, I snapped the lock shut. What the hell *was* it? Before I had a chance to pull my jacket off, I felt something new and utterly frightening under my shirt back there. The pain had stopped, but what was moving right where it had been? Something big, big as a hand, scratching and scraping to get out.

I lost control. Ripping at my clothes, I managed to pull my jean jacket off and the shirttail out in a few desperate jerks. I think I was making noise too. I'm not sure what I was doing except getting hysterical. You know the feeling of a bug or something else small and unknown under your shirt or skirt in summer, when anything has a chance to land or walk there. Multiply that by ten or twenty, make it jerk around, give it fur or something else. Play with the idea. It was that bad. Really.

And then it was out. It flew straight over my shoulder and into the mirror. The crow. My tattoo. Our skin birds; mine was alive. Off my back and alive, scared, flying in a little metal room five miles off the earth.

I broke its neck. Not thinking, I grabbed the bird out of the air and, fumbling with its sharp flutter, squeezed. *Snap!* It stopped moving: from stiff and crazy to soft and curved in an instant.

5

There is so much Weber doesn't know. Where should I begin? With Venasque and his pig and bull terrier that understood everything you said? Or with Pinsleepe and the crow tattoo?

Venasque. For thirty years of hungry customers, he was only a chatty Frenchman who made delicious sandwiches because he liked to see people eat. Other things he liked? His animals, cooking, watching television, magic.

Venasque the shaman, the most powerful I ever met. He didn't know where the magic came from, but he used it well and selflessly. He taught his animals to understand, taught me to swim (particularly through the black water of my past), taught Sasha Makrianes who she really was, taught other things to other people.

If you needed to fly, he would teach you. Yes, he could do that if he thought it necessary. But most people don't need to fly. Venasque's greatest magic was helping you discover the discipline that would eventually save your life. Often it was something entirely trivial.

Harry Radcliffe told one of my favorite Venasque stories. After he won the Pritzker Award for Architecture and was on the cover of Time *magazine, Harry had a nervous breakdown.*

It manifested itself in an original way: In the middle of designing an important building for the 750th anniversary of Berlin, he stopped all work on it and began assembling an elaborate miniature city in his living room.

At first it consisted of paper models of the Secession Museum in Vienna, Richard Rogers's Lloyd's of London building, Aldo Rossi's Teatro del Mondo. Then he added thirty or forty schlocky souvenir statues of places like the Eiffel Tower, Seattle Space Needle, and Statue of Liberty. Stir in six chrome teapots designed by Michael Graves, a modified Chinese wok that served as part of the Spaceport for visitors from other planets, assorted other models, toys, and clay figures Radcliffe made or collected, and you have a whiff of what was going on.

Through friends, Harry's wife heard about Venasque and asked him to come over. The story goes he arrived at their Santa Barbara house with the pig sitting next to him in his jeep.

In the living room, Connie crushed half of Harry's city by walking over to the table that held his lunch. Venasque kicked over the other half, saying, "He's got enough buildings. Get him a clarinet."

The old man didn't know how to play any instrument, but he made Harry learn from a four-dollar book they bought together that day, along with the used clarinet.

I have read Pauwels, Lévi-Strauss, Joseph Campbell, Castaneda, and Mircea Eliade on magic and shamans. But what they say is essentially wrong for one simple reason—those who can, do; those who can't, talk (or write) about it. When I first began to see what Venasque was capable of doing, I naïvely asked him one day if there were people who could fly.

"Yes."

"Walk on water?"

"Sure. You want more tuna salad?"

"Why wouldn't they show the world?"

"Why should they? You think they care if you know? You're smart, Phil; you want everybody to know you're a smartie?"

I smiled. "Yeah, I like it when people know."

He winked. "That's the difference between you and the guy who can walk on water. He does it to find a place on his map, not to get on the Tonight Show."

In the six months he allowed me to live with him, I learned about my "map" from Venasque and how to find certain coordinates on it. I learned I would be successful but that handling success was far more difficult than getting it. I learned how to swim. I learned how to die. I *heard the name "Pinsleepe" for the first time in a dream I had while sleeping in the ocean one night. Yes, I did that too. He showed me how. It didn't help.*

———————

Sasha Makrianes has a peculiar face. From the front she's great—thick brown hair, high cheekbones, full mouth, deep-set eyes that watch carefully but openly. Her whole expression says, I'm listening. Tell me everything before I make a judgment. Not many people do that these days. Look around and see how skeptical most eyes are, how many mouths set hard and tight into "Absolutely not!" before you've ever said anything. Sasha is the old throwback—she wants to like you. Her face says she hopes she will.

That's from the front, but her profile unfortunately says other things. A short, soft chin and down-curved nose throw your first impression off. Her forehead is not as high as you thought. It is the side view of a weak person, someone not completely trustworthy. She said that about her face soon after we met in Vienna, and she was right. In Hollywood (especially behind a movie camera) it is immensely important to notice, but I was in Europe as a *flaneur*, not *auteur*, and wasn't looking at people's angles that way. It made life easier and me less critical.

When Wyatt and I moved through the last door at Los Angeles airport and saw her, she looked exhausted and ethereal, as if she might float off the earth in the next instant. Her face was Kabuki white, her long hair swept up and gone into a tight bun behind her head. She wore jeans and a white T-shirt under Phil's only sport jacket, the one he'd bought years before at Anderson & Shepard in London. When I asked him why there, he said because it was Fred Astaire's favorite store.

Sasha knew he loved it. I felt such a smash of love and pity that I wanted to hug her until we both cried from the embrace and our loss.

She wouldn't get near either of us. "It's my hands. I don't want to touch you with them."

I noticed for the first time. They were blush red, broken out in many scattered, ugly sores, looking like she'd pulled them out of a wreck almost too late.

"I'm sorry. This hasn't happened since I was a kid. Whenever I got terribly upset, my hands broke out like this. I know it's disgusting, but the doctor said I should keep them out in the air and not cover them with gloves. I'll wear them for the funeral though. . . .

"Hi, Wyatt. I didn't know you were coming."

He dropped his bag and pulled her to him anyway. She looked at me over his shoulder and her eyes said, I'm okay. I've just been crying a lot.

Outside, the sun was an old warm friend. Sometimes I think California owns all the beautiful weather in the world—or is at least in charge of handing it out to the rest of the world after it's used there.

Wyatt bumped into a woman who'd worked on his show. When he stopped to say hello, Sasha said we'd get the car and bring it around.

She walked straight out into the traffic without looking. I snatched her back. "Take it easy, Sash. Slow down." We looked at each other, then I aimed us across the whizzing street, still holding her arm.

"Will you stay at my place, Weber? You're not going to take a hotel room, are you?"

"Not if you don't want. Sure I'll stay with you."

"Good." She wouldn't look at me. "Sometimes I sleep okay. Sometimes I go through the whole night and have no dreams. But you know what I do when I can't sleep? Watch Finky Linky tapes. Three o'clock in the morning laughing at old videos of *The Finky Linky Show*. That's why I was so surprised to see him here. It was as if he'd just stepped out of his bread shoes into my living room. They were Phil's tapes. He watched them all the time."

There was nothing to say to that. We hustled across the street and into one of the parking lots. After a few minutes of looking here and there, she stopped in front of a vintage 1969 black Jaguar XKE. Phil's car. The only person I ever knew who bought a car because it looked like a German fountain pen.

"The Montblanc is still around, huh? He always said he was going to buy something else."

"It tickled him to look at it. He and Flea used to ride around town with the top down, Flea snorting and Phil listening to his Paolo Conte tapes.

"I think he probably left the car to you, Weber. Don't be surprised if you get most of his things. You and Jackie." She unlocked the door on my side and stood very close, looking at me.

"What about you?"

"Let's wait to talk about that. I'm too nervous and edgy now. I'd like to get used to having you here before we get into any of the big stuff. Okay?"

Before I could answer, she did something that took me completely by surprise. Putting her raw, wounded hands on either side of my head, she pulled me over for a big kiss on the mouth. Her lips stayed closed and the kiss was more like a hard, reassuring handshake, but it went on a long time and I was slightly out of breath when she let go.

She looked pleased with herself. "You don't mind, do you?" Not waiting for an answer, she walked away and unlocked the other door. "I'm so happy you're here. Let's go get Finky Linky."

I have been in the houses of two people who'd recently died. When Venasque had a stroke, I went to his house with Phil to get a suit in which to bury the old man. What was most disturbing there was the incompleteness of everything. A chair in the living room slightly askew, a half-full bottle of ketchup waiting in the refrigerator, a magazine in the bathroom open to an article on Don Johnson. I remember feeling compelled to close that magazine, straighten the chair so it was plumb with the rest of the room. Things left at hurried, sloppy angles, things that would have been straightened or used up or finished if the tenant had only had the chance to return and screw caps back on, sit on the can one last time, give five minutes to finishing the dumb article on his favorite TV star.

Strayhorn's house was worse. After dropping Wyatt and Sasha off at her apartment, I took the car and drove to Phil's. I had to because, until I did, I'd be haunted by my imaginings. I had to see for myself where he'd shot himself (all I could picture was a blood-spattered copy of Rilke's poetry), the empty dog basket, a cupped dip in the blue couch where he'd sat for the last time.

I also wanted to see what was in his medicine cabinet. Was there still laundry in the washing machine? What other things did he hold in his hand the last day of his life? What work had he done? Any record on the turntable? Final glimpses, details, a clue. Is that perverse? In an autopsy, the medical examiner tells you what the person had for a last meal. Disgusting or clinical, it meant something, if only: This is what was there at the end. Pathetic or impressive. X marks the spot. It stopped here. A sweater on a chair, birdseed on the kitchen counter, a new painting I'd never seen before. The end.

I've been lying. When confronted with wonder we usually lie or shut up. We must. Impossible things demand silence for some time at least. I've said nothing about the impossible things that had been happening almost from the moment I'd heard of his death in New York. The videotape from him that never ended. Sasha's illness and miraculous pregnancy (if it were true). What Wyatt had told me on the plane about Phil and Pinsleepe, the Angel of Death. Or the coming to life of my tattoo.

I've been lying because of what I found at Strayhorn's that afternoon. . . .

This still jars me. Like admitting to some dark secret I've hidden all my life. But it wasn't *my* secret. Perhaps it's because I loved Phil Strayhorn and still don't want to admit, either to myself or the world, that what he did goes beyond any borders of curiosity or quest. What he did was unimaginably wrong. What he wanted to do was . . . understandable.

I'm speaking in ellipses. Here is what happened.

Pulling into the driveway, I remembered the day Phil and Sasha stood there with Bloodstone masks on, waving goodbye, Flea snoofing around in the bushes. I turned off the motor and sat awhile listening to the quiet: cheerful birds, the busy hiss of insects, a distant car driving off. There were all the blooming cactus we'd planted together when he first moved into the house. From the car I could look through one of the front windows and see some of the objects in the living room.

Something moved in there.

I sat up straight in my seat.

Something showed for a moment in the window and then disappeared just as quickly. A head? A child hopping across the line of vision of the window? I couldn't tell. No child belonged in the house of a man three days dead.

There it was again. Jumping. It *was* a child: short hair, yellow shirt, waving hands in the air as it bounced past.

I got out of the car and found the keys to the house and burglar alarm on Sasha's key ring. Walking down the short path, I watched for the head but saw nothing.

"Hey, you!"

I turned and saw Mr. Piel approaching, Phil's next-door neighbor.

"How are you, Mr. Piel?"

"Gregston? Well, I'm glad it's you and not some more of them ghoul groupies. You should see what we've been getting up here since the news got out. Real fuck-brains. Bloodstone fan clubs. Some fat guy even stole the arm off the mailbox! Leave the dead alone, I say.

"It's bad, bad news, Weber. He was a good fella. I liked him. His movies were shit, but the guy was nice and didn't make noise. I don't know why he killed the goddamned dog, though. A real cute thing. He could've given it to my wife. She cried for a day when she heard that."

"Has anyone been inside since the police were here?"

"Nah, cops closed it off for their investigation, and I've been keeping a close eye on things since. Nobody would've gotten in there that I didn't know about. Naturally, Sasha's been in and out, but no one else, after the cops."

"There's no one in there now?"

"No one I know of. You going in?"

"Yes."

"You got a key? Where'd you get it?"

"Yes, Mr. Piel, I have a key. Am I keeping you from anything?"

"You telling me I should take a hike?" He crossed his arms over a thin chest. He'd worked as a key grip once, but his real calling in life was professional busybody. One minute you liked his feistiness; the next you wanted to punch him out.

"My best friend blew his brains out in there, Mr. Piel. I'm about to go in and look at his blood on the furniture. I'm not in the mood to be civil. Thanks for watching the house."

He turned and started to walk away. "Some people don't know how to be grateful. I should let them tear the house down. What do I care?"

Ignoring him, I went to the door and did the necessary twists and turns to deactivate the alarm. I was curious about who or what was inside, not afraid. Too much had happened to cause any more fear. An explanation of some kind was near, and I was hungry to know it.

Opening the door, I heard a too-familiar tune.

"Whistle and hop
and blow your top,
it's the Finky Linky Show!
Your feet are long
and your math is wrong
but your head is sure to growwwwww—"

I walked into the living room just as the child came hopping in from the kitchen, singing along with the theme song.

At first I thought it was about a seven-year-old boy, the dark hair was cut so short, but the singing voice was the high and delicate bell of a little girl.

Barefoot, she skipped around the room in a pair of blue jean overalls and a black T-shirt. The longer I looked at her, the more I realized she was a *real* beauty, not just a cute little kid. This one had all the makings.

The beauty part slid away when I saw how misshapen her stomach was. Under the overalls it looked as if she were hiding a basketball. She kept looking at me until she knew I was staring at her stomach. Then she stopped in the middle of the floor and took off the jeans and shirt. She was pregnant.

It was obscene and comical. She stood with her hands at her sides and smiled at me. I couldn't take my eyes off her form. There was nothing sexual or prurient about the stares, either. It was too outrageous to be sexy, something Eric Fischl or Paul Cadmus might have included in one of their paintings. Or Bosch.

Bosch! *The Garden of Earthly Delights*. After *Midnight* first appeared, Phil said in interviews he'd gotten most of his visual inspiration from that painting. At Harvard he'd kept a large print of it over his desk. I could remember only certain details, but looking at this little pregnant girl I was somehow sure she was in the painting too. That chilled me more than anything else.

Chill two came when she spoke. It came out a deep, hoarse, chocolate mousse of a voice: Lauren Bacall's in *To Have and Have Not*, sexy and available. A voice that had smoked thousands of cigarettes and would stay out all night with you.

"This is what you want." She went to a side table, picked up a book, brought it to me. "It was the one he was reading before he shot himself." I wanted to look at her and at the book at the same time.

She offered it open to a specific page. I reached out hesitantly and took it: *The Selected Poetry of Rainer Maria Rilke*. There were red stains over the white page. "The Second Elegy." The girl walked to the television set and switched it off. Turning to me, she spoke slowly and clearly.

> "Every angel is terrifying. And yet, alas,
> I invoke you, almost deadly birds of the soul,
> knowing about you. . . .
> But if the archangel now, perilous, from behind the stars
> took even one step down toward us: our own heart, beating
> higher and higher, would beat us to death. Who *are* you?"

"You're Pinsleepe, aren't you?"

"Yes."

I didn't know what more to say. She was Pinsleepe the angel. The angel that had come to Phil before he died and told him to stop making the Midnight films because they were evil.

"Was he really reading about angels before he did it?"

Her nakedness was smooth and angular. Women have curves, little girls angles. Even pregnant little girls. She stood there smiling.

"I think so. I'd come over to make him a sandwich for lunch. When I got here, he was sitting on the patio with that book turned to that page."

"Sasha told me *she* came over to make him lunch!"

"She did. *We* did."

"I don't understand."

The girl took my hand and led me to the couch. "Do you remember a night in Vienna when you and Sasha went out to the—"

"Look, get to the point! I don't *understand* any of this, see? My best friend killed himself. Called me up to talk about thumbs, then killed himself. That doesn't make sense, does it? I've heard stories about him for two days. Tattoos coming alive. Videotapes! One of them had my mother dying on it. Now you . . . Christ! Just tell me what the fuck is going on!"

She picked up a pink pillow and put it over her hairless lap. "My name is Pinsleepe. I came because he was in trouble."

"What kind of trouble?"

"With God."

"Look, I believe in angels. Truth! But *you're* not what I believed. Understand? They don't have to come out of the sky, or—I've dreamt of them all my life. I looked everywhere for them: in friends, and on the street like lost coins. I even knew a woman once. . . ."

"You're an angel, Pinsleepe? Then show me. Fly. Or do a miracle. Angels can—"

She held up a hand for quiet, then lowered it to her distended belly. Beneath those small fingers it began to grow transparent. Healthy skin color faded in a moment to skin of glass. Inside, and easy to see, curled in on itself but showing enough face to make out, was a fetus with long brown hair: a tiny unborn Sasha Makrianes.

"Sasha and I are pregnant with each other, Weber. Whoever gives birth first, lives. Only the baby dies."

"Why? What does Sasha have to do with Phil? She doesn't even know where the baby *came* from! Is it his?"

"No. It came with her cancer. Both are wrong and unnatural things, but so was Phil's death. Both are a result of his suicide.

"I came to tell him that. To tell him the films and his whole life had gone too far. There is a human balance, and there *are* extremes. It's different for everyone, but then you reach your limit.

"If you go beyond that, the greed explodes like a bomb in all directions. Look what happened to those children in Florida. Then what happened to Matthew Portland. The same thing is happening to Sasha. It's all Phil's fault. If he'd stopped after the first warning, I think it would have been all right. But he didn't. He did those other things and then he killed himself. Maybe he thought that was the only way he could stop his greed. But I kept telling him he was responsible for what he did. Always. Now that he's dead, someone else has to be."

two

1

I remember exactly where I began writing "Mr. Fiddlehead." Only it had a different title then: "Pinsleepe."

That's right. That's something Weber will probably never know, and she'll certainly never tell him: The film was to be a slice of my childhood, like a slice of pizza when you're a kid and can't afford a whole pie. I had been using little bits all along in the Midnight films, but "Pinsleepe" was going to be the biggest. I got the idea when I was working on the video for Vitamin D.

One night at dinner with Victor Dixon, lead guitarist of the group, we ended up talking about our childhoods. Victor told me he knew a woman who'd spent her adult life illustrating her childhood because it had been so traumatic.

I asked if he thought much about his own. His answer put "Pinsleepe" in my hand.

"Yeah, kind of, man. I was one of those lonely little kids, you know? So I made up this secret friend, the Bimbergooner, who kept me company? Sort of a combination of Sheena, Queen of the Jungle, Tom Terrific, and Finky Linky. I've spent my whole damned life looking for someone like Bimbergooner to be my friend."

"It was a girl?"

"I don't know, I think so. Or at least she was a boy but had all the good qualities of a girl. Something like that."

I laughed too hard. He looked at me strangely. "I'm laughing because I had Pinsleepe," I said. "She sounds exactly like your Bimbergooner, only Pinsleepe was definitely a girl. Know why? Because my dream friend would have no hesitation about pulling her pants down and showing 'it' to me whenever I wanted. Naturally I was dying to know what 'it' looked like, but my sister would never show me. I made Pinsleepe a girl so she'd not only be my friend but would have the right plumbing to satisfy my curiosity."

Victor snorted. "Shit. I wish I'd thought of that! I don't think I even knew what my dick looked like then, much less what I would be putting it into some day."

He went on talking about his imaginary friend, but I was already spinning with a new idea and inspiration.

I'd make a film about Pinsleepe! But a Pinsleepe who comes back twenty years later to visit her old friend and creator.

What would we do if that happened? How would we handle the return of our childhood? Or a mysterious part that showed up in the flesh and wanted to stay awhile to see what things had changed in the old neighborhood?

I'd grown so weary of Bloodstone and his meager world that I knew I had to do something entirely different or go nuts. I'd done the small part in Weber's film, but I needed much more than that exotic hors d'oeuvre. Here, appearing full-blown out of the ether, was a gift from heaven!

The problem was, no one on earth wanted to do it, including my partner, Matthew. "I'll give you two words, Phil, and they say it all: Woody Allen." He sat back, as proud as if he'd just proven Einstein wrong.

"What do you mean, Woody Allen? How is that supposed to finish this argument?"

"Every time Woody Allen makes a film that's not funny, it goes right in the toilet: financially, critically, everything. Why? Because people go to Woody Allen movies to see funny. The same way they go to your movies to see Bloodstone make them wee-wee their pants. Look what happened to Coca-Cola when they tried to change their formula.

"Classic Strayhorn works, Phil. Don't start fucking around with a new formula."

"What would you do if I insisted on making this film?"

"Sell my collection of Fabulous Fifties furniture to get the dough, jerkoff. You know that. But it doesn't mean I won't put my Uzi in your eye when we go broke!"

"I'm kidding. Do it. Who cares? What are you going to call it again, 'Pin Lips'? Jesus."

"PINSLEEPE. I'll make you an offer, Matthew. I'll write Midnight Four for you and we'll do that first. Then my film. Deal?"

"Yeah, a deal! I didn't think I was going to be able to persuade you to put on that makeup again for two years, old Puke Puss. Nice name, huh? That's what they called you in the last issue of Fangoria magazine."

I made notes on Pinsleepe and my shared secret world in between drafts of Midnight Kills. It took the longest time remembering exactly what she looked like. A really clear picture emerged only months later in Yugoslavia while we were negotiating shooting rights there for part of our next Bloodstone extravaganza.

I remember making a sketch of her on a paper napkin at an outdoor restaurant in Dubrovnik. We were eating cevapcici and drinking a good Yugoslavian pivo. When I was done, I slipped the napkin into my wallet and kept it until I died. I don't know why.

Bloodstone. Going back to him and the Midnight world began as an ordeal. Not that it was difficult writing a fourth film: I knew the geography of the place by heart, and where to go, once there.

What repelled me was the necessity of going there at all. I resented most the fact I couldn't leave that part of my life behind like a hick town I'd grown up in but left after graduating from school there.

Halfway through an okay and thoroughly mediocre script, I threw the whole thing out and began again with a new goal: If, as I hoped, Midnight Kills would be the last of "those" films for a very long time, why not work as hard as I could trying to create the best of the bunch? A horror film as hot and sinister as radioactivity, full of enough tricks and traps to keep people guessing and really scared till the end. That would be worth doing until I had the chance to get down to serious work on "Pinsleepe."

I went to Matthew's house at Malibu and watched the ocean for three days. Nothing doing. No inspiration in sea breezes.

After trudging back home discouraged, I found what I needed in a postcard from Weber. In Europe he had discovered the work of Elias

Canetti and had been sending me cards with quotes from the writer, sometimes as many as three a week.

> The outer bearing of people is so ambiguous that you only have to present yourself as you are to live fully unrecognized and concealed.

I read those words three times, then turned out the only light in the room and smiled like a happy hyena. Blood was rushing into my head, and it felt like I was glowing in the dark.

What if this time I put Bloodstone out on the street in a conservative blue suit, a tattered Bible in hand: Puke Puss set in the earnest sweat hypocrisy of a television evangelist? What if this time he was worshiped for what he was, not feared?

Worshiped by a society that wants God and salvation to be as plain and filling—accessible—as a deluxe cheeseburger with French fries. A bread-and-miracles saviur.

Only in Bloodstone's case, he would present himself as the other side of salvation.

> Look at me, brothers and sisters! I went the wrong way, and witness what happened! I've seen Hell, the end, the No Exit place. Yes, it is as bad as you thought. Yes, there are devils—look at me. Flames? Look at my face. Check me out; I'm a living visa from those countries. Ground zero for your worst fears. Okay, stare, but listen to me; I've been there. I can help you through.
>
> Leo Knott. That was the name, folks, a plain American name, as American as your best friend. As American as you.
>
> Leo Knott. That was my name. That was me.
>
> Not the Bloodstone you see now. Not this human scream with a face like puke and a soul that stinks of old perfume and meat.
>
> "No, only Leo Knott, a minister of God who started out going in the right direction. But then something happened, folks. Suddenly Leo Knott saw he could use whatever powers of persuasion he had to get what he wanted. Not what the Lord God wanted, what Leo Knott wanted.
>
> Did I use it to get women? My house was filled with blondes. Had to take the phone off the hook, they were calling all day and all night. I owned two black address books!

Did I use it to get money? I had so much money in my pocket, it looked like I was carrying a couple of sandwiches in there all the time!

That's the trick, you see. Say the name "God" and good people come running. They'll sell their farms and businesses and send you the checks. When they believe, they open their hearts and you can reach right in and take whatever you want.

That's what I did. I took their best parts and didn't think twice about it. I took their love, I took their trust, and, yes, I took their money as well. Not for God, for Leo Knott.

I spent it all! Spent it in fancy stores and fancy beds. Spent it on nights I couldn't remember the next day except for the full ashtrays and pink lipstick stains on the whiskey glasses.

You know what I'm talking about?

That's how Midnight Kills *begins: Bloodstone confidently pacing the pulpit of a flyblown church in Watts, his audience a rotting array of junkies, bums, one-foot-in-the-graves, nothing-lefts on a Tuesday afternoon at the end of their lives, listening to a freak wail God at them until the free soup is served.*

We'd chosen the men and women from the worst we could find on the street. I wanted them looking as real as possible: their faces, their clothes, their broken-cup hopelessness.

As I spoke to them I felt no need to act or play. Outrageous as he appeared, Bloodstone was easy to "be" because his hatred was pure and sharp as the smell of shit. He was *shit: no subtlety, no calm, no mask. Only hatred that came in one aroma, and too bad if you don't want to smell it; it's right here in your face.*

I knew him because I knew my own wild hatred. It'll disappoint you, however, if you think I'm going to say I was my monster, that I was Bloodstone. Never. I never walked a street with curled Dracula fingers and stone heart looking for victims. Nor did I dream of his sins and wish I had the courage or kink to commit them.

But I'll tell you something. The heart of darkness or banality of evil is no more than interest. The fact we don't stand in wonder at the horrors some people do today is proof enough that the dark things interest us too much.

What did Goethe say: "I can't imagine a crime I wouldn't commit in certain circumstances"? Update that to "I can't imagine a crime that

*doesn't attract me somehow" and you have our world. People "loved"
Bloodstone and the nightmares he did because he took our few moments
of crazed, invigorating anger and turned them into a lifetime. Rest in
Piss.*

*The first day on the set didn't go well. The crew made many foolish
mistakes getting used to one another. But that was usual when you began
shooting a film.*

*More importantly, in the middle of my "sermon" one of the bums in
the audience was supposed to fart loudly. I even remember the man's
name, because he was famous in the neighborhood for being able to fart
at will: Michael Rhodes.*

*When I said, "Any man who thinks his heart well is a fool and a liar,"
Michael Rhodes was supposed to do his stuff. In rehearsal everything
had gone fine. I'd say, "a fool and a liar," and he'd let fly enough wind
and sound to flap a sail.*

*But when the cameras started rolling and Michael's big moment ar-
rived, his tail winds died. Not one toot, although the squeezed, panicked
expression on his ruined face said he was certainly trying.*

*The first few takes it was funny. But you can laugh only so many times
at a slipup. Then it gets boring and frustrating and hardens permanently
into plain failure.*

*The fifth or sixth time nothing happened, I was about to call Cut!
when someone let zap a blast that sounded like a tugboat crossing the
harbor. Everyone on the set cheered.*

*Looking out over the congregation, I did a double-take when I saw a
new face that hadn't been there before. Who's dat?*

*A little girl, but what a little girl! Short hair, gorgeous features. She
stood out from those rats like a small but brilliant acetylene flame.
Smiling wickedly, she held her nose with two fingers the way kids do
when something stinks—P.U.!*

Pinsleepe.

———————

"You were here when Phil killed himself?"

Pinsleepe shook her head exaggeratedly from side to side, a child
saying no too hard. "I told you—I came up here to fix him lunch but he
was dead."

"*You* found him or Sasha found him?"

"I *told* you, Weber, it's the same thing! We're each other."

"Explain that." It was maddening. One moment she spoke with the aplomb of a career diplomat; the next she was only a little girl, crabby from too little sleep or too much stimulus. How was I going to find out all the things I needed to know?

"I have to go to the bathroom." She jumped up and left the room. I looked out the glass doors onto the patio. There was the chair he'd died in. There was—

The telephone rang. I heard the bathroom door close just as that first ring stopped. An extension was nearby so I picked it up.

"Weber? It's me, Sasha. Are you almost finished there?"

"Wait a second, Sash. Hold the line." Dropping the receiver on the couch, I moved fast for the bathroom door. If I caught the kid on the pot, tough. I *had* to see. The door swung open onto no one there. No Pinsleepe, no Sasha. An empty room.

I have a friend whose cat always knows when the phone is going to ring before it actually does. The child jumped up right before the ring and was out of sight by the time I heard Sasha's first words. Standing there, my hand still on the doorknob, I heard the girl's last words.

"It's the same thing! We're each other."

"A long long time ago this terrible thing happened. . . ."

Dumbfounded, I looked up from the paper. Across the grave, Sasha stared at Phil's coffin, an expression of dulled, empty sadness on her pale face. Wyatt Leonard stood on one side of her, Harry Radcliffe on the other. The two men were looking at me, surprised, but Sasha continued to gaze at the open hole in front of us.

I returned to the paper and the words Phil had asked that I read at his funeral, the words that were the voice-over beginning to *Midnight*.

"A famous poet once said, 'Perhaps all the dragons in our lives are princesses who are only waiting to see us act, just once, with beauty and courage, Perhaps everything that frightens us is, in its deepest essence, something helpless that wants our love.'

"But that's not true. Dragons and monsters don't wait for courage and beauty. Only loss. Only death. There are people like that too."

If it were the beginning of his film, you would see the actress Violet

Maitland, an infant in her arms, cross an airy, pastel living room to open balcony doors. Whispering sweet goo-goo sounds to the baby, she walks out onto her wide sunny balcony. The view from this high, expensive vantage point is splendid.

After a moment to allow us to share both the view and a delectable taste of her world, the woman heaves the child off the balcony as hard as she can. The only sound is her *hoosh!* of breath doing it.

But we weren't watching the film. We were several hundred standing around a gravesite with our separate thoughts about a man who was about to be covered up with a couple of hundred pounds of dirt for the rest of time.

Why had he done this? What was the purpose? Read alone, the quote from Rilke would have been moving, both because it was his favorite poet and the sentiment was very appropriate to Strayhorn. But to include the entire opening speech from that grisly film was tasteless and perverse.

Sasha gave me the envelope as we were riding to the cemetery. When I started to open it, she put her hand over mine and said that in his suicide note Phil had asked that it not be opened or read until the correct time. I'd assumed that meant he had something to say he wanted all the mourners to hear at the same time, a final important message. But not this. Not a macabre joke at his own dead expense in the last minutes many of us would ever have for him.

What else did his suicide note say?

> At a certain point, I loaded my boat with all the important possessions I thought I wanted to take with me on the final trip to the old days of my life, across an ocean thirty or forty years long. All the things that were important—people, objects, ideas. But because of recent events (storms!), I've had to toss one after another of these things overboard until now, when my ship is so light that, amazingly, it has begun to float *above* the waters, which means there is even less control, even less possibility of reaching my previously set destination.
>
> If Weber comes, please ask him to read the enclosed at my funeral. I would prefer that no one, including you two, see what it says until the ceremony. I'm assuming you and my parents will want me to have a funeral, but it makes no difference to me. My only request is that I be buried rather than cremated.

I'm sorry about this, Sasha. Please know it is in no way your fault. You have always been the peace and intimacy of a whisper to me. I love you.

There was more of Phil's graveside statement to read. I was about to go on when the first shots were fired.

Unlike the "eyewitness" accounts you hear on television from bewildered or distraught people who "thought the shots were just cars backfiring or firecrackers going off," these sounded like gunshots. Three *pows* very fast. In the instant it took to turn in their direction, I noticed almost everyone had turned that way too. As if we all knew exactly where to look, exactly where the trouble came from.

"There he is!"

"It's fucking Bloodstone!"

He came straight at us in a slow gliding jog, black pants and shirt, silver Bloodstone face. The gun in his hand looked big as a block of wood. He was laughing and shooting at us. A woman across the grave went down, then a man. Hit? People were running everywhere. Finky Linky pushed Sasha into the grave and went in after her. I ran at Bloodstone without thinking. His high keening laugh. *Pow!*

2

We beat the shit out of him. Somewhere a woman's voice kept yelling, "Stop it, stop it! You'll kill him!" But that's what we wanted. All of us punching and kicking this son of a bitch till he died and never got up again. I love to fight but had never done anything like this—twenty (or so) to one, him on the ground, us standing over and whacking away at his unmoving form whenever we saw an opening.

"Kill the sick fuck!"

"Break his head!"

I kicked him and felt something hard go soft.

Scuffling and pushing, we were a pack of crazy starved dogs on a small prey. Each wanted a bite, our own bloody fresh piece. My dark funeral suit was dirt brown and scuffle-dust gray. Someone bent down and tore the silver mask off.

The man beneath looked like a teenager. No more than twenty. In less than a minute, his young face was a mess of ripe fruit color: shiny apple and grape, white where it shouldn't have been. Bone.

It was a blank gun. He had got off one more shot—straight at me—before I ran into him and kicked his balls. He was laughing when he shot at me, laughing on the ground being beaten down into wet rags by a lot of traumatized mourners.

I don't think I've ever been so angry in my life. When he was laughing I would have happily killed him. Pull a person's true anger out and it's impossible to put it right back in. Scare us enough and we'll do anything.

The police came fast, but there was a near riot as they tried to pull us off and get him out of there.

Who was he? I forget the name. Sasha wanted me to read an article on him in the newspaper the next day, but just hearing he was a "Midnight fan who wanted his hero Philip Strayhorn to go out 'as good as his movies' " was enough.

My anger scared me. My fear too. Riding back from the cemetery with Sasha and Mr. and Mrs. Strayhorn, I didn't say anything when the old man started piping off.

"I'm sorry, but *I'm* not surprised. He was my son but I'm not surprised this happened. You cannot make films like Philip's and expect your audience to be sane. They were depraved, both the films and the people who paid to go see them. What happened was a result of that depravity."

"What do you think is a good movie, Mr. Strayhorn?"

He wasn't used to being questioned, especially by a woman, so he looked Sasha over carefully before answering her.

"A good movie? *Citizen Kane. The Seventh Seal.* Even *North by Northwest* is a good film, maybe even a great film."

Facing him in the limousine seat, Sasha sat far forward so they were very close. "Tell me some good books."

He didn't like her closeness but wasn't about to be topped. "Oh, I don't know. Kipling's good; I've just been rereading him. Evelyn Waugh. Why do you ask?"

"What about good paintings?"

Mrs. Strayhorn touched Sasha's knee. "Why are you asking, dear?"

"Your son was trying to make something strange and new and vital with his films, but all you have to say about his life's work was it was *depraved?*"

Mr. Strayhorn crossed his arms and smiled scornfully. "You've been reading too many reviews, Sasha. Philip became a very rich man pandering to the twelve- and thirteen-year-olds in this sad country with about an ounce of imagination and a year's supply of chicken blood.

"There was nothing 'vital' about *Midnight.* Who do you think you're kidding? Yes, throwing a child off a balcony is strange, but not strange in the wonderful way of Fellini's *8½.*

"I respected Philip's success. He did what he chose to do well. But those of you who mistake his 'achievement' for something real and artistic, even worthwhile, are either blackly cynical or stupid.

"Good films? Weber made good films. Watch *Wonderful* carefully, and you see love and originality spread across the whole two hours, like good chocolate icing on a cake. The Midnight movies are cleverly filmed, and they scare the bejeesus out of you, but they stink."

"Why, because they 'pander' to our animal instincts?"

"No, because they don't *love* those animal instincts, which are so much a part of us. At best, they make fun of them. Ever think about that, Sasha? I'm sure not.

"Knowing my son, I'm sure he astutely explained their complete etiology and 'semiotic importance' to you: all the intellectually swank and blah-blah terms that are spread over society's opinions like expensive jam nowadays. But when you bite into it, it's still a shit sandwich, jam or not. People like Philip invent those terms to spread over their work so we don't realize. . . .

"Listen, I know he hated me—"

Mrs. Strayhorn put a hand on his arm and cooed to calm him down. He ignored her and kept spitting bullets at Sasha.

"—but that was his right. Maybe we raised him and his sister wrong. That could be. I'll tell you something, though—I feel sad he killed himself, but not guilty. He believed perfection was possible. All his life he said that. But that was his trouble. I'm sure he made those movies as a 'strange and vital' way of telling people they were dangerous and in trouble, so they'd better start looking inside to find out why they liked films like *Midnight.* I understand that. It's one way of doing it. But he made the money and success knowing his work was popular for all the wrong reasons. He continued to show us again and again how utterly evil and disgusting we can be to each other. *That's* what people came to see, not preposterous, tacked-on moral endings with smiling faces and false sunrises. The slime and the crackpots like that man in the cemetery ended up buying all the tickets.

"I noticed Pauline Kael didn't say anything about the last film, did she? You know who did? *Fangoria* magazine. Their review ran next to a full-color photo of someone in a pig mask covered with blood, carrying a chain saw. You know what *they* called my son's greatest creation, the being he wanted to instruct the people with? Pus Puss."

"*Puke* Puss." His wife corrected him.

"Excuse me. Puke Puss."

Sasha sat at her kitchen table while I made lunch. She'd changed into a bathrobe and bedroom slippers.

"Do you think his father was right?"

I began peeling an apple. "Yes, I think to a degree. But it's damned hard not to get comfortable inside success. It's like falling into a soft chair at the end of a hard day. Especially when you're someone like Phil who went through years of trouble before making it. He hit on a successful formula with *Midnight* and more or less stuck with it. Nothing wrong with that."

"You didn't do it. Every one of your films is different."

"Sash, don't compare us. I stopped making films. I threw in the towel."

"Why? Not because of that earthquake."

"That was part of it. Phil once gave his sister a line that stuck in my head. 'The world doesn't need me for anything, but I need to tell the world some things.' After the quake I didn't feel I had anymore to 'tell' in films.

"Something else. Remember when I shared those dreams with Cullen James?"

She took a piece of apple off the plate. "Yes. I read *Bones of the Moon.*"

"Cullen asked me not to talk about it, but I'll tell you this: For a few weeks in my life, I had a feeling for what the miraculous *really* is. It's not making films."

She was about to put the apple in her mouth when she stopped and looked at me. "Do *you* know what the miraculous is?"

"So far, all I've figured out is it's somewhere in real life, not in fantasy or art. You might be able to reach it through those things, but it's across the bridge."

She shook her head. "I don't know what you mean."

I took the salt and pepper shakers and put them near each other: the pylons of my bridge. "The only thing art can do is suggest how to cross this bridge. Better eyes than ours, better ears, have experienced things, maybe truths, that help instruct how to do it. What's on the other side? Salvation and peace.

"But you can find salvation without art. Sure, lots of artists like Van Gogh who had horrible lives found release through their art. But I don't think it was the art that saved them; it was the *work*, the love of the human act involved, that brought them peace. Their work just happened to be putting paint on a canvas, or whatever.

The miracle is somewhere in the human act. The only difference I see between an artist and a ditchdigger who loves his work is this: When the artist is working well, he's also able to control some of the chaos of his life through his work, besides enjoying the effort. The ditchdigger only moves dirt from here to there.

"But don't get me wrong—if he loves that movement, he's still a hell of a lot better off than many people."

She smiled. "You stopped making pictures because it didn't satisfy you anymore?"

"Hell, no! I loved making films. I still do. It's like having a conversation with someone you really like and admire. But when you run out of words or things to say, your listener can be the most fascinating person and you're still stuck.

"That's why I started the Cancer Theater Group. There's a million things to say there."

"Because the actors are dying?"

"No, because they're all hungry for whatever they can get. I feel that every day, and it makes me hungry too—for life, not art."

"What about art raising life to a higher level?"

"From my experience with this group, art at its best only raises life to an all-encompassing *now*. It forces us to forget time, or death, or anything and just allows us to live *now*. That's why the actors are so excited by what they're doing. For a couple of hours in their terminal day-to-day, they don't have to think about pills or chemotherapy. They're immortal."

"I have cancer too."

"That's what you said. Do you want to talk about it?" I didn't look up or change the tone of my voice.

"Not yet. Cancer, and I'm pregnant. Some combination, huh? Life and death living in one stomach, hand in hand! I don't even know where the baby came from."

"We can talk whenever you want. In the meantime, do you have any horseradish?"

When things are bad I often go into the nearest kitchen and cook. I try to make the acts of cutting and measuring, pouring and stirring, into little Zen masterpieces that, taken together, might someday metamorphose into mini-Satori. I don't close my eyes and shoot arrows into bull's-eyes, I stir-fry.

While I put things together, Sasha asked if it'd be all right to go in and lie down till lunch was ready. That was fine because good meals are temperamental—if, while preparing, you don't give them your full attention they often turn out flat and sulky, hiding in their room behind too much salt or spice.

About ten minutes later, deep into the secrets of shaving carrots, I didn't notice when she entered the room.

"Oh, carrots! Can I have one?" She wore a blue-and-white sailor-boy skirt and blouse, white knee socks, and patent leather shoes. The heartbreakers were the little white gloves and patent leather purse that looked brand new.

My first thought was to look beyond her, down the hall toward Sasha's bedroom.

Seeing this she spoke again, her voice pouty and hurt. "If you want me to go away, wake her up. That's all you have to do, if you don't want me around!"

"Come here!" Taking her small gloved hand, I pulled her into a room off the kitchen where Sasha kept a television and an old couch. "Where were you? Where have you been?"

"At the graveyard. I took Phil some flowers."

"Where did you go the other day? When we were up at his house?"

Snapping her shiny purse open and closed, open and closed, she just shrugged.

"Only one of you can be here at a time. Is that right?"

She looked at her purse, opened and closed it again, and nodded without looking at me.

"I don't understand something. You were around before Phil met Sasha. Why are you . . . *in* her now?"

"I don't know! I was with Phil when he was a little boy. I've been his friend a lot longer than *she* has!"

"Then why is she pregnant with you? She says she hadn't slept with him for months."

"What's 'slept with'? You mean in the same bed?"

"I mean have sex. They hadn't fucked for months!"

"What do you mean, 'fuck'?"

I glared at her, incredulous. Was it possible? To know so many things, to be pure magic, and not know that?

Yes, if she was really only a child.

"Sit down here. Sit next to me. I want you to tell me everything that's happened, from the minute you came back to be with Phil. Will you do that? I need to know everything, okay?"

Wonder belongs to children, so when they talk about it, it's usually in the relaxed, reasonable voice of long-time residents. More than real life, wonder is their home. They believe in miracles, people with successful wings, religion. "Impossible" is an enemy, gravity too, our mundane and inappropriate schedules for them. Many of their days aren't even spent on this earth with us. They are just very good at pretending they're here.

Pinsleepe said she was eight. I later assumed that meant Phil created her when *he* was eight and she never got older. But if that were true, how could she have written "Mr. Fiddlehead"?

"I didn't write it! I only saw it was Phil's and thought it was a good trick to change it. I touched the pages."

There was a pad of paper on the television set. I picked it up and riffled through the pages to make sure there was nothing on them. Completely blank. I needed some other irrefutable proof from her, another miracle to convince me that what Pinsleepe said was true.

"Touch this one. Do the same thing with this. Make 'Mr. Fiddlehead' again."

She took the pad, drummed her fingers on it once, handed it back.

Every page was filled with Phil's handwriting, on both sides. It must have been a very long story handwritten, because the entire pad was full. I put it down and looked at her.

"Did Phil make you up when you were children?"

"Sorta."

3

S he took the videocassette from me and, sliding it into the machine, pressed all the right buttons to get it going. Phil appeared on the television screen.

"Hi, Weber. I'm glad you got this far. I thought you would, but there's always the possibility of being wrong about people you love. That's the worst mistake you can make. But I *wasn't* wrong about you.

"Obviously you want to know about Pinsleepe. And 'Mr. Fiddlehead.' What has she said so far? It doesn't matter; I'll tell you what I can, and if you have other questions she'll answer them."

What followed was unexpected. I assumed Phil would tell the story in the concise, lucid sentences I was so accustomed to from him. Instead, for the next quarter of an hour he showed home movies, the same kind I'd seen of my mother's last minutes.

Only Strayhorn's were of a lonely child talking to an imaginary, invisible friend named Pinsleepe. But there was no real friend in his films. Certainly not the mysterious little beauty who sat next to me.

Phil (and Pinsleepe) climbed trees, built a fort, had a sword fight. Throughout, he did a voice-over about their time together: how he'd originally invented her to fill his forlorn eight-year-old life, what other purposes she served, when she went away.

"I fell in love with Kitty Wheeler when I was ten. Since there was suddenly a real girl in my life, I didn't need Pin anymore. After Kitty came Debby Sullivan and then Karen Enoch. I just stopped . . . needing her. I had real girlfriends.

"Remember them, Weber? Fourth-grade girlfriends? Who'd we ever love more?"

Pinsleepe sat next to me, watching. The only time she moved was to bang her feet back against the bottom of the couch when something bored her.

When he was done reminiscing about their early history together, the film faded expertly and came up again on Phil sitting on his living room couch.

"The first time I'd really thought of her in years was when I talked to a guy recently about having imaginary childhood friends. That's where the idea for 'Mr. Fiddlehead' came from.

"While we were in Yugoslavia filming, I wrote a few pages of dialogue. Rough-draft stuff, nothing polished or even good. I thought I'd get back to it when *Midnight Kills* was done. But when I looked at it again, a short story'd already been written. A finished story."

Some of this I knew from Finky Linky; some of it was new. The child continued to kick the couch until I put my hand on her knee and squeezed it to make her stop.

I wanted to ask questions, straighten out things that were confusing me. You can't ask a television set questions.

When he began talking specifically about her, I felt her grow tense and still beside me.

"What people don't really know, Weber, is we make up our own guardian angels. People picture angels as *New Yorker* cartoons—muses with harps, looking over the shoulders of writers having trouble.

"But it's more complicated than that. They're there, all right, but they come custom-made to *our* specifications.

"Pinsleepe wasn't there when I was a kid; I just cooked up a picture of the perfect friend I needed. I obviously didn't know I needed a real-life Kitty Wheeler more. Because as soon as Kitty arrived—*zoop!* No more Pinsleepe.

"My guardian angel, or perfect friend, came when I *did* need her most.

"We were in this shitty rundown church in Watts filming one of the first scenes of *Midnight Kills*. I looked up and there she was." He snapped his fingers and smiled wryly. "I could say she appeared out of nowhere, but that's silly. She appeared out of my own fucking head!

"Remember, I'd already started working on the idea of Mr. Fiddlehead, so, unconsciously, I wasn't completely shocked to see her.

"That, combined with the fact I knew her face from way back in my own youth. Like looking at an old school yearbook and seeing the face of someone you haven't thought about in twenty years? 'Oh, yeah. I remember that kid!' That was my first reaction.

"Only it was closer, under the skin. I didn't recognize her immediately, but I sure as hell knew that face had been important somewhere in my life.

"The first thing she said was—"

The television went black.

"*I* want to tell it." She turned to me with the remote control in her hand. "He was really in trouble! He was making those *gross* movies that made everybody sick and scared. You know what happens when you do that? You know what they do to you? A lot! They get you! Really bad!"

"Who are you talking about?"

"God, stupid! When God gets mad at you, you'd better do what he says or else you're in *big* trouble!"

"God didn't want Phil to make his movies?"

"That's right." She nodded her head exaggeratedly and handed me the remote control. The discussion was over. She'd said what she wanted.

It was another hour before Sasha woke up and came looking for me. Most of that time I listened to Pinsleepe and then, after she left, to the rest of this newest segment of my Strayhorn tape. I also spent a good while staring at the black screen trying to sort the many tangles out in my head. It wasn't easy. It was impossible.

An angel, she came to earth to warn him to stop making *Midnight Kills*. It had gone too far; he'd gone sniffing around in corners of the human and cosmic psyche that weren't his to know. Bloodstone was too close to some important truth. Strayhorn was too close to *him*.

It is simpler to combine and distill their separate monologues into a kind of split-screen dialogue. Listen.

"I don't know where or when it turned, Weber: where I tapped into some unconscious mother lode and started mining the real stuff. She wouldn't tell what was just good gore and what was the devil's lands."

"He kept making them worse and worse! They said, 'Go and tell him to stop. People are scared and killing each other."

"But all the *Midnight* films were like that. What was I doing different with this one? Why didn't Pinsleepe come before?"

"They let you do what you want till it gets dangerous."

" 'Dangerous for who?' I asked her twice: no answer. She only said, Stop making this film. Just like that. Can you imagine? Three and a half million dollars budgeted, forty people working busily away at their jobs, and I'm supposed to *stop?*

"I had this interesting plot, but I didn't think it was art or particularly . . . transcendent. So why should I stop? Horror films don't shake the world. If they're good, they scare you. You walk out of the theater feeling a little better about your own unthreatened life. That's it."

"He didn't stop! He didn't listen to me. You know how bad *that is? You know what kind of trouble that gets you?"*

"Remember when Moses had to prove to Pharaoh he was there on God's business? The miracles he performed for the Egyptians? Changing water into blood, his staff into a snake?

"I asked Pin to show me a miracle. I assume you did it too. No doubt she's the real thing, is there? You know what she did for me? Turned me into you for an afternoon.

"Remember the time you were getting out of the taxi in New York and the girl from across the street who walks around naked wanted it? You said, 'Do you want this breast?' A wonderful line. I used it in the film. Hope you don't mind.

"I was even aware of what day it was, Weber. The day you heard Phil Strayhorn shot himself."

"But he still didn't stop! He knew he was going to kill himself and knew everything but he didn't stop!"

"I didn't stop because it was too intriguing. What had I done? What was I so near that it even scared *them?*

"Prometheus, man! Maybe I'd stolen some of the big fire! Maybe I was close to figuring out their fucking Rubik's Cube!

"Would you stop if you were there? Uh-uh, too exciting. Even the fear is golden adrenaline, believe me. The more Pinsleepe said to cut it out, the more alluring it became."

.   .   .

The film was finished, despite the death of Matthew Portland (and ten other people) on one of the last days of shooting. Part of the crew went to the opening of a new shopping center in the San Fernando Valley to film the festivities for one minor scene in *M.K.*

The architects had designed the building so that all parking was up on the roof. Halfway through the local mayor's speech, one of the giant support beams twisted and gave. The roof collapsed. Six automobiles dropped instantly through the ceiling: dropped like bombs through the ceiling into the middle of everything. I saw it on the news in New York and remembered thinking, If you showed that in a film no one would believe it. There was an especially memorable picture of a green station wagon lying on its back in a large, still-flowing fountain.

The day of Matthew's funeral, the last rushes of his film came back from the lab. When Phil was able to look at them, he realized two things: *Midnight Kills* was utterly mediocre, and the most important scene was missing.

The lab said they'd returned everything but would check anyway. Sasha went down to oversee their checking but came back empty-handed.

"I closed the set for that shot. It was just Matthew, me, and the camera and sound men. Bloodstone spoke for the first and last time in any of the films. Probably the only piece of inspired writing I'd ever done. The whole series spun on that soliloquy.

"Wanna guess what happened next? Matthew and Alex Karsandi, the cameraman, were up at that shopping center when the roof fell in. That left only the sound man, Rainer Artus, and me alive to know what'd gone on in the scene.

"Pinsleepe didn't steal it. I believe that because when I told her about its disappearance, she got hysterical. Said that's why Matthew and the others died: The scene, once it was shot and came to life, was as fast and virulent as nerve gas.

"It was okay when it was only on paper, but once it was filmed, something bad in it was born and started spreading the bad all over. The only way to stop it was destroy the scene or, *I* later thought, the person who created it. So I very gallantly and guiltily killed myself. Ha-ha on me. It did no good.

"However hyperbolic and melodramatic it sounds, it's all true. That's why Pinsleepe came—to stop me from bringing that one scene to life. Seeing I wouldn't, she stayed around, hoping to convince me to dump it later.

"You've seen what's happened to Sasha and Pinsleepe. Neither of them had control over that, either. Sasha and I hadn't even slept together for a long time. But she's still pregnant. It happened the day after we shot the scene. And she's got cancer.

"Pinsleepe can't do anything to help, not as long as that film sequence is around.

"I can't tell you where it is, believe it or not, not even here. You find out some amazing things after you die, but just as amazing is what they won't tell you.

"But here's a funny thing. You know how you're allowed one phone call from jail after they take you in? Well, here too—they give someone who's still living a chance to clear you. One chance to fix something important you messed up. It's an interesting test of love, when you think about it.

"So I chose you, Weber. I asked if it would be all right if you searched for the film.

"You've got to find it before everything goes down. The first thing they showed me when I got here was what is going to happen if you can't find and destroy it. It's vile and cruel. As bad as you could ever imagine."

He stared straight into the camera.

"All my life I wanted to be a big shot and make some real art. One time I did it. Exactly one time I really brought something to life.

"Result? The worst thing a person could have done. I made some art, but it made so much noise being born that it woke up all the trolls in the cave. They're coming out now, and they're mad. Jesus, are they mad!"

4

I was staring at a lilac bush when Finky Linky drove up. Lilacs smell like they look. They could have no other scent or color. The flower simply *smells* mauve, that haunting naïve purple, mysterious and sweet, just this side of decay. When you think about it, the combination of hue and scent is first correct, then perfect.

Wyatt was driving Phil's XKE. Sasha had insisted we take it instead of renting a car to drive out to the valley to see Rainer Artus.

We'd been in Los Angeles four days before I got through to Artus. He had a telephone answering machine that gave the "not here" message in Peter Lorre's voice. At first it was macabre, then annoying, to call a number fifteen times and hear that German weasel say, "Heh heh. I'm sorry, I'm *really* sorry, but 933-5819 isn't in right now. . . ."

I asked Wyatt to go along because he knew the whole story; Sasha didn't. Why didn't I tell her? Because she had enough problems at the moment, and I wanted to find out much more before saying anything to her. That made sense.

Wyatt knew because he'd been the first to mention Pinsleepe to me. Besides, I knew from discussions in our theater group that he believed very deeply in the occult and "other worlds."

Sasha didn't. To her, life and death were good and bad enough: anything more was either unproven theory, a crutch for the weak, or straight-out silliness. If I'd told her she was pregnant with an angel who, in turn, was pregnant with her (not to mention the rest of the story), Sasha would probably have put her head down and wept in despair. Maybe something worse. The first night I spent at her house she came into my room at three A.M. and crawled into bed with me. "I'm afraid. Please let me lie with you."

Every day she looked worse. Since the funeral she'd been going regularly to UCLA hospital for tests. The people, the place, the tests scared her and made our being there even more important.

Although she knew he'd planned to stay with a friend, Sasha asked Wyatt the second day if he would stay with her too. That did some good, because they quickly got down to talking about what it was like to be grievously, finitely ill. I told her about my experiences with people in our Cancer Theater Group; Wyatt said what it was like to wake up every morning and remember two seconds after consciousness raised its curtain that today could easily be *it*.

Sometimes they wanted me with them, sometimes not. Sometimes from another room I'd listen hard to the murmurs and bursts of their voices and think they were telling secrets only they could know or fathom. Death, or imminent death, must have a language of its own, a specific grammar and vocabulary that's understood only on that side of the fence.

Theater is a positive art. At the very least, it tries to add life to words. If the words are already alive and beautiful, good drama helps lift them off the earth. I have seen that happen in the theater, more than once even with our cancer group in New York. The actors I worked with there brought enthusiasm and fear and final energy to whatever we were doing. I could direct them, but whatever talent or inspiration they had was enhanced more by the enormous threat of their ticking clocks than anything I said. I saw myself as giving them only what could fit through a small hole in a glass window or chain-link fence. For me the experience was invaluable because their energy and efforts were instructive and elemental: Everything was motivated by the clearest, healthiest greed I'd ever seen—the greed that demands another day of life.

When I heard Wyatt and Sasha talking, I thought of that fence and how unclimbable it was until you found yourself suddenly, horribly, on the other side at some unexpected time in your life.

In his best Finky Linky voice, Wyatt called out from the car, "Are we going, or are you scanning the lilacs?"

I broke off a spray and brought it with me. "When is Sasha supposed to be back?"

"Depends on whether they could do her test quickly. Probably a few hours."

Opening the door, I dropped the flowers on the dashboard. "Tell me about these tests."

He gunned the car and started away from the curb. "They take things out of you and shoot things in. They look at your guts like they're a video game but never tell you who's winning when they're finished. You drink things so your guts light up like Las Vegas, and then they say you can go to the bathroom now and flush Vegas down the toilet. It's humiliating and frightening and the worst part is, when they actually *do* show you pictures or graphs or whatever, they don't look like anything. You feel like a big fucking fool because it's *your* body in that readout, but you can't understand it. You've got to rely on all these patronizing technicians to tell you what's actually happening inside your own poor fucked-up body. You want to understand so badly that when they start to talk, you concentrate as hard as possible, but it still doesn't make sense. They say 'hemoglobins' and 'white cell counts' and so much more that your brain closes down and you can't understand any of it.

"But they even know *that'll* happen, so they stop using medical terms and start talking to you like you're retarded. One doctor I consulted had this glitzy computer game where you had to fight off the cancer cells entering your body. If you did it successfully, you won—lived. The thing made little blips: *bleep, bleep, bleep.* I played that damned game and won once. It felt so good. Here I was playing this absurd computer game, pretending the little blips were the good guys in my body."

He pulled up to a stop sign and looked at me.

"The tests are shit, Weber. The kind they're probably giving Sasha today are the second-line ones. They give you those when they know you've got it bad but want to find out just how bad before they start recommending any kind of therapy."

"What did you do the first time you heard you had it?"

"Went out and bought a pastrami sandwich. Nothing ever tasted so good in my whole life. Bought a pastrami sandwich and a pack of Marlboros. Hadn't smoked in three years, but what the hell, huh?"

On the long drive to Artus's place, we spoke about all the "something wrongs" of the last days.

"You know what else is wrong? His killing Flea. There's no way in the world Strayhorn would've killed that dog."

"Even if he was crazy?"

"Even so. I lived with him too long. He wasn't that kind of man. He used to catch mosquitoes and free them outside the window. That dog was pure love for him. He liked everything about it. Why kill it?"

"Because he'd gone mad."

We talked on and on. One of us would throw out an idea or a theory and it would be dissected or replaced or banked off the walls of possibility like a billiard ball.

Wyatt dropped his big one shortly before we arrived. "I bet . . ."

"What?"

"I was going to say something weird, but it makes complete sense. Everything that's happened, and everything we've been *talking* about . . . it's all *Dr. Faustus.*" He continued looking at the road with an expressionless driver's face. In my deepest heart, perhaps my deepest fear, I had thought about this possibility too.

"Tell me."

"What you're asking, Weber, is to tell you I believe that still happens. But you know I do."

"Tell me how you came up with it."

He rolled his head around on his neck as if he'd suddenly gotten a bad driver's cramp. "We all read *Dr. Faustus* in college. A smart guy's unhappy with his life. Nothing's worked out the way he wanted. What can he do about it? Talk to God. But God's not answering, so the guy goes downstairs.

"Lucifer says sure, I'll help. I'll make things better, but your soul's mine after you die.

"Faustus agrees and signs on the dotted line. We know what happens next—he gets the power he wants, but he uses it for all the wrong reasons. Has all the power in the natural world but uses it to make Helen of Troy appear so he can screw her.

"Is this starting to sound familiar?"

"Phil. He was so depressed back then, he would've done anything."

"He *did*—he wrote *Midnight!* But he was also smart, Weber. Don't forget that. Here's why he made his deal. It's only my theory. He signed something important over, sure, but only because he thought he could do without it. He was wrong."

"What'd he give up?"

Wyatt turned and gave me a cold look. "His moral balance. Phil made the best horror films in the world, the greatest horror films ever. But they're *too* great—too horrible.

"His fame came from making contemptible, ugly nightmares. At first it was kind of a cynical lark, but then it had him by the balls and wouldn't let go. Look at how he was *always* trying to get involved in other projects. But somehow, every time, he was pulled back down into that Midnight shit.

"Only once did it look like he was really going to get out of it. But then three things happened: An *angel* appeared, and let's assume for a minute it really was an angel and not just some strange little girl. She told him not to shoot the scene. But he did. Result? Two of his best friends were killed in an accident so bizarre no one can believe it.

"You don't think there're links there? You don't see cause and effect? In the end, the Other Guy won everything: brilliant movies that made Bloodstone a cult figure. Evil is okay so long as it's original. That's good publicity. Then Strayhorn's so eaten up with guilt he shoots himself. Finally, as a little extra perk, Crazy Phil not only kills himself but one of the few things he really loved—a completely innocent and loving dog."

"Don't forget what happened to Sasha."

"That too."

"Say you're right, Wyatt. What about the videotapes to Sasha and me? What's *their* point? How come he gets to send messages from hell?"

"I haven't figured that out yet. Maybe he's telling the truth; maybe he *has* been given one last shot at redemption through someone he loved.

"But I wouldn't trust anything now. The part of *Dr. Faustus* I liked most was watching how cleverly the Devil lured the man. He didn't grab him by the foot and drag him away. They had these fascinating conversations where he told Faustus *not* to sell his soul because Hell's a terrible place. Faustus almost had to convince him to *take* it. You think that wasn't planned? You think evil comes looking for us? Just the opposite. We run after evil until it catches us. There's no question of that."

Before I tell you what happened when we got to his house, I must tell you about Rainer Artus.

Although he had the reputation for being one of the best sound men in Hollywood, he had great difficulty getting work because he was so exacting and persnickety. He didn't check things twice, he checked them five times. He didn't want the best equipment, he wanted *two* of the best in case something wasn't just so with the original. He liked to tell the story of the pianist Keith Jarrett, who apparently demands two special pianos be made available when he's doing concerts—just in case.

Hollywood will put up all day with the bullshit demands of star actors, but it has little patience for the whims of technicians. When a Rainer Artus demands two Nagra tape recorders—just in case—you can be sure several important people are going to yell. So the man worked, but not as often as he should have.

But Phil used him for all the Midnight films, because he knew how good Artus was and because sound is one of the most important elements in a horror film. The two of them were comfortable with each other.

I'd worked with Rainer on one film but found him too aloof, too authoritarian, and always secretly wondered if he had been a Nazi in his time. Phil said no, but I wasn't so sure. I did know that Artus had had a very difficult childhood in Germany with a mother straight out of some Freudian study. She was so anal retentive she put two kinds of towels in the family bathroom—one to dry the "up" side of the body, one to dry the "down." If the kids were ever caught using one towel for both areas, she gave them a beating. It wasn't hard to see where her son got his finicky neatness. Rainer's world was all order and no dust. His car was one long shine and nothing in the ashtrays, although he smoked heavily. His house was the same. Phil said the man meditated by vacuuming the living room. That was one of the things I remembered about visiting him years before: In a closet was one of the most remarkable vacuum cleaners I'd ever seen. Yes, I peeked. The machine was immense, so enchased with buttons and switches that if someone had told me it was a Russian space probe I'd have believed it.

He lived on a sleepy dead-end street in one of those semi-"Mission"-style houses that were built by the blockful at one time in California. When Wyatt pulled up in front, the Doors' "Light My Fire" was blaring out of the house onto the street.

"Is that coming from his house?"

"I think so. But Rainer hates rock and roll music."

Wyatt gestured at the noise. "Guess he changed his mind."

"Rainer never changed his mind about anything. Let's go."

We walked across a browning lawn full of bald patches and healthy weeds. Rainer liked to garden. The last time I'd been to the house, this lawn had looked like a prizewinner. Now it looked like a skin disease.

On the porch the screen door was wide open and a number of black flies buzzed lazily in and out of the house.

"Reminds me of Flakey Foont's house in *Zap Comix.*"

"Or *Tobacco Road.*" I rang the bell. Over the crashing music inside, someone yelled for us to come in.

"Rainer?" I went in slowly.

"Yeah?"

"Rainer, it's Weber Gregston. Where are you?"

"Back here. Just keep coming."

We walked through a house that was not just dirty, it was . . . unclean. Smelling thickly fetid and disturbing, it gave you the feeling something might be dead here. Moving slowly, I felt Finky Linky take hold of one of the belt loops on the back of my jeans. He whispered, "You don't mind, do you?" I smiled and shook my head. "Good, because I wasn't going to let go anyway."

"Rainer, where the hell are you?"

"Back here. Keep coming."

We came upon what I suppose was his bedroom. At least there was a mattress on the floor with Rainer on it.

"Weber, how are you? And Finky Linky!" He was propped against the wall wearing nothing more than a pair of underpants and black socks. His hair was long and stringy, dirty. It was almost like seeing another person, because part of Rainer's Hessian image had always been steel-gray hair cut almost to the skull.

"What're you two doing here?"

"We came to talk about Phil."

"Phil?"

"Phil Strayhorn."

He squinted, trying to remember the name of the man he'd made four films with. "Phil Strayhorn? Oh, yeah, sure. Phil. He's dead. You know that? Phil's dead."

"Yes, we know that. What's the matter, Rainer? You look like hell."

He smiled. "I do? I feel good. Don't know why I look like hell 'cause I feel good."

"Are you high?"

"High? No, Finky, you know I don't do drugs. Don't even drink. Just feel good." He got up slowly, helping himself with a hand hard against the wall behind him. "I'm on vacation for a while. Takin' it easy and listening to some music." His head dropped back and closing his eyes, he began swaying slowly to the Doors' next song.

"Can I turn it down a little while we talk?" Without waiting for an answer, Wyatt walked over to the large stereo unit in a corner and turned it off. "That's better. You want something to eat, Rainer? Or something to drink?"

"No, I'm fine. Sit down, guys. Ask me whatever you want."

The next half hour was a strange experience. The man looked like Rainer, talked like him most of the time, and knew things only he could know, but neither Wyatt nor I could say for sure if it was him. The man we knew wasn't completely there—only parts. Recognizable parts, certainly, but not one hundred percent Rainer Artus. Wyatt agreed when I said later it was like those flies buzzing around the front door—they kept coming and going from the house. Only here, our man kept coming and going from the strange person we were talking with.

I asked him questions about the film we'd made together—small questions, unimportant ones, that only a person who'd been on the set would have remembered. He knew everything and laughed at some of the memories. It was Rainer. No. No, it wasn't.

"Listen, please. This is an important question. Remember when you shot that sequence in *Midnight Kills* when Bloodstone did his monologue? I guess it was the only time he ever said anything."

"Sure. What do you want to know about it?"

"Do you know where the film is? It seems that section has kind of disappeared."

"You check with the studio?"

"We checked with the studio, the lab, Sasha Makrianes, everyone. The whole piece is gone."

"That's mysterious." He said the word, but his tone of voice said he wasn't interested in this mystery at all.

"You don't know where it is?"

"No."

"Do you remember the scene? What he said?"

"It was a closed set, and when we were through with the shot Phil took my tapes and Alex Karsandi's film and said he would take care of the processing and the lab himself. He'd never done that before but he's the boss, so we gave it to him." It was the most Artus had said at one time since we'd been there and appeared to tire him out. It was plain he didn't have much more in him, and we'd have to get whatever other information we needed fast.

"What did he say, Rainer? What kind of things did he talk about in that scene?"

He rubbed his face with both hands and looked at us vaguely, as if only having just gotten up for the day. "He did it ad lib. None of that scene was in the original script. We all got the feeling he was making things up as he went along. He talked about evil and pain . . . but nothing you haven't heard already. A bad guy telling why he's bad. Nothing special.

"What *was* bad came at the end of the scene when Bloodstone killed the little girl. Christ, it looked real! None of us knew how he did it. This great-looking kid, maybe eight or nine. He went through this 'Why I'm bad' spiel and then brought her out from the wings, like a magician about to do a trick on someone from the audience.

"None of us knew what he was up to, but Phil was a good ad libber so we just left him alone. Matthew Portland had brought the girl on the set, but she'd been hanging back in the wings so quietly I'd forgotten about her."

"What was her name? Do you remember her name?"

He rubbed a hand over his face again. "Yeah, I remember because it was a funny name: 'Pinslip.' He didn't call her anything else. Brought this little Pinslip out and a moment later, with the camera rolling, Bloodstone cut her throat while she was singing this song he told her to sing." His mouth started moving as if he were chewing gum. "In my town when I was a kid there was this crazy woman we called 'Salad.' I don't know where the name came from. We used to go around scaring her whenever we could." His mouth kept moving. He looked at me, and his eyes cleared for a moment. "Ever since we finished that film I haven't felt so good. I don't want to make another Midnight. The money's good and Phil's a king, but I'm not going to do it again. I've got to call and tell him that. Is he back in town yet?"

"There she is—by the car."

Shading his eyes against the sun, Finky Linky looked toward the street. Pinsleepe was standing by a tree with a bright orange ball in her hands. Seeing us, she waved happily.

"If she's an angel then she can save me, can't she, Weber?"

"I guess so, Wyatt. Maybe she can."

We started off the porch toward her. She moved toward us.

"Hello, Finky Linky. Yes, I can save you."

He looked at me. She looked at me.

"Why didn't you tell me about that scene?"

"I can't tell you everything, Weber. Phil told you that on the tapes, didn't he?"

"Why do you talk like a child sometimes and like a grown-up others?"

"Because I'm both. Today I look like a kid with an orange ball. What did you find out from Rainer?"

"What happened to him? What's the matter?"

"*Midnight Kills* is the matter. So you know about me being killed in the film?"

"Yes. Did Phil know he was going to do it?"

"I think so. When he asked me onto the set, I thought it was to show how he'd decided to change the scene for the good. But he was too far gone by then. Whatever little good was left in him, he had to kill and show the whole world. No better place to do that than a movie."

"Is the scene gone?"

She tossed the ball into the air, caught it. "The film's gone, but that's not important. He burned the film and the sound tapes before he died, but it was too late and he knew it. He'd done the scene, so it was alive. It still is. *That's* why he killed himself."

"Then what am I supposed to do? What *can* I do?"

Pinsleepe tossed the ball to Wyatt. She looked at me. "You have to shoot another scene, Weber, one to replace Phil's. If it's better, things'll be all right again. Sasha will be okay. So will he."

"That's it? Is that what you want?"

"Yes."

"How do I make it 'better'?"

Someone screamed behind us. We turned around to see Rainer on his porch, still in his underwear, waving. "Hey, thanks a lot for coming, guys! Love your show, Finky. If you ever need a sound man, let me know!"

When we turned back to Pinsleepe, she was gone.

5

L ook at this splendid room. Come, I'll show you around.

Sasha's always been a big collector. When you have money you collect "objects," when you're poor you collect "things." Sasha has objects. I bought her some of them. By the time that happened, I was so rich and untroubled by money I could walk into a gallery or antique store and not haggle over price, not turn the thing here and there, pretending to look for flaws or hidden cheapness. I'd say how much. They'd say some crazy price. I'd say all right.

That Maris York skyscraper, over the fireplace, and the painting by Jorg Immendorff were from me. I brought the painting over in my car with the top down. It was so big, it flapped in the wind like a sail. The gallery owner was horrified, but I wanted to give it to Sasha immediately and see her reaction. She put it down on the floor and walked around and around it for minutes, checking from all angles.

Sasha is . . . oh, don't worry, she won't be back for a few hours; she's still at the hospital having tests. We have time to appreciate her place: the two Chinese carpets, one the color of dusk, the other of dessert; an old ink bottle my father would love on the desk next to the round stone she found when we were in New Mexico. . . .

A woman who can demand or coerce millions of dollars from hard-edged money people, she also likes to laugh while fucking. When she wakes up in the morning, she's usually in a good mood. Sasha buys hard-cover copies of books people recommend she read. It's ridiculous making a list of someone's good qualities. Anyway, I'm supposed to be giving you a tour of her apartment, not her personality. But our books, the two pairs of black running shoes, how often and how carefully we water the plants . . . haruspication. Remember the word? Study the order, find the answer. Why did she pick up that round rock and not another? Here, would you like to hold it? The size is unimportant, I can tell you that. Size, color, where exactly she found it: not those things. Rather the totality, the dots of a life connected by a smart eye. The stone and ink bottle on her desk, a bad drawing of a dinosaur that hangs in the bath-room. A little nothing that amuses her and which she can never take down, even when she thinks of doing it. Because I gave it to her.

Nothing I gave her has left this house. Not before, not after I died. I check every day, take a walk through the house when she's not around to see if some of me is still alive here. If even one thing were gone I would worry.

Sometimes when she's here I'll sit in a near room and listen to her going about the small acts of her life. The whish of her shower, the way she often hums, the quick click of channels when she tries to watch television but finds nothing—nothing to put an hour of her life into because there is nowhere else to put it right now.

I almost never sit in the same room with her. Too close. Too sad. From the looks on our faces, you wouldn't be able to figure out which of us was sadder, the pregnant woman or the dead man.

Can I tell you about this? Do you mind? I'd be very grateful.

Relationships begin with the delicate, scared use of big words you hope will apply someday soon: concern, commitment, love. Sasha and I were in the Hamburger Hamlet on Hollywood Boulevard when I said the first one, honesty.

"I have to be honest with you."

Sasha looked quickly away and I thought, Uh-oh. When she looked back, she wore a suspicious, unhappy expression. Said I didn't owe her anything, she'd gotten something "out of the fuck" too. The word sounded silly. I took her hand, but instead of responding or squeezing mine, she only looked at our two clasped hands on the table and asked if my "honesty" meant I was telling her thanks for the roll last night but go away now.

"No, my honesty meant admitting right away I'm in love with you."

"I wasn't ready for that. I'm still getting used to the idea of our sleeping together."

"Yes, get used to it. Get used to me."

We were each other's big, real hope and luckily recognized it fast. When good fortune pulls up in front of you too quickly, it can make you suspicious. You hesitate before getting in. But both Sasha and I had been through enough lonely times to know there were only so many chances at contentment with another person. In other words, don't think too long before acting.

In his Letters to a Young Poet, Rilke copies down one of his correspondent Kappus's poems and sends it back to the young man.

> And now I am giving you this copy because I know that it is important and full of new experience to rediscover a work of one's own in someone else's handwriting. Read the poem as if you had never seen it before, and you will feel in your innermost being how very much it is your own.

For some reason, the idea of this great man hand-copying a fan's poem and sending it to him has always touched me deeply. What generosity! Who would ever think of doing that?

But then I met Sasha, and she took much of what I was or believed and, putting her own stamp on it, handed it back to me as if I had never seen it before. Perhaps that is what love is—another's desire to return you to yourself enhanced by their vision, graced by their script.

I asked her to live with me.

She looked at her feet. "I've never been very successful at that." Her smile was over just after it began to grow.

I reached out and stroked her hair. "I don't care what your won-loss record is. I want you for what you are, Sash, not for what I want you to be."

"Me too. And that's the best place to begin.

"When I was out walking Flea tonight, I saw this man on a big motorcycle with his girlfriend on the back. He started dragging his boots on the ground, and I guess he had metal heels or something because sparks flew in all directions. The girl laughed and did it too. It looked so impressive and magical: the big ruuuuum of the bike, her laughing, all those sparks. . . .

"I couldn't wait to get back in and tell you about it. But then when I came in, after only ten minutes outside, I saw you and was so glad to see you that I forgot what I wanted to say. Those are sparks too, aren't they, Phil?"

Relationships that begin in your late twenties or early thirties have a dimension that doesn't exist when you're younger. Besides knowing more, you're also more grateful for the good things, forgiving toward the bad. What drove you nuts at twenty is only a crumb, at most a small stain on your sleeve, ten years later. It can be cleaned. It can be overlooked as long as the rest of the jacket hangs well and feels right.

From the beginning of our relationship, I didn't see great sparks flying up from our boots. I'd never have said it to Sasha, but it was enough to put my hand under her skirt in the dark at a film and feel the soft down of hair and stipply gooseflesh on the inside of her thigh. There was love and respect. We discovered we had a world of things to talk about.

When Weber came over for dinner one night, he said we felt like a couple. "Some people live together for years, but you never get the feeling they fit very well. It feels like they live on separate floors of their house. Not you two."

We agreed. What was odd was going to my office every day and working on something as vile as Midnight Kills, then home to Sasha and Flea at night and a life that had become so full and good.

In retrospect, I realize it couldn't have lasted a long time. I knew Midnight hadn't gotten me this good luck. Sasha admired my Esquire column about life in Hollywood, not Bloodstone. Yet, like it or not, he was my bread and butter and I spent a good part of my life thinking about him.

In bed one night as we watched Flea walk around on top of us, looking for a place to lie down, Sasha asked where Bloodstone came from.

"You mean really, or in the film?"

"Really. Where did he come from in you?"

Flea plumped down and, coincidentally, looked straight at me, as if she too were waiting for the answer. My two girls.

"Rock and Roll."

"Music?"

"No, not exactly. When I was a boy, my father took us on the first and last vacation we ever had: to Browns Mills, New Jersey. The only distinguishing things about it were it had a muddy lake and was near Fort Dix, one of the big military bases on the East Coast. We had a bungalow in the middle of the woods and were surrounded by army families from the base. One of them was named Masello, and the father was in the military police. My sister and I spent a lot of time in their house that month because they had three kids around our ages.

"One day after swimming we were out on their back porch eating brownies and listening to the radio. It was a station in Trenton. Remember the song 'Monkey Time' by Major Lance? That was on when it was cut off by a news bulletin. A man had walked up to a military police car on the base, leaned down, and shot the two policemen inside, point-blank. One of them was Mr. Masello.

"All of us kids looked at each other. I remember that very well, because we all had brownies in our mouth and were chewing."

"You used that scene in one of the Midnights!"

"Right, Midnight Too. I shot it exactly the way it happened: The oldest Masello kid's mouth dropped open and big chunks of brownie fell out. He closed his eyes and started screaming 'Rock and Roll! Rock and Roll!' and kept screaming until his mother came and dragged him on his knees back into the house."

"How could you use that, Phil? What if one of those kids saw your film?"

"They did. One wrote a letter and called me a motherfucker."

"Why did you do it?"

"Let me finish the story. My parents got so scared that this killer might come and get us that they packed us up that night and drove home. In the car I fell asleep and had a dream where a man with a silvery, featureless face chased me, screaming 'Rock and roll!' I've had that dream all my life. It still scares the bloody shit out of me.

"After that I was traumatized by Rock and Roll. Every time I heard of a murder on the radio or read about one, I thought of Rock and Roll. That was his name, and he must have done it. My mother read The National Enquirer, and every crime in there, brains on the floor, blood on the walls, was done by him. Everyone has their vision of evil, and he was mine. A war in Africa? Rock and Roll did it. A baby disappeared in

Darien? Rock and Roll. He was everything bad. He covered the field. And every time I had that dream again, he got bloodier and more frightening because I'd given him credit for something else."

Sasha sighed. "How much of your films is from your life?"

"More than I like."

"Does it help to film it? Is it a catharsis?"

"Sometimes. Sometimes it's too far down. Like those glass-bottom boats you ride in Florida that let you see the big fish below? Sometimes doing this brings me close to the things, but I can only see them, their dark shapes. I can't get them out."

There are nights in a relationship when you come as close as you're ever going to get to another person. It usually begins with a few doses of wonderfully all-out sex, but then it blossoms into something much more profound and transcendent. You start by doing things to each other physically you'd only fantasized before. Then, when it's calm again, you start telling secrets about yourself or your life you never thought would come out. Weber called them "Holy Nights," which is an apt description. To him, there are few times in our adult life when we are "simply" honest. It is either unnecessary or detrimental to tell the truth in our everyday life, so we don't.

That is one of the reasons religion suffers so in our century: To really find God, you must be honest. To be honest you must begin by looking clearly at yourself, but that's too distressing. So we learn to worship material things instead, because not only are they attainable but how we attain them doesn't require virtue or virtuous behavior, as some higher goals do. We don't want goodness, we want a Mercedes. Who needs a relationship when you can have all the fun of one without making any of the commitments? In the end, even AIDS is the perfect consumer's disease: It comes from either bad sex or bad needles. None of this "wrath of God" stuff in our time. Plagues are for the Dark Ages.

I'm rambling. But why are we so honest on Holy Nights? Because we're so close to death then. That night Sasha and I discussed death. We spoke of how we imagined it to be (we were wrong), how we imagined we'd die (I was wrong), of how we wanted to be buried. We spoke as if the other would be there at our end to see to these last wishes. After that *we made love again, because talk of death always makes you feel more fragile and hungry.*

Look, I can say this: Death is the minimum. The minimum of anything. In those hours when you're so close to another person, you go from being two to almost one. The minimum. Love is death: the death of the individual, the death of distance, the death of time. The delightful thing about holding a girl's hand is after a while you forget which is yours. You forget there are two instead of one big one. Death. It is not a morbid thing.

Let me tell you one more story. When I was twelve, my friend Geoff Pierson and I were down at the river in our town, fooling around. We'd smoked all the cigarettes we had and gotten bored enough to be in the middle of a stone-throwing contest. It was a hot July day, and the only sounds around were a lawn mower somewhere off in a far distance and the ker-plunk of our stones hitting the water. He threw one. I threw one farther. He threw one farther. I threw one that hit something.

Slowly, languorously, the thing turned and became an elbow, a crooked elbow sticking like an inverted V out of the water. It stayed there a few seconds and then, just as languorously (as if tired), turned back over into the water.

I told Geoff to go call the cops while I leapt wildly into the water, like a dog jumping off a boat. Nothing more had surfaced there, but where that elbow had appeared was so burned into my consciousness I didn't need any landmarks to find the place again. Thirty feet out, I saw something light, something dark, something large in front of me. There was the elbow just under the surface! Taking it, I started swimming with one hand back to shore. It took a long time and the thing in my hand was hard and cold. I didn't look back until I could put my feet on the bottom and pull it in to shore.

It was a woman. She was almost naked. Only bra and underpants. Both were white, and I could see her dark nipples and pubic hair through the thin material. The body was frozen in rigor mortis—one hand cupped under a breast (thus the crooked elbow), the other held rigidly against her side. Her face was completely covered with what looked like mucus. After pulling her up onto the grass, I bent down and tried to wipe some of the scum from her face. It all came off in one big shiny piece.

I didn't know her but even in death she was very good-looking, her body especially. What else is a twelve-year-old to think? There it all was in one living dream in front of me—sex (I'd never seen the real thing before), death, horror, excitement. Who she was isn't important nor is how she got there. The point of this is to tell you how disappointed I was when Geoff came back and I began to hear the wail of a police siren. For one of the only times in my entire life, I had everything I wanted in front of me. Everything I knew, wanted—was—had reached consummation here. In a few minutes (I can still hear Geoff Pierson's sneakers running hard across the grass toward me) life would take it—take her—back into its hands and I would be only me again; twelve, confused, hot, thrilled.

If possible, freeze that moment in your mind. Freeze the look of greed and desire on my face. For the only time in my life, I knew the greatest secret of all—the dead love you.

We'd been on the set of *Burn the Gay Nuns!* for only an hour before I'd had enough and went for some coffee. If Strayhorn had been alive, what we were doing would have been a good subject for his *Esquire* column. The people on the set of the film were named Larry and Rich, Lorna and Debbie. They were professionals and went about their jobs with brisk efficiency. When Debbie was about to have her clothes (and head) ripped off by a samurai-sword-wielding priest (recently back from the dead), she stood patiently for minutes in her underwear while two chatty women sewed a rip-away habit around her scrumptious figure. Phil's article could have been about a day in the life of the filming of a Grade D horror/sex film. Or an interview with "star" Douglas Mann, who walked around with his second head under his arm, eating one gooey French cruller after another.

Since films like *Friday the 13th* and *A Nightmare on Elm Street* became such smashes, people have been trying to make similar low-rent slash-and-gore junk that sells like potato chips to the crowd that fucks at the drive-in or rents four films a day at the video store.

The motion pictures I'd made were certainly not calm affairs (especially the last one), but looking at the script for *Burn the Gay Nuns!* made me feel like I'd done *The Finky Linky Show.*

A few nights before on television, we'd watched a program about the popularity of horror movies. They began by showing stomachable clips from the most popular video in the United States at the time. Titled

Faces of Death, it was a badly put together feature-length documentary of people actually dying in front of a camera: suicides jumping out windows, a man being eaten by an alligator (his dropped camera took it all in), firing squad, electric chair. An out-and-out snuff film you could rent for three bucks most anywhere.

Later in the program, a twelve-year-old girl who had just seen something called *I Spit on Your Grave* was asked why she watched things like that. She beamed and said, "I love all the blood!" That was really her answer. When I was a kid, seeing *The Tingler* with Vincent Price had given me big nightmares for months.

Speaking of Finky Linky, his arrival on the set caused a happy furor. Actors with melted eyeballs like lava running down their faces or hatchets buried in their backs came up for autographs or only to say hello.

Wyatt was Finky's charming, wacko self and, as a big favor to the director, even did a five-second cameo appearance in the inevitable "walking dead" scene.

What were we doing there? My excuse was it happened to be the only horror film being made in Los Angeles at the time. I hadn't directed a movie in over two years. If my next work *was* going to be horror—Phil and Pinsleepe's wish fulfilled—I wanted to see what these guys did. Wyatt said he was along because he'd always wanted to see how shit was made.

What I'd seen in our hour on the set was disappointing. They were using a new, more sophisticated camera from Austria, but other than that the scene was a thoroughly familiar one. It reminded me of why I'd left this life.

Movie people, even the most invisible gaffer or best boy, have a self-importance that is understandable because everyone seems to want to be in the movies. It's an interesting phenomenon: Ask ten people if they want to be President, and surely some of them will say no. Ask them if they want to be in the movies in some capacity, and you can bet most if not all will say yes. The irony is, filmmaking generally has to be one of the most boring ways to spend a day. Nothing is done quickly, and everything is done four, five, six . . . endless times. There is not much sense of community either, because everyone's task on a set is so specific and time-consuming that you do your job right up until a shot is made, then run like hell to get going on the next one.

But as is true with so many jobs, the consumer only sees the final product, and that is so glamorous and exciting it's hard not to want to have a go at it.

Standing with a coffee in hand, I looked back at the set and remembered my last set: how, when filming *Wonderful*, I frequently had the feeling I was watching my life more than living it. It was a haunting, ominous thing to experience and took time to go away. Part of it returned the day I heard Phil was dead. As mentioned, some of my first thoughts after I had the news was to picture his death cinematically. That could be attributed to shock, but not many months before, I was seeing everything I knew through the lens of an inner camera. *I Am a Camera* is a wonderful title, but isn't healthy when it's your life. Looking at the set of this film made me remember my last days in Hollywood.

"Mr. Gregston? Weber Gregston?"

I turned around and saw a nice-looking thirtyish woman. "Yes?"

"You don't know me, but I sort of know you. My name is Linda Webster. I did wardrobe for Phil Strayhorn on the Midnight films?" She put out a tentative hand to shake. Without really looking, I reached for it but a second later yelped. Looking down, I saw a big needle sticking into my thumb.

She snatched it out and stuck it back into a pin cushion she was wearing on her wrist—the giveaway sign of a person doing costumes. "I'm so sorry! I always forget . . . I'm sorry."

"It's okay, it's okay. Really!" Her expression was so stricken and concerned I felt more protective of her feelings than my beaming thumb. "Come on. Let's have a coffee." I held up mine.

"You were in Europe awhile, huh?"

"What do you mean?"

"Europeans say 'Let's have *a* coffee.' Americans say 'Let's have coffee.' Singular and plural, depending on which side of the ocean you're from. How long were you there?"

"About a year."

"Tha-a-at's right, I remember! Phil talked about you a lot and was always wondering where you were that day. He used to bring your postcards onto the set to show us. They were really funny."

"What do you think of his stunt? Did he tell you what he's doing now?"

"What he's *doing?* He's dead."

She smirked and shook her head. "That's not what I hear."

"Lol . . . Linda, is it? Linda, I'm staying with Sasha Makrianes. She found the body. He's dead, you know?"

"I know Sasha. She found a man with his head blown off, but that's all."

"Linda, what are you telling me? He was my best friend."

She had the eyes of someone who thinks they're more cunning than they are. Yet those eyes also said she knew something, maybe a secret, that I didn't. Her expression said she was going to stretch it out as far as it would go.

Finky Linky came up from behind and put a hand on my shoulder. "Hi, Linda! I didn't know you were working on this."

She made an exaggerated pout and stuck out her bottom lip. "I saw you before and said hello, Wyatt, but you were too busy with Debbie and the others."

He made a Finky Linky laugh and, speaking in the famous voice, said, "I saw you, but I told you: We've got to stop meeting here like this."

"Tell Wyatt what you just told me."

She shrugged. "I said everybody knows Phil isn't dead. That the thing was a whole big ugly setup."

The Finky voice disappeared and Wyatt's came back, soft but on edge. "What are you talking about?"

"He's been showing up all over town since it happened. I mean, come on, Wyatt, what about that shootout at the cemetery? Do you really think that was spontaneous? The whole thing's a setup."

"Where was he seen?"

"Someone saw him having a hotdog at Tommy's, Walt Plotkin saw him on Melrose at L.A. Eyeworks, I don't know—I've heard a lot of people saw him in different places."

"Doing what?"

"Hanging around. Drinking, eating dinner. Normal things."

I looked at him. "Sounds to me like a *National Enquirer* headline: 'Philip Strayhorn Found Alive and Shopping on Melrose Avenue.' "

"But it would explain your tapes, wouldn't it? Instead of being tapes from the dead."

"Wyatt, for Christ's sake, do you really believe that bullshit? They say it about every celebrity who ever died! Elvis lives. JFK lives. Howard Hughes."

"Bullshit? Thank you very much!" Linda turned and walked away.

Neither of us paid attention. Wyatt counted things off on his fingers. "It would make complete sense, Weber. A horrible, melodramatic sense. The little girl, an *angel* messenger, if you please, comes with warnings from God not to make these movies. And we know he didn't want to do them anymore. And we know he was very much on edge, maybe even sick. And it wouldn't be the first time this has happened out here. Either as a publicity thing or because someone cracks and winds up in Lu-Lu Land."

"What about Sasha?"

"What about her? Somehow Phil knew she was sick before she did."

"Come *on!* What about her pregnancy? Did he know that too?"

"You can tell when certain women are pregnant by the look on their faces. That's nothing new."

"What about my tattoo, then?"

He took my coffee and had a sip. "That may be your magic and not his, Weber. We haven't even talked about that yet. Remember, you were the one who went to Rondua, not Phil."

6

Whenever a dream comes true, you take one step closer to God. But the closer you are, the better you see him, and he may not be at all what you imagined.

I fell in love with Cullen James the way I'd always wanted to fall in love: with the joyous enthusiasm and devotion of a teenager, the grateful appreciation of experience. I wanted her the moment I met her. She was someone to fight for, someone to long for. I spoke to *her* too fast, wanting her to know everything. Her smile said she understood my hurry. My dream came true.

We never went to bed. I never tasted her thin mouth. She was happily married to a man I had no quarrel with, a man who was capable and strong and essential for her. I wasn't, and that is where my dream came true too much. I'd finally found what I wanted, an invaluable coin in the street, but there was no image on the other side of that coin. Cullen wanted a friend, not someone else to share her life with.

Why Danny James and not Weber Gregston? An array of reasons, some of which you'll find in her book *Bones of the Moon*. But what I remember best (and most painfully) was a conversation we once had where I asked her that very question. Why him and not me?

"Because you and I drive each other crazy too much, Weber. I drive myself crazy enough with all my nervousness and eccentricities. You and I fan each other's flames. Right now that's okay—it's wonderful!— but we're only just beginning. You always smell good and are on your best behavior at the beginning of an affair. But what happens later when you know from one glimpse the other's in a shitty mood and has no way to get out of it? Or the best way to retaliate is to stay silent for three days? You and I would do that to each other. We'd fight too long and be mean, even when we didn't really want to. We're too alike, Weber. The person who drives me craziest is me. What happens when two me's or two you's get into bed at night? Sure, we make great love and have the best conversations in the world, but we also know the tenderest parts, like karate masters. All the most dangerous pressure points. Hit them here and they die in a second. Hit them there and destroy their ego.

"Danny gives me peace. It's not a dull peace, either. We balance each other. Isn't that what we should be doing—looking for balance?"

"How do you know all this without even trying?"

"Because I'm afraid I'd like living with you too much, and then I'd find out way too late it was a terrible mistake ever to try."

"That sounds cowardly."

"Being safe and being loved is not cowardice. We'd love each other, but there's no safety between us, Weber. We'd be flinging each other across trapezes without a net. That's all right when you're young and have nothing to lose but your heart, but when you're older and know your heart is only a piece of the whole, then you pull back and say I'd rather have a family than the air. I'd rather lie on my back on the earth and look up at the stars than try to fly to them with little chance of getting there."

"You think we'd have a chance of that?"

"Of course. But only a small one, and I don't want to gamble any-more. I have a good man, a baby, and a pretty charmed life right now. What am I supposed to do, put all those chips on the table in hopes of winning a jackpot? How many jackpots are won? How many people walk away from the table rich?"

That conversation isn't in her book, but the reason I remember it so clearly is because that night I had my first Rondua dream.

What was Rondua? Take a child's perception and experience in a toy store at six or seven years old. Where the stuffed animals are as big and all-encompassing as skyscrapers; where you want to see and touch everything, even when it frightens or repels. That was Rondua. A place where dreams you once had, creatures and situations that knew you (yes, situations knew you in Rondua) all returned to visit, instruct, astonish. But those were only part. It wasn't only things you knew but a world where new wonder and surprise were common currency and certainty had no place.

People dream of strange lands all the time, but the difference here was Cullen James and I dreamed the same view, saw the same wondrous landscapes and creatures, and could thus compare notes and draw maps the next day.

What did it mean and why did it happen? Nervously, I asked a number of people, but the explanation that sounded truest came from Venasque, Phil's shaman and our one-time neighbor with the pig. The only proof I knew of the old man's power was Strayhorn's unequivocal belief in him, which didn't remove my skepticism, however. But when the Rondua dreams came more and more frequently, I thought it could do no harm to ask him.

"You know the joke about the thermos bottle? A bunch of researchers are interviewing people to hear what they think is man's greatest invention. Someone naturally says the wheel, another the airplane, the alphabet . . . then one guy says, 'The thermos bottle.'

"Thermos bottle? What are you talking about?

"The guy says, 'Look, in the winter when it's ten below out, I fill my thermos bottle with hot soup and go to a football game. Two hours later it's still cold as hell out, but when I open up the bottle there's hot soup in there. Right?

"'Okay. Then in the middle of summer, when it's ninety out, I fill that same bottle with ice-cold lemonade. Two hours later when I'm dying of the heat, I open it up and there's still ice-*cold* lemonade in there. I got one question for you: How does it *know?*' "

Venasque took a handful of M&M's and handed them to the pig.

"I don't understand your analogy."

"*Love* is the greatest invention of human beings, Weber. It's such a great invention that man made it and brought it to life, but then it got so strong and smart it took itself out of our hands and now runs its own affairs. It's like that thermos bottle—It *knows.* How it knows can be applied all over the place.

"You want this woman and you know she's the right one for you, but it just can't be. So love takes over. If you can't have her, you can know her better than any other person on earth does, including her nice-guy husband. You can't sleep together, but you can 'know' her better than any hundred nights together would ever teach you.

"What's the place called? Ron-dua? Enjoy it, Weber. Even the bad parts. Love's giving you a present. The two of you."

As suddenly as they came, the dreams left. According to her book, Cullen thought I stopped dreaming because she put her hand on my forehead and said a secret word. I think they stopped because, like some kind of deep alpine tunnel that goes on for ten or twelve miles, I'd gone into and through my improvident love for her and finally come out the other side. By the time she touched my head and said that word, 'Koukounaries,' I'd gotten through this tunnel and emerged, blinking and disoriented but safe in another country.

I would always love her, but not with the same unhealthy need and hope as before. That was suicidal. If Venasque was right and Love *had* given us Rondua, losing it as I did meant a loss too of the damaging obsession I had for Cullen James, which had badly affected whole months of my life.

A couple of hours after Wyatt mentioned Rondua, Danny James called to see how things were going. I wanted to talk about the videotapes and the tattoo moving off my back, but Sasha was home and I didn't want her to hear any of this yet. Wyatt was the only one who knew the whole story, and we'd agreed not to tell her anything until we were more sure ourselves. What if Strayhorn *was* alive? Or Pinsleepe really was an angel come to earth to right his wrongs? Sasha was pregnant and full of cancer. When I said Wyatt had cancer too, he blithely brushed it off, saying, yes, but he wasn't pregnant. What's more, he *did* believe in impossibilities like angels and atoning for a dead man's sins. Sasha didn't, which made it difficult in case other queer things would have to be done to resolve these matters.

"Danny, you never told me why Phil went to New York the last week before he died. Would you now? I think it's important."

"He was with a little girl named Pinsleepe. About eight or nine. Said she was his niece, but I don't know. That was the first thing that worried me. The two of them were in and out of town a lot, because every time I called I had to leave a message. When I saw them they'd just come back from New Jersey."

"Do you remember where in New Jersey?"

"No, but Phil said he'd spent a summer there when he was a kid."

"Not Browns Mills?"

"Yes, Browns Mills. That was the name."

"What was he like when you saw him?"

"Very up, like he was on dexedrine. He kept telling jokes so the little girl would laugh. Almost as if he were babysitting and felt compelled to entertain her the whole time. It was odd. I felt uncomfortable."

"Why didn't you bring Cullen?"

"Because he specifically asked me not to. No Cullen and no Mae. Which was strange too, because you know how much he liked both of them.

"We spent a few hours together and then I had an appointment. As we were saying goodbye, he told me to tell you he'd be sending you some very important videotapes soon."

"How come you *didn't* tell me?"

"Because he was dead a few days later."

If you've seen *Midnight Too* you know about Browns Mills, New Jersey. Only in the film Phil called the town Levrett, after the dormitory we lived in at Harvard.

Why would he want to go back there with the child? There are singular events in life that shift or determine our direction forever. I'm not only talking about marriage or the loss of loved ones. In Strayhorn's case, it was the death of two strangers that did it. Both happened the summer he was ten in Browns Mills.

His family rented a cabin by the lake there. Because the town was near an army base, lots of military families lived nearby. Phil became friendly with the children of one and they all hung around together.

Their father was a military policeman. One day when all the kids were sitting around listening to the radio, a news bulletin came on and said two M.P.s had been shot to death by an unknown assailant. When they gave the names and the father of his friends was one of them, Phil snapped. For some reason, he started screaming 'Rock and Roll! Rock and Roll!' They took him to the hospital and put him under observation.

That would have been enough for one summer, but a few weeks later he was down at the lake with another friend throwing rocks into the water, and one of them hit something. It turned out to be a girl's body. Strayhorn stood on the shore and watched his friend drag her in. Then he ran away, screaming 'Rock and Roll did it!'

For years afterward, he was haunted by this "Rock and Roll" monster. Whenever anything bad happened he was sure who did it. If he woke in the night gasping and sweaty from some lunar struggle, he knew who must have caused it. We all have our demons, but Phil's was linked to real death and one real body.

Even when we were at Harvard he sometimes had screaming Rock and Roll dreams. He told me their origin and how over the years the thing had taken on a face and body that he later used as the basis for Bloodstone.

When I got off the phone with Danny my head felt like it was going to spout steam: Sasha, Pinsleepe, Strayhorn (alive or dead), angels, devils, Browns Mills. . . .

What the fuck was he doing with Pinsleepe in Browns Mills, New Jersey?

He'd been seen at El Coyote, so we went there and asked questions: nothing. He'd been seen in the valley at a gay bar called Jack's, so we went there: nothing. He was seen on Rodeo Drive. . . . We asked for three days before turning up anything. I had repeatedly gone back to the videotapes to see if anything new would appear, but it didn't. Both Wyatt and I called people we knew and then people they knew until our ears were red and bored. There are so many stories and counter stories in Los Angeles that we were constantly comparing notes to see if we already had certain information or if it ran counter to what we'd learned.

What emerged was this: A man who looked and sounded like Philip Strayhorn was going around town in Porsche sunglasses, a black silk suit and shirt, and alligator shoes saying Ha-ha, it was all a big publicity joke: Here I am, and rumors of my death have been greatly exaggerated.

The problem with this description was Strayhorn was one of the most unfashionable men I knew, unlike Mr. Alligator Shoes.

Phil bought clothes the way some people buy whatever's nearest when they're hungry. When his underwear got holey, he went down to Thrifty Drugs on La Brea (a favorite Strayhorn hangout) and bought three six-packs of plain BVD white underpants. While there, he might go on a shopping spree, which meant including some white T-shirts and cotton basketball socks. Top that off with sneakers and jeans, and you had the well-dressed Strayhorn.

Besides that, he almost never went out. Chic restaurants and "in" places made him nervous and uncomfortable. His idea of a good time was to stay at home and talk to Sasha or play with the dog. His house was one of the coziest I knew.

I called my friend Dominic Scanlan in the Los Angeles Police Department and described what was going on. He said he'd look into it. Two hours later he called back and said to meet him at an address downtown. When Wyatt and I got there, a small yellow house was partially roped off by Police Investigation tapes. Dominic pulled up a few minutes later.

"The kids in these neighborhoods tear down our tapes so fast. We got a call a couple of days ago from the next-door neighbor saying something fishy was going on in there. Strange loud noises, crashes and bangs, that sort of thing. There are a lot of crack houses around here, so we thought maybe some dealers were having a party.

"Fuck us and our premonitions. Nothin' is ever simple, huh? The first cop goes inside, takes one look, and calls back to his partner, 'Hey, come here! We got 'Ripley's Believe It or Not.' " Dominic took a manila envelope from under his arm and opened it. Sliding out some pictures, he handed them over.

"Holy God!"

"James Penn, ex-out-of-work actor, ex-waiter at Jack's—"

"Ex-human being!"

"You got it, Finky. The guys in pathology are still trying to figure out what happened to him."

"What was the cause of death?"

"Electrocution, blood loss . . . shit, I don't know. Everything. Ha! That's one for you—guy died of everything!"

"And this is the same man who went around pretending to be Strayhorn?"

"Look at the other pictures."

There were some of Penn alive and smiling. He did look like Phil, and it was easy to see how some might have mistaken him for the other.

Something ball—shriveling came to me. I looked at Dominic.

"It's a scene from *Midnight Always Comes!*"

He nodded. "You got it. The ultimate Hollywood crime: Guy goes around impersonating Philip Strayhorn, then ends up getting killed the way Bloodstone did a guy in one of *his* movies. Cinematic justice. Other places you got poetic justice, out here we got cinematic justice!"

"Can we go inside?"

"Speak for yourself, Weber, I'm not going in there."

"Yeah, you can go in, but don't touch anything, huh? They're still checking the place out. I'll stay here with Finky. I want to ask him a couple of questions about the old show. I got this great Finky Linky T-shirt at home. Wish I'd brought it with me so you could sign it. Here's the key, Weber."

There was a brick path up to the front porch. The lawn smelled fresh-cut. Two of the steps creaked when I put pressure on them. I thought about walking up to Rainer Artus's house a few days before. Inside his place had been a vague madness; inside this one was the bitterest kind of death.

I unlocked the door and stepped in.

Eerily, everything was in perfect order. Clean wooden floors, a smell in the air of some kind of pine disinfectant. Spotless, ordered. When he was technical adviser on one of my films, Dominic had taken me to other murder scenes. They'd reflected the chaos of the act—blood, scatter, curtains torn from windows in the desperation of the soon-dead. Not here. James Penn's house appeared ready for a party to arrive any moment.

I walked into the living room and saw Pinsleepe sitting on a blue couch eating a red ice-cream cone.

"Hi, Weber."

"How long have you been here?"

"I don't know. I've been waiting for you. I just finished cleaning up."

"Did you know this man?"

"James Penn? No. But it's another part of the Phil thing."

"Penn was killed the same way Bloodstone killed someone."

"That's right. It's what I told you: When Phil did that scene, everything bad got loose."

"You mean Bloodstone's alive?"

She smiled and licked a corner of her cone. "No. Phil thought up that scene, not Bloodstone. All the Midnights are Phil."

"He's alive?"

"No. He's dead. But what he *was* is still alive. Do you get it? If we could put all the children we have been across the sky, we'd understand ourselves a lot better.

"No matter how many times Phil killed himself, by making that scene in the movie after I told him not to, he was only killing himself *then.* All the other thirty years of Strayhorn were around and alive: the little boy Phil who ran away from the bogeyman Rock and Roll, the Phil who thought up Bloodstone, all of them. Who you are now controls all the people you *were.* If this now-you dies for the wrong reason, the other ones get to do what they want. And if they don't have any guide, they go crazy."

"They killed Penn?"

"Sure. Maybe it was the eight-year-old Phil with the bad temper who was angry at the man for impersonating him. Or the twenty-six-year-old Phil who was stoned all the time and did strange things. . . . I couldn't tell you which one. Maybe it was a combination. Maybe they ganged up on Penn.

"Did Sasha ever tell you why they really broke up? Ask her. Ask her about 'A Quarter Past You.' She still has it. Don't let her tell you she doesn't. That'll show you some of the different Phils you didn't know.

"You're the only one now who can do anything about it, Weber. If you don't film that scene, everything's over. Other things too, besides Sasha dying."

"Like what?"

She shook her head.

"If I film it . . . right, then Sasha lives, and her baby—*you*—die. Right?"

"Right. I go away. I don't have to be here anymore."

A QUARTER PAST YOU

It began innocently enough, sort of. They loved each other. They wanted to grow old together, and that is the only real proof of great love. But recently there had been one thing, one large speck of dust on their otherwise clear lens: sex. It had always been fine with them, and there *were* times when they reveled in each other. But sleep with another person a thousand nights, and some of sex's phosphorescence rubs off under the touch of familiar fingers.

One time, as they worked to catch each other's rhythms, she'd uttered something inadvertently that made him smile and want to talk about later, during those fading soft moments before sleep.

"You shouldn't!" was what she'd suddenly said.

He hadn't been doing anything new or special, so he had to assume she was fantasizing a naughty scene with someone else. The thought excited him, particularly because he himself had often done the same thing.

Afterward, in the blue dark, he touched her hand and asked if he was right.

"I'm embarrassed." But then she giggled—her sign she was willing to talk.

"Come on, don't be embarrassed. I've done it too, I promise! It's just another way."

"You promise you won't misunderstand?"

"I promise."

"Okay, but I'm really embarrassed."

He squeezed her hand and knew not to say anything or else she would shut right up.

"Well, it's not anyone in particular. Just this man. It's a fantasy. I see him on a subway and can't stop looking at him."

"How's he dressed?"

"The way I like—jacket and tie, maybe a nice suit. But he's also wearing fresh white tennis sneakers, which throws the whole thing off in a great way. It's a touch of humor that says he wears what he wants and doesn't give a damn what others think."

"Okay. So what happens then?"

She took a deep breath and let it all out slowly before continuing. "I see him and can't stop looking, as I said. He's sexy and that's part of it, sure, but there are other things that make him more special than just that.

"He has these great Frenchman's eyes and is carrying a book I've been meaning to read for a long time. Finally he looks at me and I'm hooked completely. The best part is, he doesn't check out my body or anything. Just looks at me and I know he's interested. I love that. He doesn't go over me like I'm a new car in the showroom."

Her story was much more detailed than he'd have thought. In his own fantasies, he'd make eyes at waitresses in high heels or shopgirls with thick lips. Things were arranged. They'd go back to her apartment. Once there, they'd leap to it with instant heat and curiosity.

Moments pass before he realizes she's begun speaking again.

". . . follows me when I get off the subway. Knowing he's there behind makes me incredibly excited. I know what's going to happen and I know I'll do it, no matter what."

She talked on, giving the most minute, loving details. She and Mr. White Sneakers never speak, not once. As things get more intense, they slow down until it's all movement under water.

The single sentence ever said aloud is the line "You shouldn't!" This is something she says each time, but only once it's actually happening and she feels a momentary pang of guilt. But that passes quickly because the experience is simply too rare and extreme for guilt to enter into it.

When she was finished, there was a silence thick as fur between them. Under her breath, she mumbled something about its not being a very original fantasy.

"Don't say that! Don't degrade it! What do you care, so long as it excites *you?* What difference does it make how original it is? I bet three quarters of most people's sexual fantasies are either about taking or being taken.

"What's his name?"

"Who, the man? I have no idea. We don't talk. He never tells me."

"What do you *want* his name to be?"

"I never thought about it. What a funny question."

He went into the kitchen for some wine. When he returned, the light on her side of the bed was on and she was sitting with her arms wrapped around her knees.

"Peter Copeland." She smiled at him and shrugged as if a little embarrassed.

"Peter Copeland? Sounds like a Yalie."

She shrugged. "I don't know. It's just the kind of name he would have."

"Okay. Is it always the same fantasy? Do you ever make up others about him?"

She took a sip of wine and thought about it. She no longer seemed uncomfortable talking about Peter Copeland now that the fact of him was out in the open and he had a name.

"Usually the same—the subway, what he wears, how he follows me. It's enough."

That last phrase hit him hard. He'd had so many different fantasies with so many different predictable faces and settings. "It's enough." He knew then he was jealous of her and her Peter Copeland, content with each other and their silent mutual fever.

The next day, walking to work, he stopped in the middle of the street and started to smirk. At a florist, he bought ten tulips, her favorite flower, and arranged to have them sent over to their apartment. On the enclosed card he wrote, *I hope you like tulips. They're my favorite. Thanks for putting the comet over last night's sky. Peter.*

And in bed that night, he changed everything. He became an entirely different person in the dark. She couldn't see him so he could have been anyone. He wanted to be Peter Copeland but didn't know how.

Usually they spoke, but in this half hour when they owned each other, he said nothing. From the beginning she understood and responded eagerly. Whenever they sailed toward something familiar, their own from their years together, he steered them away. Then she took over and was strong or passive when he least expected it.

It was all better than he had imagined, and once again he grew so jealous of Peter Copeland. No stranger, however wonderful, deserved what she offered now. The only things he had ever given *his* dream lovers were both anonymous and forgettable.

At the end, when she again said, "You shouldn't!" he was thrilled she was saying it both to him and to someone else. A moment later he wished it were only him.

The next day he bought the book he knew she had been wanting to read. Inside he wrote, *I think you'll like this. Peter.* She discovered it under her pillow. Sitting down on the bed, she held it on her lap, both hands on top of it and very still. What was he doing? Did she like it?

Their electricity and willingness to go in so many new directions both awed and scared them a little. Both wondered who they were doing this for—themselves or the other?

That week their nights were long exhausting experiments. He couldn't ask her what she liked because it all had to remain silent, spoken only through touch and movement. By eight every night they were excited and looking at the clock. Whatever they'd been used to doing before was unimportant and forgotten. Now they would slip into their new second skins, and whatever was left of the day would hide because it did not know them.

On Thursday she was out walking and decided to buy him a present. In a store, a salesman spread beautiful cashmere sweaters over a glass counter: lilac, taupe, black. She couldn't decide. Only after leaving the store did she realize she'd chosen one that would look better on Peter Copeland than her husband. That startled her, but she made no move to return it. She simply wouldn't tell him.

. . .

At work he realized he'd written the name *Peter Copeland* three times on a pad of paper in front of him. He didn't even know he was doing it. Each time the script was completely different, as if he were trying to forge rather than invent the other man's signature.

"What's for dinner?"

"Your favorite—chili."

He didn't like chili.

There was no chili—her little joke—but the tulips he sent were in a new black and yellow vase on the dining table between them. They were like a third person in the room. He wanted to tell her about writing Copeland's name, but the vivid flowers were enough of the other's presence for the moment.

He looked at them again and realized he was not looking at the same ones he'd bought. Those were pink, these were deep red. Where did she put his?

"It's tulip season again, huh?"

She smiled and nodded.

"I saw some great pink ones the other day. I knew I should have gotten them for you. Somebody beat me to it, huh?"

Her smile remained. It said nothing different from a moment ago. Or was it the slightest bit pitying?

He liked to shave before going to bed—a personal quirk. Standing in front of the bathroom mirror scraping off the last bits of snowy foam, he suddenly pointed his razor at the mirror.

"I heard what you two are doing. Don't think I don't know, you bastard!"

"Are you talking to me?" She called from the bedroom.

"No, Peter Copeland."

He smiled his own weird smile when she didn't say anything to *that.*

. . .

Her fingers were moving lightly across his face when he saw how to break it. Pushing her hand away, he took over and started touching her much too hard, hurting her. To his surprise, she jerked and twisted but remained silent. It was always silent now. Somewhere in these recent days they had both accepted that. But why wasn't she protesting? Why didn't she tell him to stop? Did she like it? How could she? She had said a million times she couldn't understand how people could like hurting each other in bed. Or was Peter Copeland allowed everything? Worse, was the pain he gave pleasant to her now? That was insane! It meant he knew nothing about his wife. It made him breathe too fast. What parts of her did he know, for sure? What else had she held back from him over the years?

He started saying brutal, dirty things to her. It was something they both disliked. Their sexy words to each other were always funny and flattering, loving.

"Don't!" It was the first time she had spoken. She was looking straight at him, real alarm on her face.

"Why? I'll do what I want."

He continued talking, touching her too hard, talking, ruining everything. He told her where he worked, how much money he made, what his hobbies were. He told her where he'd gone to college, where he grew up, how he liked his eggs done.

Soon she was crying and stopped moving altogether. He was in the middle of explaining to her that he wore white sneakers because he had this bad foot infection. . . .

Sasha wouldn't tell me specifically which parts of Phil's short story were true (or why he'd even written it), and I didn't ask. She wanted to know how I knew about it so I lied, saying Phil had told Danny James about it in New York. She said the events of "A Quarter Past You" were only part of the problem and the reason why they'd separated. Since the middle of filming *Midnight Kills*, he'd become bizarrely temperamental and awful to live with.

He was a good-natured man who rarely showed that he was out of sorts, even when he was. His father hadn't liked moody kids, so Mrs. Strayhorn taught Phil and Jackie to either camouflage their distress or put it in their rooms behind a quietly closed door. Phil didn't like his father, but he agreed with this way of concealing pain. In the years we'd lived together at college, I almost never saw him grumpy. If it happened, he would go out of our room and not come back until his spirits had lifted or he'd worked out whatever it was. I couldn't imagine my friend as selfish and mercurial as Sasha went on to describe. But in the end, something Pinsleepe had said came to me: "No matter how many times Phil killed himself, by making that scene in the movie after I told him not to, he was only killing himself *then*. All the other thirty years of Strayhorn were around and alive."

Was this schizoid, unpleasant man already fragmenting before he committed his final act? Was the person who treated Sasha so strangely the same one who shot himself? The same one who caused the death of Matthew Portland? The same one who was on my videotapes, the same one who talked with Danny James in New York, the same one who took Pinsleepe to Browns Mills, the same one . . . ?

7

U h-oh. *What can you believe—or rather, who—the angel or the dead man?*

Pinsleepe has really outdone herself this time. And obviously taken unfair advantage. She's the star witness for the prosecution, always conveniently on the scene to steer the jury (Weber) in the right direction.

What am I allowed to do in my own defense? Nothing but make a couple of absurd videos for him and Sasha where I wasn't allowed to say anything other than a few hints. Like being on some bad TV game show, Celebrity Charades. Guess what the ghost is saying!

Did I lie to you before? Yes. I lied about where Rock and Roll came from. And who went for the cops when we found the dead girl. But I'm not lying now.

So much of what she says is almost true or just a little wrong. If you gave her a lie detector test she'd pass. But truth doesn't come in percentages. Eighty percent true. Ninety-nine. It either is or isn't.

Here is the official Pinsleepe version: Philip Strayhorn got so carried away making his silly little horror films that along the way the poor man signed his soul over to the devil. For what? For power, kids! What else? Power enough to make audiences go out and kill each other, power enough to sell millions of tickets and make lots of money, power enough, finally, to use real *dark forces!*

Yowee! Get your real dark forces here! Get 'em while they're red hot!

Now could we please have a cavalry charge or a heavenly choir? Because at this turning point in our tale, an angel comes to warn Phil not to be naughty anymore because he's making God upset. Stupid Strayhorn, so full of pride, ignores the warning and goes on making the utterly half-assed Midnight Kills. As a result, little Phils come bursting out of the past like maggots and everyone nearby gets killed or cancer.

There was one good scene in the film, and that's the one they—she—wanted me to cut. I didn't. Bad things happened afterward. Were they a result of the scene? I honestly don't know.

But I had to tell Weber they were, because I was forced to. Tell him this. Tell him that. Make him believe. . . .

It's odd how you're allowed to lie here. I can lie to Weber, to you, to anyone alive.

But I'm not going to lie to you anymore. I want you to know as much as I'm allowed to divulge. Why? Because we have a long way to go yet, and I want you to know some of the anger and frustration I've experienced watching Pinsleepe (and the gang) and their manipulations.

Besides, like me, there is nothing you can do about what happens to Weber, Sasha, and Wyatt. Sit here next to me. I've saved a place for you. We'll sit up here in the expensive seats and watch the game together. If we yell very hard, they might barely hear us down on the field. But they won't pay any attention because they're too caught up playing.

Later, during halftime, I'll tell you about what happened in Browns Mills. Or about the scene they wanted me to cut. This time I'll tell you the truth. Take it however you want.

One of the nice things about Los Angeles is it's close to the ocean. Just get on Santa Monica Boulevard and drive till you see the water. It takes about half an hour and is a pleasant drive, especially if the top is down and you're with people you like.

Sasha and Wyatt had argued about who should sit on the uncomfortable tiny back seat of the Jaguar. Finally I suggested they shoot for it. Both of them lit up and they played Rock, Paper, Scissors until Wyatt won three out of five and hopped in the back. He was wearing a pair of khaki Bermuda shorts and matching khaki bush shirt, thus looking more like he was going lion hunting than to the beach.

"I never really swim, you see. Just put my feet in the water and browse."

Sasha had a bag packed with sandwiches, drinks, tanning lotion, a Frisbee, a book. . . . "I like to keep my options open." She wore a chic dark blue swimsuit that showed off her good figure. Seeing her so nicely revealed reminded me of our time in Zermatt; how generous she was in bed, how much fun we'd had that trip.

She also wore a promotional *Midnight Kills* baseball cap, which was disconcerting in light of what had been happening. But maybe it was good she could wear it and seem to ignore its implications. That meant there were corners of her life still untouched by the shadows Phil and his movies had cast over her.

It was time we all did something light and unimportant. When the night before I suggested the beach, Sasha shrugged, but Wyatt and I talked her into it. From the way she was acting today, it was plain she was happy.

Although nothing had been said, there was a silent agreement among us not to talk about Strayhorn or the other related things flying around our lives. We needed a rest. Jump in the water. Get a little sunburn. Lie on your back with the million-year-old sand under you, hard and hot and familiar.

We must have looked very California that day. The black convertible, good-looking woman wearing a baseball cap and dark glasses in the passenger's seat, friend in the back with his knees up and big smile on. I think we all felt good. The day promised to be clear and fresh enough so we could get out the paints (or toolbox) and touch up (or readjust) small parts of our lives. I remembered Saturdays as a boy that were like that. Today I'll lift weights or run *two* miles, clean up my room and help Mom shop. Maybe mow the lawn without being asked, do my homework carefully. You were too young to understand it, but the energy came from gratitude. Thank you for letting me be alive, young, healthy. I don't know any other way of showing it but to do more of everything and do it better today.

That's how it felt driving out to the beach with my friends.

Sasha said something I didn't hear.

"Excuse me?"

She leaned over and said loudly, "I asked why you stopped directing films. I always wanted to ask but never had the nerve."

I looked in the rearview mirror and saw Wyatt leaning forward, the wind blowing his wild hair back. He was trying to listen.

"I wanted to live in Europe awhile, and not just at the Crillon in Paris for a couple of weeks while making a film.

"One day when we were working on *Wonderful*, I was in the farmer's market buying fruit. These two old guys stood next to me. One of them said, "Aaron tells me I gotta finish two Dynasty scripts before we leave, not just the one. So I told Frances, 'Honey, we gotta skip Italy this time and just do the two weeks in Germany.' "

"Hearing that made me so fucking depressed. I didn't want to be sixty years old, writing Dynasty scripts instead of going to Italy. That happens too easily when you live out here too long and forget there are other things in the world."

"Why didn't you go on living in Europe?"

Pulling up at a red light, I looked at her. "Because you have to come home sometime. The longer you're away, the harder it is to return. I wanted to come back to America, but not to the life I had before. That's why I went to New York."

Finky Linky put his head on Sasha's shoulder as I accelerated away from the light. "Tell her about your half/half theory. That has something to do with it too."

"Not really a theory. It's just that I'd like to live the second half of my life better than the first."

Simultaneously, the two of them said "What's 'better'?" and then laughed at the coincidence.

The trip to the beach was all sun, wind, and shouting. We couldn't agree on what good was, but everyone disagreed so vociferously that it was obvious each of us had a damned good idea of what *we* believed it was.

We arrived at Santa Monica jazzed up and ready to go. Wyatt took our things and told us to go ahead while he set everything up. We didn't need any more encouragement and ran straight out into the cold ocean. It was early afternoon in the middle of the week, and very few other people were around. We swam out from shore together until the waves were really bobbing us up and down.

"You look like a beautiful blond seal!"

"And you look like a lifeguard!"

She paddled over and, coming behind, wrapped her arms and legs around me.

"This was a great idea, Weber. Thank you."

"You're welcome. Look at Finky!"

Back on shore, Wyatt had taken off his shirt and was doing what looked like t'ai chi. The quick cold slap and pull of the water around us was such a contrast to the slow delicacy of his exercises.

"Give me a piggyback ride." She bit me on the back of the neck. I bent down and bit her on the arm, then began moving slowly through the water at an old man's pace. It felt good having her around me like that. It had been too long since I'd been with a woman and the press of breasts against my back, warm breath on my neck and ears. . . . Something would have to be done about that when this was over; it was time to find someone who mattered. Besides my masochistic love for Cullen James, the only women I had serious, intimate contact with were those in the Cancer Theater Group. Their needs were very different from mine. When I began working there, I made the mistake of sleeping with one but quickly and painfully learned that pity is not a good substitute for support.

"Do I feel heavier?"

"I don't know, Sash, I haven't given you many piggyback rides."

"You know—from the pregnancy. Maybe I just think I float better now."

"What did the doctor say about your being pregnant?"

"He said the conditions were strange but things like this have happened."

"How do you feel about it?"

"If it's Phil's child, I want it. It could only be his! I haven't slept with anyone else since you and I were together in Vienna."

I paddled us out a ways. There were so many things I wanted to tell her and talk about with her.

"Weber! Look at that, over there!" She pointed off to our right. Coming up from behind a flipping wave was the large golden head of a dog. It moved fast toward us, head straining hard out of the water. Sasha let go of me and I went for the dog, thinking it must have fallen off some boat and been swimming since.

"Here, boy!" I tried to whistle but got a mouthful of salty water instead. It saw me but wasn't interested. Sasha called and it saw her too, but no thanks. The dog (it looked like a vizsla or golden retriever) paddled by both of us and kept right on going. We looked at each other and made the same face—What can you do?

Treading water where we were, we could only watch.

"I thought it was drowning!"

"It sure didn't want *our* help. The loneliness of the long-distance swimmer."

Reaching shore, it trotted right out of the surf, looking supremely successful. One good shake and it was on its way again down the beach.

Sasha laughed. "I love that! Where did it come from?"

"Neptune."

She beamed. "Yes, Neptune's dog. Right!"

I moved over and took her in my arms. She hugged me. "That's so mysterious! It just came out of nowhere and didn't want to have a thing to do with us."

"Mysteries of the deep."

"Sometimes they're nice. Let's swim some more. I want another piggyback."

When we got back, Wyatt had laid everything out and was on his back sunning, but with an expression on his face like something smelled bad.

"What's the matter, Finky Linky?"

"I always like the *idea* of suntanning, but when I do it I get itchy and impatient."

I sat down next to him. "Isn't the idea to relax and let the sun do the work?"

He sat up, saw how wet I was, and moved away. "The idea that people spend hundreds of dollars so they can sit in the sun and *sweat* is beyond me.

"Look at what our friend made for lunch."

While we ate, Sasha told him about the dog. I'd thought it was a funny, oddball thing that made for a five-minute story. But she was enraptured and couldn't get over what had happened. I think Wyatt saw it my way because he kept encouraging her to go on while looking at me with what-*is*-this? eyes. Hours later I realized she was so starved for something light and good and amusing in her life that a swimming dog was reason enough for wonder.

We spent the day at the beach trying as subtly as possible to keep Sasha happy. When she laughed we wanted her to laugh more, louder, longer. We told stories and jokes and moved around as if putting the show on right here. Maybe we were. Sasha was really one of the good ones, a person who deserved every bit of our energy and concern. We knew she appreciated whatever we did and, if necessary, would give it back in duplicate one day. That's why she and Phil had gone so well together. They were both inordinately generous people who, quite touchingly, never really realized why their friends liked them so much.

At dusk we took a long walk down the beach. People were walking their dogs; lovers held hands and looked even more romantic than usual; a surfer missed a wave, and his board, flying up in the air, caught the orange of the setting sun and threw it over us a moment. On our left side, the ocean was all pound and rush. On our right, cars hissed by on the Pacific Coast Highway. A distant helicopter arched across the horizon.

Wyatt was an exceptional mimic and had done most of the voices for the creatures on *The Finky Linky Show*. Walking down the beach, we kept asking him to do Fiti, Elbow, Pearl, and the others. The funniest part was, he did them deadpan. Hands in pockets, face expressionless, he kept mixing the high birdy *wheek* of Pearl with, say, the bass-drum *clump* of Elbow. They had conversations, they sang songs together. Passing a man fishing in the surf, Wyatt broke off long enough to make the sound of line whizzing crazily off a spool, as if the guy had just caught Moby Dick.

After one of the voices demanded and got a round of applause from us, Wyatt stopped and, taking Sasha's arm, pulled her to him. She looked at him but he only shook his head and put his hand behind her back.

"What's your name, dear?"

Sasha opened her mouth, but before anything came out a voice very much like her own said, "Mrs. Bubble."

"Where do you come from, Mrs. Bubble?"

"The sea. I am her sea self."

"Did you know you had a sea self?"

Grinning, Sasha shook her head. Such a great look on her face: a child at a magic show, a kid sitting on Santa's knee at the department store.

The next day Wyatt and I had two appointments. The first was with the man who had taken over as producer of *Midnight Kills*. Our meeting with him was short and to the point. We told him we'd be willing to edit *M.K.* and, if necessary (I wanted to leave that door open), rewrite and film a scene to replace the one that had disappeared since the deaths of Strayhorn and Portland.

When he got over his false astonishment (we knew Sasha had already told him our plan), he asked how much we'd want to do this. Nothing; we were doing it for Phil. Then what kind of line in the credits did we want? None.

The meeting took as long as it did because it ended up with the producer threatening that if we *didn't* let him put both of our names high on the credits, he wouldn't let us do it. "You know how many more ticket and video sales I can make with your two names up there on the screen? The triumphant return together of Finky Linky and Oscar-winner Weber Gregston, writing the latest installment of *Midnight!* Jesus Christ, are you kidding? The press'll go crazy with this!"

Neither Wyatt nor I cared about a "triumphant return" to Hollywood, but if using our names was the condition under which things would be done our way, all right. We tentatively agreed and made a date to sign papers and see what was left of the film at the end of the week.

Our other meeting that day was with Dominic Scanlan and a friend of his on the police force. I knew of this other man only through Dominic's stories. His name was Charles something, but no one ever called him that. They called him "Blow Dry." Apparently even his children called him that.

As we were getting out of the car in the garage of the Beverly Center, Finky Linky asked, "Why are we having lunch at this dump with a man named Blow Dry?"

"Because Dominic says he's the most terrifying man he knows."

"Why do we want to meet him?"

"Because I have an idea. Actually, I have two ideas and he's going to help us on both."

"Don't you know enough horrible people?"

"Listen, Scanlan was a SEAL in Vietnam. You know about them?

They made Special Forces look like sissies. He's also gotten four commendations for bravery from the police. When he says this guy is something, I want to meet him."

"Why here?"

"Because Blow Dry likes to come here on his lunch hour and shop."

"Please register my dissenting vote."

"I will. Let's go."

We rode the escalators up the side of the building with what seemed like everyone else in Los Angeles. Coincidentally, the first store we saw on entering the place was the pet shop where Phil had bought Flea.

"Where are we meeting Mr. Dry and Company?"

"At a computer store on the second floor."

"Changing the subject, have you thought about how you want to film the scene?"

"Yes. That's why I want to meet this guy."

Wyatt looked at me with his head cocked to one side. "Are you telling me something?"

"Not yet. I want to meet him first. Then I'll let you know what I'm thinking."

Clothes, food, intelligent toys, cutlery . . . you could probably buy everything you needed for the rest of your life at a big shopping mall. All the things for the different stages you'd go through would be included too. Want to be a hippie at fifteen and wear bell-bottom pants, eat whole grains, and listen to Vanilla Fudge? Third floor. Cut your hair at twenty-two, wear only black with rolled-up sleeves, and carry a black aluminum briefcase from Germany, don't forget the Ray Ban glasses? Fourth floor. Et cetera.

"Hey, guys!" We turned and there was Dominic with a big chocolate-chip cookie in his hand. "Don't mind this. I know we're going to eat lunch, but I can't resist these things."

"Where's Blow Dry?"

"Playing a computer game. Come on, I'll introduce you. I brought my T-shirt with me this time, Finky Linky. Will you sign it?"

"No."

"No?" Both Dominic and I looked at him.

"No, because I brought you something better." He handed over a bag he'd been carrying. Inside was a turquoise sweatshirt with a picture of Finky and his whole crew across the front.

"Hey, wow, that's wonderful! Thank you very much! I don't know what to say."

"You already said thank you once, Dom."

"Hey, B.D., there you are. We were just coming for you."

He was plain-looking, nothing more. A little bit over middle size, black hair, very round slightly pockmarked face framed by steel glasses over nothing eyes. He shook hands hard but not a crusher. Suit, white shirt, tie. If I saw him on the street I'd've guessed real estate salesman or insurance. Definitely not a policeman. Definitely not scary.

"What do you like to eat? They have everything here: Chinese, deli, whatever you want."

"I'd love a corned beef sandwich."

"You got it."

Wyatt and Dominic trailed behind us as we walked toward the restaurant.

"Should I call you—"

"Call me B.D., Weber. That's all right."

His voice was calm, uninteresting. I kept wanting to look straight at him but didn't.

"How come you wanted to meet me?"

"Dominic says you're the man I'm looking for."

"Looking for how?"

"I asked him to introduce me to the scariest guy he knew."

Dominic came up from behind. "What he *really* said was, 'Who's the scariest motherfucker you know?' B.D., I couldn't tell a lie."

Lunch was corned beef and talk about the LA Lakers. The scariest man Dominic knew dabbed at the corners of his mouth with a napkin after every few bites and seemed bored by us.

"B.D., what was the most frightening thing that ever happened to you?"

"I saw some stuff in Vietnam that gave me something to think about. And you work for the police long enough. . . . No, wait a minute! I can tell you exactly what. The most frightening thing that ever happened to *me* was when I was a little kid. This is going to sound crazy, but I think you'll get what I mean.

"When I was six or seven, my mother took me for the first time to spend the night at my grandma's house over on Wilcox. Nice old woman. Anyway, I was all excited because I'd never slept anywhere but my own bed. This was a big thing, you know? Well, after Mom went away, Grandma and I stayed up late watching *The Untouchables* and eating these big caramel sundaes she made for us. I was in heaven: watching *Untouchables*, staying up past nine, ice cream. . . . Finally it was time to hit the sack. I was sleeping in the same bed with her, and about as soon as I got under the covers I was out like a light.

"Now, maybe half an hour later I woke up hearing this giant fucking monster *right next to me!* You know? I mean, it was right *there!* Going *rrraaawww . . . gllllllkkkk . . . rrraaawww.* . . . I came out of sleep like a shot, but what could I do, run away or something?"

I started smiling, which turned into chuckling, which I tried to hold back by putting a hand over my mouth. Impossible. The three of them looked at me. Blow Dry smiled.

"You know, huh?"

"I know, and I understand! How old were you?"

"Six. You remember how it was then."

Dominic looked at us. "So what the fuck happened? What's with the monster?"

B.D. looked at me and winked. "The monster was my grandma snoring! That's what the growling was. I'd never heard anyone do that before. Can you imagine what a loud snorer sounds like in the dark to a six-year-old kid?"

"Aw, come on, B.D., get the fuck out of here! You're telling me you were more scared in that bed hearing your grandmother snore than—"

"I was never more scared in my life, Dominic." The way Blow Dry said the sentence was like a guillotine blade coming down. Whatever charm and sweetness the story had had died right there and left us looking at the man who'd told it.

I was with him often after that day but never saw any of the malevolence Dominic attributed to him in story after ghastly story. The only part of his menace I experienced was hearing the feral tone of that one short sentence. It was enough. I'd found our Bloodstone.

8

Sasha couldn't believe I was leaving. Both Wyatt and I had to re- peatedly reassure her I'd be back in less than a week. What was I going to do in New York? Some business that had to be taken care of before I could start work on *Midnight Kills*. Why couldn't it wait till later? Because some of it had to do with filming; I needed to talk to some actors there because we wanted them in the film.

The day before I left, Wyatt and I made a list of the people in the cancer group who would fit what we were going to try and do with our scenes. I say scenes, because after seeing the rushes of the film we knew it needed at least two more to make any sense.

Midnight Kills was by no stretch of the imagination good. The idea was half interesting: Bloodstone comes to life this time as an evangelist who starts convincing crowds that his "philosophy" is not only valid but correct. Halfway through, we discover it isn't really Bloodstone, but. . . .

The plot had more twists and turns than a snake on fire. What Phil had done was substitute surprise and tricks for real story. Although you were constantly being electrified with new shocks or jolts or severed body parts, there wasn't no story. It was that simple. The first thing Wyatt said after we'd sat through the thing was, "It doesn't need a scene, it needs a proctologist!" I agreed, so we spent a hell of a long time working out what needed to be done.

Another problem was what to tell Sasha. We took the easiest and most dishonest way, which was to say we were simply fulfilling Phil's contract for him. Too much time and money had already been invested. Since there was so little left to film, why not do it right ourselves instead of letting some jerk at the studio ruin it?

Phil hadn't liked Sasha to look at his work until it was finished, so luckily she hadn't seen any of *M.K.* yet. What would she have said if she had? Agreed with our opinion that it would have been best for the film to be destroyed and forgotten?

"Is it any good, Weber?"

"No. But I think we can make it better."

"I'm not surprised. When he liked something he was doing, Phil never worked on anything else. After he wrote 'A Quarter Past You' and showed it to me, I knew everything was going down the tubes: our relationship, the movie, everything. Why would he want to write a story about that, Weber? Wasn't he ashamed, or at least embarrassed?"

Chewing a fingernail, Finky Linky said, "The last time I saw him in New York, he was way beyond being embarrassed. He didn't have both oars in the water, Sasha. Really pretty crazy. That's what Weber and I were saying about the movie—it's so scattered and confusing—"

"A crazy man's film?" She wanted us to say yes, *Midnight Kills* was a crazy man's film, and the Strayhorn who wrote it and a short story about their sex life and ended up with a gun in his mouth wasn't the same man we'd known and loved.

Wyatt said, "Before my father died a couple of years ago, he was so mean and impossible to be around that he made everyone's life miserable, especially Mother's. Whenever I'd call and ask how she was, she'd say, 'Weary, dear, I'm pretty weary,' because she was giving him every last bit of love she had left, like blood. Whatever she'd kept stored up for maybe her grandchildren, or us, whoever, she was giving him. It was like a transfusion: If love could keep someone alive, he could have all of hers. I've never stopped thinking about that.

"But the sad thing was, it didn't do anything for my father. He only got sicker and more demanding.

"You did what you could, Sasha. It's egotistical to think we can always save the person we love. Even if you were the perfect mate, after what happened to Phil you end up with all kinds of unlocatable guilt. My mother did, and she behaved like a saint with her man.

"Push it away; you made Phil happy. By being with him, you increased the odds in his favor and built something winning and good."

"But what if I drove him crazy?" She looked from Wyatt to me.

"Making *Midnight* drove him crazy, Sasha. Let's finish this damned film and get on with the rest of our lives."

As the blue airport shuttle waited in Sasha's driveway, I put my arm around Wyatt and walked with him to the van. "You'll call Blow Dry and explain what we want?"

"The only reason you're going to New York is so *you* don't have to ask him. Yes, I'll call. What else?"

"You have an idea of how this has to go. What I really want from you, Wyatt, is humor. The whole thing is so much fucking dreck and blood now, we're drowning in it. I want the first scene to lift us completely off the earth and put us somewhere else."

"Where, Disneyland?"

"No, not that far, but somewhere we can . . . rest from Bloodstone awhile. Somewhere we can get a little fresh air."

He nodded and we shook hands.

Sasha was at the door to the van, standing over my suitcase. "I still wish you weren't going."

I stepped up and hugged her. "I won't be gone long, and when I'm back it'll be for a while."

"That's then; this is now. Oh, Weber, I hate missing everyone. It takes up so much energy and makes you so sad. . . . Go ahead. Wyatt and I are going to Larchmont for lunch. Have a good trip and come back soon. Sooner than you said!"

Driving away, I turned around and saw the two of them standing on the sidewalk, arms at their sides, neither of them moving an inch. Both had cancer. At least one of them would be dead soon.

The trip east was uneventful. I made notes for an hour and then fell fast asleep for the rest of the flight. There are so few times or places where you're forced to turn your energy down and simply sit still for a few hours. That's why I enjoy flying, where you can only think or read or sleep. Watching a film or eating a meal on a plane is torture and not even to be discussed.

Since Phil's death I'd been on the run, so thinking long and hard about any one thing was impossible. Boarding the plane, I vowed in the next hours to try and put some of the events together in understandable order. But being away from the Strayhorn hurricane for the first time, my body shut right down and said, "Later. Now take a nap."

I awoke over upstate New York, feeling both refreshed and guilty. I'd be flying back to California in a few days, but in the meantime it felt good to be on my way home.

There were so many things that had to be done. Close up my apartment, talk to the actors, see if I could reach my old cameraman and then convince him that making a couple of scenes for a horror film would be an interesting challenge. . . .

One of the most important qualities a person needs in order to direct for a living is to be a great coaxer: money from producers, performances from actors, special angles from cameramen. . . . When I was directing movies I'd usually be exhausted by the time we began filming because of the days already spent coaxing and wheedling, stroking and reassuring so many people that what they wanted I wanted, and vice versa.

The same was true for stage directing, but in New York I was working with intense, eager people who weren't in unions or up for Oscars or scared they'd lose their shirts if we produced a bomb.

But I'd be flat-out lying if I didn't say I was also intrigued and excited about what we were doing.

The night before, Wyatt and I sat up and talked about it.

"What are we supposed to do, Weber? Fix the film so it's moral or immoral?"

"I don't know. You were there when I asked Pinsleepe the same question."

"Then what are we going to do?"

"All I know now is Blow Dry will play Bloodstone and we're going to use three from our group. Maybe we'll just put everyone together and let them talk."

His look said that wasn't the answer he wanted to hear. "Weber, I've seen all of your films many times and I think they're superb, but this *isn't* the same thing."

"Hold on a minute. Do you think this is real; that once we film whatever is necessary, and do it right, it will save Sasha?"

"Yes, I think it's real! But most of the craziness has been happening to you. Don't *you* think it's real?"

"Anything's real, Wyatt, so long as it's happening to you at the moment. Dreaming Cullen's dreams was real once, the tattoo flying off my back was real. Videotapes from the dead that are there now but weren't a minute ago are real." I stood up and threw my hands in the air. "But then tell me what the fuck is 'real'? Weren't we brought up recognizing boundaries . . . definitions of what was reality and what wasn't? We were, goddammit! That's where we got our sanity!

"So what do we do when everything goes beyond those bounds, like right now? Does it mean the old rules were bullshit and we have to make up new ones, new definitions for reality?

"And if *that's* so, if all boundary lines are down and we've got to start redefining everything, what's 'good' and what's 'evil' now?

"I'll give you a stupid example. When I was in Munich a couple of years ago, a baron I met invited me to an auction of some of the possessions of Princess Elisabeth of Austria. You know, Sissy? It was a ritzy affair, invitation only, and the crowd was mostly royalty with lots of money.

"One of the things for sale was Sissy's bathrobe. Just that: a white bathrobe with plain red stitching up the side. Know how much it went for? Two thousand dollars. If it had been a painting, something unusual and valuable, I'd've understood, but it was a white bathrobe that sold for two thousand bucks! What was it, Finky, a bathrobe some fool paid too much for or a valuable piece of memorabilia?"

"Obviously it sold for that much because of who wore it."

"That doesn't answer the question! We're not talking context here. We're talking bathrobes! What was sold for two thousand dollars? Do you get my point?"

I was so loud he put a finger to his lips. "Shush! No, I don't."

"A robe looks like this; you use it to dry off; it costs about this much. Okay, that looks like one! But the guy just paid two bills for it and then put it in a safe or in a frame. So what is it?

"*Midnight Kills* is a film about evil. But that was evil by the old rules and definitions. The old bathrobe. That was before little pregnant angels, home movies of my mother dying. . . .

"Pinsleepe isn't going to tell us what to do. We have to figure that out ourselves. I think that's the point. But first we have to figure out what—

"You know what I think, Finky? We've looked at that film and the other three now, and none of them are very good. *Parts* are, but even the first one is overrated. It's not nice to say, but I think Phil did something new with *Midnight* but then just coasted through the other three, particularly this one.

"I can't imagine what Pandora's Box he might've opened, or what new 'evil' he unleashed, based on what we saw. It's all the old robe, and people are paying the same price and getting the same product they expected.

"First we've got to redefine some of these things and then make them new. After that we can think about what Pinsleepe wants from us."

My apartment smelled stale and familiar. The furniture and few doodads were old friends who silently said hello. The mail said I owed people money, that I didn't want to miss some terrific opportunities, that sad-faced children needed my help. A Cullen and Mae James postcard from Rockefeller Center said it was time we all went ice skating together again.

Cullen! That's where I'd begin. I called and luckily she answered. In a few short sentences I told her a little of what had happened in California and said I needed to see her as soon as possible. We made a date to meet later that afternoon at a bar near their apartment.

After we finished speaking, I spent ten infuriating minutes looking for my address book, which for some reason turned up under the kitchen table. I called two people and got two answering machines. I told both beeps something interesting was up and please call me back soon. That was all I could do for the time being (the third person didn't have a phone), so I got ready to go for a quick sandwich and beer.

Walking to the door, I passed the window that looked over onto the nudist girl's apartment. She wasn't there, but for the first time since I'd seen his tape, I thought of what Phil had said about the time he was me when I got out of the cab and bumped into her. The phone rang.

"Weber? Hi, it's James Adrian. I just got your message. You're back! What's cooking?"

"Hi, James. Want to go to California and be in a movie?"

"Are you kidding? Sure! What movie? Are you going to direct?"

"Yes. The latest *Midnight.*"

"You mean like in Bloodstone *Midnight?*"

"That's the one. We want you and Sean and Houston to be in this—"

"Houston died, Weber. While you were away."

"No! Oh, God. What happened?" I knew what his answer would be —I'd heard it five times already—but I never got used to it.

"He just felt sick and weak and went to the hospital. What else is new? Tell me about this film."

I sighed and rubbed my forehead. "Finky Linky and I are doing it, and we agreed you three would be great. But Houston's dead. I can't believe it." James gave a small snort on the other end. Of course I believed it. "Anyway, you know, Philip Strayhorn was our friend and he'd almost finished this film before he died—"

"I read he committed suicide."

"Yeah, well. Anyway, we were asked by his production company to wrap it up for them and we agreed."

"You and *Finky* are going to do a *Midnight* film? Man, that's the most astounding thing I've heard in a month. You bet your ass I want to be in it. What are we going to do?"

"Can you come to my place tonight around nine? I'd like to explain it only once."

"Sure. Sean and I were going to the movies anyway, so I'll tell her when we meet.

"Weber, this is really fantastic. Thank you so much for asking me. It'll be the first time I've ever done any professional acting."

"It may not be the best place for you to start, because we don't know exactly what we're doing yet. But I think it'll be interesting. Look, I'll talk to you later. I've got to call Wyatt and tell him about Houston."

"Weber, I just want to say one more thing. Houston told me one time what you did for him was the only good thing that ever happened in his life. He knew he wasn't a great actor, but he said you were the only one who ever gave him a little pride in himself. I think he had it the worst of all of us—his life, I mean—but you know all of us, the whole group, are indebted to you for what you've done. We don't tell you that enough, and I'm not just saying it now because of what you're doing for me. You've saved our lives in a lot of ways. Even if we don't have that much longer to go with them."

I called Wyatt and told him about Houston Taff. We talked for a while and agreed on someone else. Either because he was in the same relative situation as Houston, or just because he took things more calmly than I do, Wyatt seemed unfazed by the sad news. "He died looking forward to something. Lucky him. He had a main role in the play. You gave him that, Weber. You gave him his last future."

I was early for my date with Cullen, so I stood outside the bar, enjoying the New York cold on my face. Looking the other way, I felt someone tap me on the shoulder and say, "Nice jacket. Where'd you get it?"

It was Cullen, wearing the same jacket as I. I'd given it to her as a surprise in the beginning of our relationship as a spur-of-the-moment I'm-crazy-about-you present. She looked a lot better in it than I did.

"I've been in the house all day with Mae, Weber. Would you mind if we just walk down to the river and get some fresh air? Maybe after, we can come back and drink some rum or something?"

We walked down to the park along the Hudson and kept going because the cold was breezy and insistent.

Cullen likes to talk and often interrupts without thinking. It can be exasperating, so I told her to hear me out completely before asking questions or making any comments. It was a long story and would be hard enough to tell anyway. "It's a little bit like Rondua, Cullen."

She put her arm in mine and pulled tight. "Give me a kiss before you start. A good one." She put her hand behind my head and pulled that to her too. Her kiss was strong and loving.

"That's the first time you've ever kissed me like that."

She shrugged and gestured with her head to keep walking. "I can't help it, you look so sad and tired. Are you going to tell me now or keep making ground rules?"

"Now. Remember the day Phil died and I came over to your place?"

We walked for two hours and I talked straight through. Although she'd promised not to interrupt, she did. We got cold and went into a diner for coffee. Stomachs warm, we went back outside and walked down Broadway. I saw a dog that reminded me of the dog in the ocean. I saw a girl who looked vaguely like Pinsleepe. We passed a used bookstore that had three copies of *Bones of the Moon* in the window. Next door was a place that sold the same chocolate-chip cookies Dominic Scanlan was eating the day we met Blow Dry. It was a walk where everything reminded me of something else and thus helped make my description to Cullen sharper and more intricate.

Nevertheless, it's impossible to tell someone about extraordinary or scarifying experiences in your life after they're over. It's like describing a smell. I once went to a lecture by a writer who was famous for having written about exotic places. After the lecture, someone asked why he always went to these places before writing about them. Couldn't he just use his imagination? "No, because if you don't go, you won't catch the invisible smell of the place, and that's its most important feature." The same is true about the high or low moments of your life; invisible smells permeate these important times, and if other people are not there to smell them too they can never really know or understand.

It was frustrating and enervating to try and explain, but I wanted to hear what Cullen, more than anyone else, had to say about my last days. She was my best friend now that Phil was dead. Because we would never be lovers, I could listen to the angular, interesting logic of a woman while generally disregarding the sexy sword of Damocles that usually hangs over such conversations.

When I was finished we were once again having coffee at a Chock Full O' Nuts somewhere in the fifties. Cullen was eating a donut and had powdered sugar all over her upper lip. When she started to speak, a white fall of it dusted her jacket. I reached over and rubbed it into the leather.

"Did you ever listen to Bulgarian music? While I was with Mae this afternoon it came on the radio, and I listened to the whole show. Very strange and mysterious, sad, but I kind of loved it too. Something in you recognizes it, you know?

"What are we talking about here, Weber? Angels and devils: they're Bulgarian music. You have contact with them and it throws you off, but you also recognize them. Not as themselves but as part of *you*. I think any person who has visions—"

"I didn't have a vision, Cullen. Wyatt was with me when I saw Pinsleepe."

"And you were with me when I saw Rondua. Let me finish what I was going to say. What you saw and experienced is Bulgarian music. At first you pulled back and made a sour face because you never heard anything like that before, but then you started tapping your foot and thinking, This stuff is all right! That was me with Rondua. But do you remember the last words of my book? They're the only ones I can still quote because I still feel that way: 'It's hard convincing yourself that where you are at the moment is your home, and it's not always where your heart is. Sometimes I win and sometimes not.'

"You should've seen your face while you were talking, my friend. Whatever is going on now fascinates you. It's everything you love—ghosts, movies, helping other people. You've just never heard it played like that before and it sounds fucking weird.

"You want me to tell you something practical? Okay, get back there fast and see what you can do to help. I think the angel wants you to make a scene that so derides horror and evil that people will only laugh when they see it shown like that in a movie. Sounds like, whatever Phil did, he made bad look good—too good—and that was what let all the cats out of the bag.

"But I think you're right. I never found any of those *Midnight* films very scary. They creep up on you and make all the right howls and screeches, but in the end they're just so-so.

"Did Finky Linky ever tell you about his popcorn meter for films? No? It's really true. You go to the movies and buy a box of popcorn, doesn't matter what size. Even a candy bar. If the movie is great, you get so caught up in it you forget about the food and just hold it in your lap. If the film is only good you eat about half or a third. Et cetera. You know how much popcorn I ate when I saw your last film? Not one piece, so help me God. Ask Danny. You know what I ate when I saw the last *Midnight*? *Two* boxes of Raisinets, my own and most of Danny's. You know why I remember? Because when he discovered I'd taken most of his, we had a little fight in the theater and I had to go get him some more. Terrific film, huh? You eat two boxes of candy and have a fight in—"

"And you know what I say to *that* fuckin' shit, Larry? I say, Fuck you!"

A few seats down, a little Puerto Rican guy was sticking his finger in the chest of the big black man next to him.

"Well, eat my dick, Carlos, 'cause that's the way it is!"

This got louder, but what else is new in New York? I was in the midst of turning back to Cullen when the first plate crashed. Turning again, I saw the two men shoving each other. Then little Carlos fell off his stool and, getting up, punched big Larry in the face. Everyone nearby got up fast and moved away, including Cullen, who danced to the other side of the counter.

"Weber! Get over here!"

"I've still got my coffee."

I sat there and sipped while David and Goliath tried to pound each other. Carlos was little, but Larry kept missing.

"Weber!"

A saucer landed about a foot away, so I picked up my cup and walked over to join Cullen. When I got there she frowned and called me a macho ass.

A policeman came in and things calmed right down. When the three of them had left, Cullen blew up. "You were just going to sit there and drink that coffee! Two guys slugging it out a foot away from you but you don't move? I've seen you do things like this three times, Weber. It's not impressive and it's not courageous; it's stupid."

"I wasn't trying to impress you, Cullen. There wasn't any reason to move."

"That's why you and my husband get along so well: Neither of you know the difference between being brave and being dumb."

The meeting at my apartment that night was good. I told the two men and one woman what *Midnight Kills* was about and what direction we wanted to take with the scenes we did. Nothing else.

One asked why couldn't we just splice what was already there together and release it? No one ever paid attention to plot in a horror film anyway.

Because it was Strayhorn's last work and we wanted to do everything we could to save it.

Another smiled and said, from the sound of it, Wyatt and I didn't know what we wanted to do in our scenes. I agreed and told them it was extremely important they think very hard about what *they* thought real evil was and how—or if—it could be portrayed. Was cancer real evil? Was the pain and despair they suffered from the disease evil? I read them the dictionary definition—"something that brings sorrow, distress, or calamity"—and asked if that satisfied their own visions of what it was. Unanimously they said no. I asked them to tell evil stories; to talk about evil people they knew and why they thought they were evil; to tell about evil things they'd done.

We did this constantly in our work in the group. Theater is just group therapy with an audience much of the time, so no one was hesitant about doing it now.

Nothing astonishing came out of that first session, but I hadn't expected it to. What I wanted, and felt after several hours, was their hunger to begin again. Dedication and enthusiasm are important qualities, but what you really want is addiction to the work. No matter what else they're doing, you want them thinking about it day and night like drug addicts. Once you get that, you've started. Not before.

The three of them went out the door arguing about the difference between cancer and Hitler. I said good night but no one heard me.

The next day was errands and a general meeting with the theater group to explain why I had to leave them high and dry right before their first production. It wasn't a pleasant or comfortable scene. All of them knew this could well be their first and last production. They had worked very hard to get it to where it was. How could I just leave them at the three-quarter point and waltz out to Hollywood? Didn't I think that was pretty selfish and shitty?

Unfortunately I had no stirring Sydney Carton speech to give about far far better things. I *was* leaving them flat. Some of them *would* die before we had time to put up another show. When I asked if they wanted to delay *The Visit* until I was finished in California, someone laughed nastily and said sure, *he'd* be happy to delay but would his body?

When everyone had had a say, we all sat there and looked at one another. My eyes filled with tears. I didn't have to look closely to see many of theirs were too.

The garage where I picked up the rental car also had an "exclusive car wash service." While waiting for the papers to be processed, I asked a man how much the car wash cost. One hundred dollars. What did they *do* for one hundred dollars? Use toothbrushes. On what? Everything, man.

Driving downtown, the thought of men swarming around freshly washed cars with toothbrushes reassured me. A hundred dollars for a car *that* clean? I'd pay.

It was like those wonderful advertisements on television for toothpaste or vacuum cleaners where decay or dirt are semipersonified into funny/evil cartoon creatures that love to dig holes in your teeth or spread foul muck around the house. Suddenly the Tooth Patrol (fluoride in a police uniform) or Vacuum King comes flashing down like lightning and "kills dead" all the baddies. Where else was good so clear-cut, thorough, and effective?

Racketing through the lights and lead-thick fumes of the Lincoln Tunnel, I fantasized spirits you could hire to come in and give your *self* a complete cleaning, millions of brushes scrubbing white effervescent foam into every obscure or hidden corner of your soul.

Then I remembered a thought I often had about smoking cigarettes: If there were some kind of wonder pill that would clean your lungs out so they were like new, but in taking it you could never smoke again because you'd die, would you take it?

Inevitably my answer is no. Whether it's clean lungs, car, or soul, what happens when you have to breathe again, knowing the air is full of brown pollution? Or drive the car out of the garage, back into the filthy world? Lungs are prepared to breathe bad air, cars to drive on dirty streets.

Maybe souls too were meant for hard wear and rough adventure. To make one "toothbrush clean" was a commendable goal, but unless you planned to live in hermetic seclusion forever afterward, it made little sense.

However, if Phil Strayhorn had done what I thought he'd done with *his* soul, he was inexcusably wrong. Some part of him decided he liked the taste of dirt (or shit, evil, pain) so he decided to see how much he could eat before exploding. That was the only Faustian element I saw here. Souls are made for rough adventure, but not such alarming and cruel ones. The warnings from Pinsleepe, the sexual Kabuki he'd played for Sasha . . .

Once past a certain point, he didn't want to clean his soul. On the contrary, he wanted it dirtier and dirtier, all along asking, like a child, "Will you still love me if I get this dirty? Yes? *This* dirty?"

Thinking about these things, I emerged from the tunnel into the afternoon light of New Jersey realizing something important: Magical and haunting as they were, I didn't fully believe what Strayhorn said on those videotapes.

Why should I, knowing only some of the things he'd done before killing himself? Had death given him redemption? It didn't sound like it, according to his plea that I straighten out part of his ongoing mess. He was calm and solicitous, but asking favors.

It reminded me of playing with a Ouija board. If it works, a board can be both disturbing and frightening. But whatever dead spirits you do raise are so easily accessible because they've been condemned to some ominous place between life and death where they are eager to talk to anyone who will listen—much like people in prison who, with so much time on their hands, learn to be both extremely eloquent and patient.

The car I'd rented shivered and shook if I took it over sixty-five, so we eased by the smoke and strong chemical smells of Elizabeth and the white and silver lift of planes taking off from Newark Airport.

It was a long trip to Browns Mills, and I had no idea what I'd find there. But something said it was necessary to go, even if only to spend an hour or two looking around and getting a feel for the place. That invisible smell again.

When Cullen and I had returned to her apartment the other day, I spent an hour talking with Danny about what Strayhorn was like on his last trip east. He had nothing new to add except to describe Pinsleepe in greater detail, but that only agreed with what I already knew.

"Did he say why he was taking her to New Jersey?"

"No, only that she'd asked."

"*She* asked? That's interesting. Nothing else?"

"Only the name of the place. Browns Mills."

The New Jersey Turnpike is pretty once you get by New Brunswick. There's still a lot of traffic, but it feels like that's where the country begins; if you were to get off at any exit you'd soon see cows or small towns where people were friendly and owned trucks.

I hadn't had anything to eat, so I decided to pull off at the next stop and get a hamburger. What more American a tradition is there than the turnpike rest stop? I don't mean those Mom and Pop pretty-good-food one-shot places somewhere off the interstate that sell homemade pralines. I'm talking about a quarter-mile lean on the steering wheel that curves you into a parking lot the size of a parade ground, fourteen gas tanks, toilets galore, and Muzak. The food can be pretty good or pretty bad, but it's the high-torque ambience of the places that make them so interesting, the fact that no one is really there—only appetites or bladders, while eyes stare glazed or longingly out the window at the traffic. These places differ from train stations or airports because you go to such terminals to leave. A turnpike stop is a break in the flow, the concrete island where you can supposedly rest, tank up, get your bearings, and take a few deep breaths before rushing back out into the pack.

They are particularly American because, although the same kind of stops exist on European highways, there people tend to linger. Real meals are served and enjoyed, white tablecloths and flowers are often on the tables, and people eat slowly and talk. When I was in Europe it struck me the driving, and anything associated with it, was regarded as a good part of a vacation or trip, not just the means to get somewhere.

But I liked the feeling of eating in no-man's-land where you didn't really know where you were except, as the signs said, sixty miles from here or a hundred from there. I liked knowing I was sharing the same experience as every person in the place that day. Where do we have that kind of community? At a movie. At a rest stop. In church.

I parked the car and climbed out slowly. What postures we get into when we're driving! No, that's an excuse. When you're young there's never that cranky, stubborn slowness in the muscles. If you're fulfilled or at least busy, there's no reason to think about growing older—that is, until little things like that tap you on the shoulder to remind you. I had my eyes closed and my arms stretched overhead when I heard, "I could tickle you, but I won't."

That stopped that stretch. She was wearing powder blue: a powder-blue sweat suit that said RIDER COLLEGE in about five different places, powder-blue sneakers.

"Hello there. I haven't seen you in a while."

"You didn't need to. Everything you've done so far is perfect. Choosing that man to play Bloodstone and the actors from your group was a great idea."

I leaned against the car and crossed my arms. The sun was behind me so she not only had to look up, she also had to squint to see me. "How come you're here? Are you keeping an eye on me?"

"No. Yes, sort of. I came to tell you not to go to Browns Mills."

"Why?"

"Because there's nothing there."

"Then why can't I go?"

"You *can*, but . . . all I'm saying is don't waste your time. What you want isn't there. It's back in California."

"What'll happen if I go?"

"Listen, do you believe who I am?"

I thought about that while the low *whomp*ing sound of turnpike traffic behind high hedges filled the air. A little pregnant girl in a blue sweat suit, hands in her pockets and eyes squinted to fight off the sun.

"Driving out here I realized I don't trust Phil's tapes."

"That's your choice."

"I have no reason to trust you."

"That's true. But then you have to be afraid of me. Either way, you have to finish this film."

"Why?"

"Because you want to save the lives of the people you still care about. That's the only thing *you* think is evil, Weber—the pain or death of the ones you love. The problem is, you know there are so few left. You've been leaving everything behind for a long time, friends included. Now you realize it's time to stop thinking about yourself and do something for them.

"I can guarantee that if you don't finish the film, Sasha and Wyatt will—"

"Don't threaten me!"

How strange and evil it must have looked to anyone watching. A fortyish man stabbing his finger and yelling at a little fat girl in a blue sweat suit in a parking lot in Somewhere, New Jersey.

"I'm not threatening, I'm telling you the truth. They'll die. I have no control over it." Her voice was a real plea.

"What *do* you control?"

"Nothing till you finish the film. Then you'll see."

I wanted to say something more, but what? We watched each other a bit longer like two fighters in a Mexican standoff; then I got back into the car. "I'm going to Browns Mills. Do you want to come?"

She shook her head.

I nodded mine and, from out of nowhere, smiled. "This would've made a good scene in a film, wouldn't it?"

"I'm not going there again. I asked him to take me out there so I could see it for myself. Browns Mills was where he grew up. That was the summer he saw the dead people and met his first girlfriend." She made a bitchy face. "Kitty Wheeler. Such a little asshole! He didn't need me anymore after that."

"Not until he started making the *Midnights*."

"Only the last one." She rubbed her belly and looked at it. "None of this would've happened if he'd listened to me! Go out there and look for yourself! It's just a dumb town!"

She turned around and ran very fast away across the parking lot; like children when recess is over who are afraid if they don't run they'll be late for class.

Getting out of the car in New York ten hours later, I felt like the Tin Man of Oz before Dorothy found the oil can. After I paid and was walking away, one of the men called and told me I forgot my postcards. I went back for them: three postcards of Browns Mills, New Jersey. I got nothing else from my trip there. Pinsleepe was right—if only Strayhorn and I had listened to her in the first place.

three

*"It was
my favorite hour—
Midnight—
that perfect hour when
struggling day has
been completely devoured,
its tail
disappearing down
the throat of night."*

COLEMAN DOWELL,
My Father Was a River

1

An out-of-work actor is approached by the devil.

"If you come with me, I'll make you the greatest star that ever was. Handsomer than Clark Gable, sexier than Paul Newman—"

"Yeah, yeah," the actor says. "But what do I have to do to get all that?"

"Give me your soul. And the soul of your mother, your father, your wife, your children, your brothers and sisters, and your grandparents."

"Okay," says the actor, "but what's the catch?"

Nice joke. Matthew Portland told it to me not long before a car fell on his head. Nice joke, but it doesn't work that way. They don't ask you if you want more, they ask if you want to put what you've already got to better use.

Weber and the others can say what they want, but the first Midnight was a very good film. The others weren't, I admit it, but that first one did the job. I asked people for months what scared them before I put a word down on paper. You can't imagine how boring most people's fears are: I don't want to die, I don't want to get sick, I don't want to lose what I have.

Midnight came out as well as it did because at the time I had one great idea, no idea of how to write a movie, but nothing to lose by trying. Some people create best when they're sure, others when they're not.

Weber thinks the chain of events went like this: I was a walking basket case due in equal parts to failure and doing killer drugs with my girlfriend. Luckily I met Venasque the shaman and he saved me. Returned from the brink, I was able to clear my summa cum laude head and begin work on the project that ultimately made me famous.

Sounds like a testimony at Alcoholics Anonymous. Or the way we all wish life would work. "Let us all now bow our heads and pray God lets life make sense from here on out."

That's one of the first things Venasque taught me. We were sitting out on the patio feeding Big Top, his bull terrier, sour-cream-and-chive potato chips.

"He doesn't like barbecue ones. Or nacho. The pig eats anything, like me. But not Big. He's the chip connoisseur, aren't you?"

The old white dog lifted its head and looked at Venasque, then lowered it again to the big spread of chips in front of him.

"No, you got it all wrong, Phil. What's that word, 'teleology'? Screw teleology. People don't want things to make sense. Know why? Because if they did we'd all be in trouble. You drive too fast down the street because it feels good or you're in a hurry. If things made sense, a cop'd stop you and give you a ticket. But what happens when a cop does stop you? You get angry. That's not fair! Sure, it's fair. It also makes sense. If life made sense we'd all either behave ourselves a hell of a lot better or be walking around scared for all the bad things we do every day.

"We want things to make sense only when it's to our advantage. Otherwise, it's interesting not knowing what's coming next. Maybe you'll get heads, maybe tails. People do wrong things and get away with them. The wrong people get their necks broken. Would you prefer it if only the good people got rewarded? How often are you good? How often do you deserve the good you get?" He put his hand deep into the crinkly green-and-yellow bag and brought out more chips. The pig was drowsing a few feet away. The dog was slowly and delicately eating his pile.

"What you told me doesn't help."

He was about to eat a chip but stopped it an inch from his mouth and said, "You didn't ask for help. You asked me to tell you some of your future."

"What can I do?"

"First, stop worrying about what's going to happen to you. There's a

long time before it comes. In the meantime you're going to be famous. Isn't that what you've been wanting?"

He didn't tell me about Pinsleepe or that I'd kill myself, although I'm sure he knew. Venasque knew everything but gave you only what he thought you needed.

"Wouldn't you rather have an interesting life than a fair one?"

"I don't know. Not if it's going to be as short as you said."

"Bullshit, Phil! Don't make me angry. You're talking about time, I'm talking about quality. I heard a very funny line in a health food restaurant the other day. Two old guys were sitting near me drinking carrot soup. Is that disgusting? Carrot soup? *Who on earth thought that nightmare up? Anyway, one says to the other, 'Steve, if you drink this soup for a hundred years you'll live a long time.' That made me laugh, but later I thought about it different. You probably* would *live longer if you drank carrot soup and took naps. Notice I said 'probably.' "* He shoved a load of deadly potato chips into his mouth and smiled around their crunch. *"But some people* learn *more from chips. You learn how good bad things taste, what guilt feels like. . . . Eat a few of these delicious sins and you really learn how disgusting carrot soup is. Perspective! You learn perspective. The only thing you learn drinking carrot soup is how to get used to it."*

"What are you telling me?"

"I'm telling you to eat the chips and learn from them."

"I should write this horror film?"

"Definitely. It sounds interesting. You're enthusiastic. It'll teach you about evil. It'll teach you evil doesn't make sense either but is still interesting."

He held the bag out and shook it for me to take some. We both smiled at the gesture.

"What about good? Shouldn't I be learning what that is?"

"Why? Good doesn't interest you. You're the one who likes reading about trips to Hell and looking at Bosch's pictures. How come no madonnas or Last Suppers?

"What's important and interesting is not what evil is, Phil, it's what we do *with it. Bosch took it and painted those incredible pictures. Stalin took it and wiped out a third of his population.*

"That reminds me—I saw something on TV the other night that fits this. They were showing old documentary films about life in Russia in

the twenties and thirties. One scene was of all these hot air balloons at a celebration for something. You don't know what's going on, except for all these beautiful balloons lifting off the ground and pretty girls cheering. As they rise, you see they've got strings attached and are pulling something up with them. What is it? A giant poster of Stalin! How about that? Balloons, pretty girls, celebrations, Stalin! That monster. The same thing with good as with evil. It's not what it is—"

I took some potato chips. " 'It's what we do with it.' How many more years will I live, Venasque?"

"More than me. Don't ask that question. It doesn't do any good to know. If I said twenty years you'd say 'Phew.' If I said twenty minutes you'd shit. Either way of thinking doesn't get you any farther toward where you need to go. One's too relaxed and the other's desperate. Find out about evil and write your movie."

"Is that what's going to make me famous?"

"Yes."

So you see, I already knew. I trusted Venasque so implicitly by then that if he had said I'd become famous as the coach of the Burmese Ping-Pong team I would have believed him.

That was the most intensely enjoyable time of my life. I was full of energy, sure of what I was doing, and so enthusiastically critical of every word I wrote that I drove myself crazy, but loving it, loving it. Venasque gave me five thousand dollars and told me to write and give him back six when I became famous. I took it without hesitation, knowing I'd give him seven: knowing I would soon have seven. I wrote, read, walked with Venasque and the animals, and thought about what man does with good and evil.

The only part of Midnight that is not wholly my own creation is the scene with Bloodstone, the child, and the magnifying glass. That was something Weber had said in passing many years before in a completely different context and which miraculously came to mind when I was writing the script. He never remembered or even realized it was his but, both ironically and innocently, always contended it was the most effective and appalling scene in the film. In any of my films. Great minds think alike, eh?

It was so galling because everyone talked about that scene. When I *asked Venasque about it he shrugged it off like nothing important, but it was damned important to me. Horror film though it was, I wanted Mid-night to be mine, but here was this little brilliant bit of not-mine on the screen attracting everyone's attention. And even before it got to the screen, it was the flash that caught Matthew Portland's attention when I was just another putz in Hollywood with his first screenplay and a well-known friend trying to push him.*

Weber didn't mention, either, that when we were filming he came up on three separate occasions to help the director. I remember him pulling into that little mill town at three in the morning in his silver Corvette, looking fresh and alive yet vaguely funny with his curly red hair that never stayed brushed and green eyes that were so smart and serious you couldn't look away from them without feeling something like regret. Was he the model for Mr. Fiddlehead? No, Weber was too real to be anyone's dream friend. Weber was too real to . . .

He never mentioned winning an Oscar, did he? He also won a Mac-Arthur Award (the genius award, for those unfamiliar with it), a Golden Globe, New York Film Critics, and the Golden Palm at Cannes.

Some people look good in clothes. Whatever they wear, they effort-lessly give it a look and originality that is like a beautiful signature. The same is true with achievement. As long as I've known him, Weber Greg-ston has worn his accomplishments with style and modesty. When The New Yorker accepted one of his poems our junior year in college, he was genuinely shocked they'd taken it. At the Oscar ceremony, he took his statue from the famous star presenter and said, "The real reason I came up here was so I could meet Jack Nicholson."

As he became more and more famous, the only thing that changed in him was a new, understandable guardedness in his manner that grew out of the demands Lost Angles (as he called it) made on him. He enjoyed the goodies fame gave him, but like most decent people who make it big, he felt guilty and uncomfortable.

When he wasn't working on a film, he was somewhere helping. A course in directing at Los Angeles Community College, ads for Amnesty International, work with the terminally ill at Veterans Hospital. Always free, always voluntarily. The only thing he asked was that there be no publicity.

Once when they were both over at my house, Venasque looked at

Weber and said, "You got too many different kinds of fruits on your tree. It's time to cut 'em all off and just grow the oranges."

Later, when I asked the old man what he meant, he told me doing a lot well didn't always mean you were doing yourself a favor.

"You guys were raised thinking you've got to know how to play a solo on every instrument in the band. But you ever see one of those one-man-band characters standing on the street? He's got cymbals between his knees and a harmonica wrapped around his head. . . . You know what I'm talking about. Looks silly as hell, and the music stinks."

"Weber's music is pretty good, Venasque."

"Yeah? You want to trade places with him?"

"I don't know. I never thought about it."

"Think about it. I'm going to the toilet."

The scene must be set here because of what happened next. The two of us were sitting outside. It was twilight. The air was full of the heavy perfume of flowers and the high dynamo sounds of insects. It was warm enough to have my shirt off. As I reached for a Coke I had under the seat, the question of whether I wanted to be Weber moved through my mind.

In an instant, less, I answered out loud, "I don't want to be anybody else. I'm all right."

Almost as soon as I said it, I felt something like sticks on my back. Lots of little sticks moving on me. Half straightening, half turning, I came face to face with a small black bird that was just standing on my shoulder. It was such a shock that I lurched and the bird flicked off and flew away. The direction I'd turned was facing the door, and when I calmed a bit, I realized Venasque had been standing there with his hands in his pockets.

"Hey, did you see that? The bird on my back?"

"Did you see your tattoo? Take a look."

It was gone, of course. My tattoo had flown away.

"Weber's still got his, Phil, in case you're interested."

"What does it mean?"

"It means you know who you are. You just said it—you're all right."

If only it had been that simple.

. . .

Time passed. Midnight *was a hit. Weber met and fell in love with Cullen James. She said no. He dreamt of Rondua. She still said no. He came back to California to prepare* Wonderful *but couldn't stop talking about this woman. When I met her she was very nice and in some ways special, but not the end of the rainbow. I liked her tall husband and child more.*

Venasque died during the filming of Wonderful. *A stroke in a motel room outside Santa Barbara. The last time I saw him we'd watched* Miami Vice *on television, his favorite show, and then taken the animals for a long walk. I already knew he was going away for a week of training with one of his students. He had no school and never taught classes as such, but there were students, and I assumed they learned from him the same way I did.*

"Are you going to the ocean?"

"First to the ocean and then the mountains. Maybe just the ocean. Maybe it won't take that long. I don't know yet."

"Have you ever failed with a student? Not given them what they needed?"

"Sure. I wanted to work with Weber but he wasn't interested."

"Will he be all right?"

"I don't know, Phil. He's still got a bird on his back."

He was dead a couple of days later. One strange thing was the pig died very soon after Venasque. Harry Radcliffe kept Big Top at his house in Santa Barbara afterward because there was a yard for the dog to enjoy. I guess it's still there, the last living magic of the great Venasque.

Have I ever seen the man here? No.

The earthquake came, Weber finished Wonderful, *I began* Midnight Always Comes. *He left for Europe as soon as post-production was done, saying he'd be back when there was reason to come back. That turned out to be over a year later and only long enough to pack boxes for his move east.*

You've heard the rest. You've heard most of this story from Weber, but as you can see, there were small details to be filled in. And what of Pinsleepe, vis à vis the gospel according to Strayhorn? Or Sasha? Even little Flea? Later.

I will *tell you one thing—I didn't kill the dog.*

"Yes, you did!"

"The fuck I did!"

"Okay, Sean, James, that's enough. B.D., you wanted to say something?"

"I wanted to say this discussion is bullshit and boring."

I don't know what it was about the man, but whenever he said anything, the room went silent for a few beats before the noise picked up again. Maybe it was his reputation. Or else all of us kept sizing him up. This was the strongest thing he'd said since we began work.

"Go on."

"There's nothing else. All this about what is the 'real evil.' You sound like Jehovah's Witnesses. We've been here two days bullshitting around and getting nowhere. You want to know what evil is? Evil's a gun. Evil's a creep who puts bullets in it. Evil's a tree that's been split in half by lightning.

"It isn't some *thing*. It's everything, turned bad. A kid's bicycle is okay, but when you see it turned over and blood on the ground nearby then it's something else."

Sean, angry at having been interrupted in her yelling bout with James, asked aggressively, "What was the worst thing *you* ever did?"

B.D. sneered. "I wouldn't tell you, even if I knew you. Because something that bad, I don't want *anyone* to know."

Wyatt leaned over and said quietly in my ear, "This is going nowhere fast."

I nodded and stood up. "Let's break for the day."

No one needed urging. The room emptied in about twenty-five seconds.

"What am I doing wrong, Finky Linky?"

"B.D. is right—we *are* boring ourselves with so much talk. It sounds like kids sitting around a campfire telling their best gross-out stories. 'What's the worst thing *you* ever did?' Who cares? I'm sure Blow Dry has the most hideous tale, but even if he does, we'd react to it like kids, say 'That's really gross,' and wait for someone else to one-up him."

Walking out of the rehearsal room, I thought for the hundredth time of what I was trying to do. Was our purpose to make a couple of frightening, black scenes which, when slipped cleverly into the greater context of *Midnight Kills,* would finish the picture satisfactorily? Or did "they" want a clearly moral statement, something saying Bloodstone and anything he stood for was sick and rotten?

What Phil had succeeded in doing in three films was to make a monster into a kind of perverse antihero. Kids loved Bloodstone. They wore T-shirts of him holding a magnifying glass. Over a hundred thousand posters were sold. *People* magazine did a cover story on him. According to the article, *Midnight* was one of the most popular films in Beirut. Soldiers on both sides would go into theaters with their guns and, when favorite parts came on, wave them and shout his name.

Cullen believed we should make an anti-Bloodstone, anti-*Midnight* statement.

Wyatt was convinced that if Phil *had* touched some heart of darkness, it was by lucky mistake. Whatever he'd created to do, it had since been destroyed. As a result, our job was to finish a film that, without those special Strayhorn scenes, would just be another silly horror film destined to go nowhere a few months after it came out and thus effectively defused.

There were other possibilities that only added to the confusion. One of them, which was seductive, came from a literary critic I'd recently been reading. According to him, "The genre to which a story belongs can be changed just by adding or subtracting a few lines." Before leaving for New York, I'd told Wyatt to try taking *Midnight Kills* in a humorous direction, just to see what he'd do with it. What he came up with was funny and surreal, but inappropriate and too much like his old television show. Yet the idea of changing the whole direction by "adding or subtracting a few lines" stayed with me and kept coming up in my thoughts.

I still believed that by sitting around and throwing out ideas with the people who'd be involved in the scenes, we'd find something important. So far, we'd come up with nothing.

Wyatt asked if I wanted to go to dinner, but the worthless afternoon had taken away any appetite I might have had.

"Then let's go to a movie. What do you want to see?"

"No, thanks."

"You want to go dancing? We can go to Jack Nicholson's—"

"Wyatt, don't worry about me. I'm all right. Discouraged, but all right. Thank you for your concern."

He dropped me off at the house and took the car to visit a friend. I let myself in and, without thinking, walked to the kitchen for something to eat. Not that I wanted it, but it was something to do until I could come up with something better.

"Weber? Is that you?"

"Hi, Sash. Yeah."

She came in smiling widely. "The results of some of my tests came back today, and the doctors were really positive."

"That's good news! Oh, Sash, I'm glad to hear it."

"Something else, too! I guess I should let Wyatt tell you, but he keeps saying he will and then he doesn't. He went to the lab and had a blood test when you were in New York. *His* blood count is the best it's been in almost two years!"

Ever try looking happy when you were suddenly scared shitless? Good luck trying. Sasha's news sent a hundred ants crawling over me. Their better health *had* to be linked to what we were doing. But what happened if we failed? What happened if the new scenes were lousy, or 'only' good, and didn't reach the level that had been prescribed?

"You know, the strangest memory came to me today. After I got back from the doctor's, I felt like seeing a film, something positive and hopeful. First I put on Fellini's *Amarcord* but then realized I wasn't in the mood for that. So I put on your film *Babyskin.* I forgot how funny and generous it is, Weber.

"The scene at the end when the two old people go swimming naked in the moonlight? God, that went straight through me! But you don't feel sorry for them. You know why they're there and that it was inevitable, but you just want them to be happy swimming and face what has to come later.

"But that's not what I wanted to tell you. About halfway through, you have a scene where they put the party hat on the old man's dog—"

"That was Nicholas Sylvian's idea. The one where he goes into the man's room and wakes him up with licks?"

"Yes, but you know what it reminded me of? When my father was dying he told me one day that the sicker he got, the more his breath smelled like our dog's. When I remembered that, it was like someone threw a rock through a window in my head. It's always so crazy what sets off memories."

The same thing happened to me a few hours later. I don't look at my films very often. If I do, I see only mistakes and missed chances. But *Babyskin* was my first "European" film and had all the glamour and excitement that goes with that phrase. I worked with a superb team; my life was heavenly.

That night I'd planned to look at all the Midnight films yet again (Finky Linky refused to do it anymore and Sasha fled to the other side of the house when she heard the first notes of the Steve Reich score), but it had been such a down day that I decided to put on *Babyskin* and watch that fortunate part of my history instead.

I couldn't have watched more than fifteen minutes before I saw something that made me jump up, eject the film, and slide in *Midnight Always Comes* in its place.

After searching, I found that clever scene where Bloodstone walks into the young couple's bedroom with a small tape recorder. Turning it on, we hear the very loud, unmistakable sound of people having a great time fucking.

"He took that from me!"

Out came the Strayhorn tape, in went the Gregston.

The night of the old woman's birthday. Her husband goes outside to piss, or so he tells her. He's given her no present that day and she's heartbroken. Suddenly from out there we hear very faintly the sound of Bix Beiderbecke's orchestra playing "That's My Secret Now." The woman, scared but curious, gets up and goes to the window. Her husband is outside on the lawn, kneeling next to the gramophone he's bought for her birthday.

"He took that from *Babyskin!* I'll be damned."

I put his film back in and watched the tape recorder scene again. Same blue and blinding white lighting, Paul Delvaux shadows, room set up exactly the same way. . . . It was the whole look and mood of my scene.

"I'll be damned."

What else had he snitched? Was that the right word, or was I only miffed at myself for not having realized it till now? Filmmakers steal from each other like pirates, but this rubbed me the wrong way somehow.

It was one in the morning. When Finky Linky came in at four, I was still watching Midnight movies and taking notes.

"Why didn't you tell me about your blood test?"

"Because I don't know what it means. I've had more remissions than Loretta Young's had face lifts."

"But you heard about Sasha's results?"

"Yes. I know there's probably a connection, Weber, but I didn't want to start thinking about it because it might be nothing and then I'll have gotten excited for nothing.

"Listen, I was with a friend tonight who has AIDS. You know what's most pathetic about him? His hope.

"He's heard they've found a cure in Czechoslovakia using carrots. Laetrile is back in if you have the money to go to Mexico for the quack treatments; he's considering it. And he has a friend who's considering getting injections of Interferon in his *brain* because he heard that's how they cure rabies sometimes. Can you imagine making that kind of insane connection?

"I don't want to be like this guy, crazy with hope and strange possibilities. I was like that when I first got cancer, but they're not good friends to have in this situation. That's what I've been telling Sasha: You can be optimistic, but don't be hopeful."

"What's the difference?"

"Optimists know they're going to die, but they look everywhere for a cure right up until the end. People who're hopeful are convinced there's a remedy; they just have to find it. That's why they're so bitter when they realize it isn't always true."

"You mean you're a realist?"

"Hell, no. A realist knows when he gets leukemia he's going to die."

I told him about the similarities between Phil's films and my own and showed him some samples. He was amused.

"So? He knew a good thing when he saw it."

Early the next morning Sasha woke me because there was an urgent phone call from the police. It was Dominic Scanlan asking if I'd seen Charlie Peet.

I might have slept two hours. "Dominic, who the fuck is Charlie Peet?"

"Blow Dry, asshole. That's his real name. Have you seen him?"

"No, why?"

"Because he didn't go home last night and didn't report for duty this morning. He doesn't do things like that."

"He was at rehearsal yesterday afternoon."

"We know, but that's the last anyone saw him. All right, Weber, I'll get back to you if anything comes up. Hey, how is he as an actor, anyway?"

"He's playing Bloodstone, you know. He'll probably be perfect."

"You ain't kidding! He's the real thing. Take it easy."

Trying to go back to sleep was impossible. I lay there thinking about the dead actor who'd gone around impersonating Strayhorn until he ended up looking like a French fry left in the microwave too long. Then I thought about the psychopath at the graveyard the day of Phil's funeral who got his fifteen minutes of fame doing Bloodstone with a blank pistol. Next came the kid in Florida who'd killed two kids à la Bloodstone in one of the films. Now the disappearance of Charlie Peet.

Can evil be created, or does it always grow alongside the road like some poisonous mushroom, waiting to be picked and eaten?

Had Phil created evil by inventing Bloodstone?

I got out of bed again and went back to the television room. The windows there faced onto the small backyard where a redwood picnic table and two benches sat under a palm tree. I heard quiet voices and recognized Sasha's and Wyatt's.

She was asking him why we were so concerned about finishing *Midnight Kills*. Wyatt said because all artists want their work completed, even if it's a horror film.

Even.

2

A strange yet sure sign that my work is going well is that I often forget to pray at night. Since childhood, I have always tried to say the Lord's Prayer, with a few postscripts added at the end. I pray every night but I don't ask for much. I just say thank you. Sometimes it's habitual, like having to get in a certain position before being able to fall asleep, but that's rare. I thank Him for giving me a good life and for keeping the animals at bay.

Whatever was happening with Strayhorn and Pinsleepe was only further proof to me that there *are* other "animals," yet life and death are the only domesticated ones we know and will touch.

It was about a week after we'd started filming that I realized I hadn't been saying my nightly thanks. It had happened before when I was working and I didn't like it; didn't like myself for being ungrateful.

But the neglect meant a blindness toward everything but the work. I'd be staggeringly hungry because of forgetting to eat, unusually grateful to sit down because I'd been standing for six hours.

When Blow Dry still didn't show up, I decided to try something else until he returned. Along with the cameraman for my other films, Wyatt and I went around shooting what I call "object scenes": the sun over an alley at six in the afternoon, an empty gas station at three in the morning. We were looking for a variety of moods—the open-air loneliness of a used car lot, the excitement of a woman taking three dresses with her into a try-on room in a department store.

We didn't specifically know where we'd use these shots when we were finished, only that some of them would be in our scenes and it was important to have them. Then, as we moved around town filming bus stops and gun stores or people passing out flyers for massage parlors on Hollywood Boulevard, the three of us fell into a kind of unspoken understanding and enthusiasm for what we were doing. Once while having lunch at a hotdog stand, Wyatt said "Griffith Park!" and we finished as fast as we could so we could get over to the park and start looking immediately.

When we weren't out filming, I was either working with the people who'd come from New York or looking through art books in the library, particularly photography of the 1930s.

The New York group lived in adjoining rooms at a hotel in Westwood and spent most of their time together, which meant when Wyatt and I joined them, they'd already come up with some intriguing possibilities. We'd shown them *Midnight Kills* and, although their initial reactions were disgust and disappointment, they'd since taken it upon themselves to come up with something that they hoped would raise the level of the film via their contributions.

There were Sean and James, and the third was the amazing Max Hampson. Max was probably the best actor in our group, but the reason Wyatt and I hadn't first considered him was because of his physical condition. He was about forty but had had cancer for over ten years and at least as many operations in that time. One of his legs had been amputated and he usually had to use a wheelchair because neither his arms nor his "good" leg had the strength to support him.

When you heard his story, you knew here was one of those human beings whose lives are one long bruise. His twin sister contracted meningitis when they were children and became little more than a vegetable. Max's parents were alcoholics who found a way of blaming him for the girl's hopeless condition. Somehow he survived this environment and went to college, where he studied business. On graduating, he started a small travel agency that specialized in trips to exotic places. It did well, and he opened a second office. It succeeded too, and he was considering opening a third when a broken leg from a skiing trip didn't heal and it was discovered he had cancer.

What was so amazing about Max was his good nature. He and Wyatt were good friends, and apparently Max had always wanted to be an actor but had never had the courage to try. The disease pushed him toward it, and besides being one of the founding members of our group, he was also one of the great cheerleaders and spirit lifters.

But, like all of them, he knew what constant pain and fear were and his acting displayed them. Recently, when I'd asked Max and Wyatt to do a scene from *Waiting for Godot,* his performance was so reminiscent of Charlie Chaplin at his saddest and most beautiful that it made me cry.

Wyatt got me onto the photography books. One day he handed me one by someone named Umbo.

"I don't know exactly what I mean, but I think we should make it look and feel like this."

The first photographs were surreal black-and-white still lifes or portraits of women with black lips and bobbed hair, very Louise Brooks. Nothing special. But when I got to the middle of the book it was immediately clear what Finky Linky was talking about.

In the late 1920s this Umbo had taken a haunting series of pictures of show-window mannequins. Using their exaggerated facial expressions and a kind of Expressionist lighting, the photographer had caught something both shadowy and compelling about these mundane figures.

But there was more. A few pages on, Umbo had done another series on a clown named Grock: Grock putting on his makeup, Grock's violin half out of its case, Grock in full costume with a cigarette in his mouth. The power of these pictures was the dust-in-the-corners, bare-bulb sadness of Grock the man's life. We have no idea if this clown is successful, but even if he is you wouldn't trade with him for anything. No matter how many laughs or coins he puts in his pockets, he always comes back to these small dressing rooms with soiled wallpaper and mirrors with his own picture stuck in them (as if to remind himself who he is supposed to be).

Besides the expected horror of Bloodstone, Wyatt wanted the still, almost-real, almost-threatening quality of the mannequins and the yellow sadness of an old clown with a cigarette in his mouth.

Wyatt was right, and that vision led me excitedly to other photographers of the period: Kertesz, Paul Strand, Brassai. But I kept coming back to Umbo and his Grock.

Almost every day I put in the tapes Phil had sent me before he died to see if they would say more, but there was never anything. However, I must have watched my mother's death twenty times. I grew to know every detail, the few words she spoke to the man in the next seat, the small spot on her skirt. . . . It was never comforting to see, not even the twentieth time. I'd been wrong to think if my questions about her death were answered I would feel more at peace with it.

I watched my own films too. It had been years since I'd made them, but generally they held up. Would I have changed parts? Yes, but I'd honestly forgotten so much that when I saw them again and realized how poignant and funny they were, I was proud. There are different kinds of pride, but being able to look back on something you did and know it's still good or important is the best.

I also watched Phil's video *The Circus on Fire* and many episodes of *The Finky Linky Show*. Wyatt started to look at the first with me, but it made him depressed and he left the room.

Sasha asked why I was watching so much TV. The only answer I had was that something was *there* but I couldn't figure out what—yet.

The studio lent me a camera, three video machines, and three televisions. When I had them set up at Sasha's, I'd often put three things on at once to see if I could find what I was looking for. No luck. In the end I felt a little like Lyndon Johnson when he was President, watching the news on three separate channels.

"Christ! What's all that?"

Sasha came into the house with bulging armfuls of grocery bags.

"There's lots more in the car. Would you help?"

"What's going on?"

"Finky Linky and I decided we're going to have a dinner party to-morrow."

"Tomorrow! That's short notice."

"I know you hate socializing, Weber, but you like all the people who are coming, so please don't run away." She stopped putting groceries away and counted off on her fingers. "Dominic and his wife, Max, Sean, and James, Wyatt, you, and me. Eight. Will you make your potato salad?"

"How come a party?"

She took a deep breath. "Because I'm sick of sadness. Wyatt said it's time we laughed some more, and he's right. We even bought a *Best of The Supremes* tape so we can dance if we want. Okay, Baby Love?"

"Okay. Did you buy lots of bacon? I'll need that for the potato salad."

Finky Linky walked in with more bags. "We did not buy bacon and we forgot sour cream. You're elected to go, Weber. Get you away from those fucking television sets for a while." He held out the car keys, but I said I'd walk.

"Has everyone said they'd come?"

"Yes. We called them this morning. We knew you'd have to come if they all said yes."

"Come on, I'm not that antisocial."

"Really? When was the last time you went out?"

"I went to your birthday party, Wyatt!"

"Yes, six months ago. You've become such a recluse in New York that the only time we ever see you is at rehearsal."

"It's like Phil before he died."

Both of us looked at Sasha. Her last sentence drifted slowly across the kitchen like a well-made paper airplane. I remembered once saying about Strayhorn, "He wanted to be famous. He wanted to be left alone." I'd already had my fame. It was like a too-sweet dessert. Did I also want to be left alone? No sane person wants to be left alone in any real sense.

"Don't fall into that, Weber. Let the people who love you see you now and then."

An ice-cream bar slid across the counter to me. "We even bought your favorite disgusting ice cream, so you have to come."

The market was jumping with after-work shoppers. The place was so large it took fifteen minutes to find the things I'd come for. I was standing at the express checkout line, trying to read the headline on the week's *TV Guide*, when a voice behind me said, "Word is, you're making a new movie."

I didn't know the voice, and when I turned I didn't know the person: a woman with a nothing face and pulled-back blond hair. But Los Angeles is a friendly town and more often than not, if people know who you are, they speak as if you're old acquaintances. There wasn't much else I could do, standing there with my bacon and sour cream.

Radiating a new "I'm not antisocial" charm, I said, "Not really a *whole* one. Just helping out on a friend's."

She had four cans of whipped cream and four cans of deodorant. Something was up in *her* life. When she spoke, everything came out sounding like an accusation. "I heard you're working on a horror movie."

"Something like that, yes."

"Another one?"

"Another? I've never made a horror film."

Smirking as if she knew better, she accused me, "You mean you never made one *all-out.* Only little pieces here and there. Because horror movies don't win Oscars, do they? Come on, move, huh? I want to get out of here."

When I got home, we had a ball preparing for the party. Wyatt put on the Supremes tape full blast and we danced around while we cooked, set the table, cleaned the house, discussed. At midnight, Sasha decided we needed balloons, but not tomorrow—now. We got into the car and drove around until we found an all-night drugstore that sold balloons. Then we were hungry, but Wyatt said the only place to go for a real hamburger at night was a place in his old neighborhood.

No matter how old or jaded you are, there will always be something exciting and cool about cruising around at three in the morning with a bunch of good friends. All the old duds are asleep but *you're* still awake, the windows are down, the radio's glowing green and playing great music. Life's given you a few extra hours to horse around. If you don't grab them, they aren't usually offered again for a while.

"I want to be fifteen again and still a virgin!" Sasha had her head out the window, and the wind whipped her hair.

"At fifteen the only thing you thought about was losing your virginity!"

"You know where it happened? On a beach in Westport, Connecticut. There were three other couples around making out, and a full moon shining down so they could see everything. When it was over, I

185

was so scared and ashamed I ran right into the water with all my clothes on."

"Scared of what?"

"That that was all there was to it. 'You mean this is it?' *That's* what was supposed to make the world go round? Shit! Your turn, Wyatt."

"I'm driving. Weber's next."

"Barbara Gilly. Affectionately known in our town as 'The Tunnel.' "

"You slept with a tunnel?"

"Everybody slept with her. We did it on the hill behind John Jay High School. I used a rubber I'd had in my wallet for six months. You can imagine how comfortable and exciting that was. And you?"

"My cousin Nancy."

Both Sasha and I cried out, "You slept with your *cousin?*"

We drove another hour, telling old secrets and funny stories. It was like a late-night bullshit session in college, when you felt so close and wise, sure you'd remember these people and these discussions for the rest of your life.

When we got home we gave each other big kisses and hugs because the evening had been such fun. I kept smiling and chuckling as I washed up and got into bed, thinking about some of the things that had been said.

Sometime later, just after the first morning birds started to sing, the door opened and I turned in time to see Sasha standing there. Gesturing to close the door, I held up the blanket for her to come in with me. She was there in an instant, sliding close, naked under a thin silk nightgown.

She took my hand and ran it across her stomach, up over her breasts, up the thin curve of her neck. Opening her mouth, she slipped my fingers into it and started licking them.

I took the hand away and caressed her face, her shoulders, her arms. Neither of us talked, although when we'd been lovers in Europe, years before, we'd always said things and made lots of noise.

But tonight needed to be different. We weren't here as lovers but as two longtime friends who loved each other and had had the luck to share a wonderful night together.

We fucked in silence, trying not to make even the slightest sound. The secrecy made it hotter, more exciting.

When we were finished and the early light lit the floor, she lay half across my stomach, her breath tickling my chest. Loving the feel of her there, I whispered, "I wish I'd been that guy in Westport."

She lifted her head and grinned. "Really? You wish you'd been my first?"

"Not so much that. I don't know if I would've done it any better. But I would have . . . gone swimming with you. I wouldn't have let you go so easily."

She touched her head to my chest and slowly got up. Standing, she tried to find where the armholes were in the knotted tangle of her nightgown. Her hair was fluffed and flying out in all directions and she looked as beautiful as I had ever seen her.

Giving up on the nightgown, she threw it over her shoulder and sat down again on the bed. I took her hand.

"Will you always be my friend, Sasha?"

"I promise."

"Even if we don't do this again?"

"We think differently about it. I could be happily married for twenty years and still have no hesitation about going to bed with you. I love you, Weber. I sleep with the people I love."

"What would you say to your husband?"

"I don't know. Maybe nothing."

Leaving the room with the gown held carelessly in front of her, she was a Bonnard painting: faint pink, cream, curves, a small backward wave goodbye.

I caught Dominic and his wife, Mickey, getting out of their car.

"What the hell are you doing, Weber, *filming* this? Wait a minute!" He stood up, ran his hands through his hair, and straightened his Hawaiian shirt. "Is this a shirt or what? Mickey got it for me. Okay, now you can roll 'em."

We started around to the back of the house where the others were.

"What's with the camera?"

"I'm trying to get used to using one again."

"You're going to film the party?"

"Part of it."

Some American must have invented barbecues. I know mankind has been grilling meat over a fire for tens of thousands of years, but Americans made it into a religion.

For all the words they wrote about my pictures, no film critic ever noticed how in every one of them I stuck in a barbecue somewhere. Even in *Babyskin* it is the American visitor who shows the old people how to do it "right," thus unwittingly bringing on their fall.

Meals cooked in the open, food eaten with the fingers, smoke, grease. Paper plates, loud voices; if you don't have a napkin use the back of your hand. Even if it's only family, things are louder and more raucous usually, freer. People get sexy or they drink too much; they cry.

After introductions were made and everyone had a drink, Wyatt suggested we play Time Bomb, the game he'd invented and made famous on his show. I got paper and pencils while Sasha took people's orders for how they wanted their steaks done.

Dominic and Max were so fast and clever with their answers that none of us had a chance after the first round. I was the second to "blow up," which was fine because all I really wanted to do was film the exchange between the two men: Max weakly curved into the pillows of his wheelchair, Dominic up on the edge of his seat like a football center about to snap the ball.

They were still at it by the time the medium rares were served and Sasha was forking the mediums off the fire. Wyatt said they should call it a draw and both men agreed.

"You're the first guy I ever played that game with who knew what he was doing, Max."

"You should see him play at rehearsals." Sean waved a piece of bread to make her point.

Dominic looked at me. "You play Time Bomb with your actors?"

"Say that again, Dominic, but look at Max this time."

"Weber, we're having dinner conversation. Will you put the camera down?"

All of them grumbled he was right, so I did as I was told, but under protest because it had been such a pleasure. Sometimes we used a video camera in New York, but that was like shooting game films for athletes; we watched them to see what mistakes we'd made. The stuff I was shooting now was only "family" and fun and addictive for someone who liked to look through a camera anyway. I had an idea in the back of my mind to make a little film of the night's festivities and then send copies of it to everyone there.

"What's the newest on Blow Dry, Dominic?"

"Wait a minute. I got to get some more of these baked beans. Who made them? We gotta get the recipe, Mickey."

"Max."

"Max? Shit, you make beans like this and play Time Bomb too?"

"Dominic?"

"What?"

"Blow Dry?"

"Oh, yeah. Nothing! Creepiest thing about B.D. was he had no vices. No girlfriends, didn't gamble, drank a beer once a month. Usually when someone disappears, you try to find out if they bought a ticket to Vegas or Acapulco. This guy didn't do those things."

"He just scared people."

"Yup! And that's the only thing we have to go on. He didn't have vices, but he had a fuck-load of enemies. There are a number of people down at the department who think B.D. might have seen his last Dodger game."

"Does that bother you?"

He wiped his mouth with a napkin. "Normally it would, but Charlie Peet . . . Christ, if you even called him Charlie by accident he'd give you a look that'd make your toes curl."

A that's-the-end-of-*that*-subject silence fell over us—until James laughed loudly. "Yeah, but he would've made a gr-r-eat Bloodstone!"

Dessert was Mickey Scanlan's Poodle Cake, which was an astounding piece of work. She told us not to ask the ingredients or else we wouldn't eat it, but no one had any trouble doing that.

After two pieces and a cup of Sasha's weak coffee, I picked up the camera and started filming again. Going from person to person, I asked them to guess what *was* in the cake.

Wyatt smiled at the camera while squeezing chewed dessert through his teeth. I moved on quickly.

Sean said chocolate and prunes and shrugged. James said chocolate and raisins. Dominic said chocolate and Blow Dry.

Mickey threw her spoon at him but laughed as hard as the rest of us. I panned from face to face, going in as close as I could on each, then pulling back and moving to the next but trying to catch all their faces before the first real waves of laughter had crested and begun to fall.

When I got to Max I thought he was laughing so hard he had lost all control and simply dropped his plate and fork into his lap.

But it was worse, and that moment of recognition was where one of those feared animals I spoke of before suddenly rose in me and leapt.

For seconds, long important seconds, I knew something was terribly wrong with my friend Max Hampson, but I did nothing—besides filming him. I needed a few more seconds of the camera at my eye before I could help him. Before I *would* help him. That's right—before I would help him.

Wyatt yelled, "Hey, what's the matter with Max? Look at him! He's sick!"

I dropped the camera but way too late. In the following chaos, no one knew what I'd done. But did it matter? I knew.

Driving to the studio the next morning, I saw her standing at a bus stop.

"Why aren't I surprised to see you?"

"Max is going to be all right, Weber. I promise. You didn't do anything bad."

"I didn't help."

"You were doing your film. Don't you understand yet that's the most important thing you *can* do? If it's good in the end, then everything else will be okay. I can help you now. I've been allowed. Since you came back here, I've been able to do some things. Max will be okay."

"Prove it."

"Call the hospital. Get Dr. William Casey and ask him about Max's condition. I'm *not* lying, Weber."

"What about Blow Dry?"

"He's dead. He was killed in east Los Angeles by a gang called the Little Fish. They'll find his body today."

"Did it have anything to do with this? With *Midnight Kills?*"

"No."

"Pinsleepe, tell me what it is they *want.* Please."

"I can't tell you because I don't know. I was told to come talk to Phil and I did. Unsuccessfully. Then I was told to talk to you."

"Who sent you?"

"The 'good animals.' "

I pulled into an abandoned lumberyard and turned off the motor. "You know about that?"

"The more work is done on the film, the more I know you. The image of animals isn't far from the truth; it's just a lot more complicated than that. Remember what Blow Dry said the other day? About evil? That it's not some *thing;* it's everything, turned bad? He was right."

"I don't understand."

"Midnight Kills. You saw it—it's not very good. Nine tenths of it is a normal Saturday night horror film. But then Phil did something, found a trick or a piece of genius, and wrote a scene that turned everything bad—"

"He made a work of art."

"He made three minutes of art, but it was enough."

"I don't believe that. I don't believe art comes to life."

"It doesn't. But do you know about binary weapons? Nerve gas is usually built as a binary weapon. You have one chemical here and one over there. Separately they're harmless, but combined they become nerve gas."

"Those killings in Florida—"

"That was nothing compared to this."

She asked me to drop her off at a flower store on Sunset. As I was pulling away from the curb, the first idea came to me. I began talking fast and urgently into a little pocket tape recorder I carry whenever I am working.

I stopped once on the way at a telephone booth and called the hospital to find out about Max. A Dr. Casey said it was one of the most unbelievable recoveries he'd seen in his entire medical career. He was about to go on when I thanked him and hung up.

3

I reached over and started to turn on the light, but Wyatt stopped me. "No, don't do that. I want to see it again."

"What do you think?"

"I think it's brilliant and sick. It's what those films should have been. But show it to me again." He put a hand on my shoulder. "You really are a director, Weber. Your style is *so* distinctive. God, I wonder what Phil would have said if he'd seen that."

"Look again and tell me what else you think." Leaning forward, I pressed the play button.

For days I'd worked both at the studio and at home cutting and pasting and generally rearranging the three and three quarter Midnight films into one rough Gregston version.

Why? Because I was sure Pinsleepe was hinting at something important when she'd repeated Blow Dry's "evil is everything, turned bad." Phil may have found the magic to create the lost scene, but who was to say there wasn't another magic in what he'd already made?

In college, Strayhorn and I took a course together called Ancient Rome. One of the few things I remember about it was the haruspex, a kind of diviner who based his predictions on inspection of the entrails of sacrificial animals. Study the order of the world carefully, and you'll be able to figure out its secrets.

What if I studied the order of Phil's work? Moved it around like a designer or an architect, giving it new angles and edges. Were the answers there? Enigmas to be solved, or only the corny splatter and glop of horror movies?

There are two inherent problems with the genre. The first is the moment the monster is shown for the first time. Invariably half the tension of the film is lost right there. Until then, the audience has created their own nightmare images of a monster. So no matter how ghastly or unique you thought yours was, it couldn't possibly be as bad as their individual bogeymen. People are scared of different things— blood, rats, death, night, fire. . . . There is no way of combining them into one all-encompassing creature without being funny or falling flat.

Bloodstone was good because he was a kind of indistinct blur, despite the silvery face and small child's hands with no fingernails. Yes, you knew something was very wrong with him but the image was so delicately underplayed, he could just as easily have been a man going to a costume party.

The same was true with what Phil had him do. No heads were torn off or stomachs ripped open with a single long fingernail. Bloodstone was a presence from somewhere else. Like a creature from another planet a thousand times more advanced than ours, he had wondrous ways to make man suffer. That was part of the fun of the Midnight films: What's the son of a bitch going to do next?

But that was all. The films opened, Bloodstone went around hurting people in interesting, novel ways, and then the story ended. Every time it was the same, and that introduced problem two: the Endings.

Traditionally, there are two ways to end a horror film—happy or sad. The monster wins, the monster loses. That's it. And the audience knows that when they walk into the theater. They'll be scared, but they know how it will end, always.

Great films keep you guessing; you don't know who's going to get to the finish line first, if anyone.

In my version of the film (Wyatt quickly titled it "Midnight's Spills"), we rarely even saw Bloodstone and the end was inconclusive.

"Hey, that's one of the scenes we shot downtown!"

"Right. At the shoeshine place on Hollywood Boulevard."

"I didn't even realize that. Did you put many of those in?"

"A few."

"No wonder the film feels tilted, you know what I mean? It's like looking at something you've seen before, a painting or a building, but something's off about it. It's basically the same as before, but now it's better and you don't know why."

"What about the order of the scenes and the way they're moved around?"

"Don't even ask me about that, Weber. You know they're wonderful. Don't fish for compliments."

Halfway through the second run, Finky Linky turned on the lamp and looked at me while the video was still running. "I have a very strange suggestion to make. Before you hate it, think seriously about it.

"If you're going to put other scenes in here besides *Midnight,* add some from your own films. I'm thinking specifically of *Sorrow and Son* and *The Night Is Blond.*

"What you've done is redefine the mood of *Midnight.* It's your mood now, Weber, the one that's in all your work. But if you're going to do that, go all the way. I keep thinking of little sections of your movies and how well they'd fit in here and here and here and here. . . . I can't imagine what you'll end up with, but I'd love to see the result.

"I just thought of a funny story that reminds me of this. When Billy Wilder made *Double Indemnity,* he was nominated as Best Director of the Year. He was convinced he should get it, but another director won. Wilder was so pissed off that when this other guy was walking down the aisle to get the Oscar, Wilder stuck out his foot and tripped him. I wonder if Phil would trip you after he saw this.

"It's damned good, Weber, but I think I'm right about what I said. *Midnight'*s never looked better, but even with your rearranging and the other scenes added, it's still basically *Midnight.* Make it that, plus *Sorrow and Son* and *The Night Is Blond,* and you're going to have something wild."

Dear Weber,

I want to tell you this to your face, but I can't because it's still very embarrassing for me. I want to tell you what happened between Phil and me at the end and why we decided it was better that we not live together anymore, at least for a while.

I know I've told you some things, and you can get an idea of what it was like at the end after you've read his story "A Quarter Past You."

But this tape tells the rest. Give it back to me when you're done and *please* don't tell Wyatt about anything you see. I wish I could watch with you to hear what you think, but I can't. Maybe sometime. But maybe I should just let you watch and then throw it away. It's been in my drawer for weeks, and every time I think about it I get jittery. Why did I keep it? I don't know.

Sasha

I didn't watch it all. You got the idea in five minutes.

In real life, Strayhorn had not only re-created whole scenes from *Midnight* to scare Sasha, he filmed them too. An example? She's fast asleep when he brings a tape recorder into their bedroom and turns it on to the sound of people fucking. You can barely see the expression on her face when she comes awake and realizes what's happening, but for the viewer it's embarrassing and provocative at the same time. Her life has suddenly become a movie—how *will* she react?

How could he have done it? How could she have put up with it after one experience like that? How could he have shot some of those scenes without her knowing about the camera?

I put the film back on her bed with a note: "You were right to leave. Get rid of this thing."

Wouldn't it be easier if life worked that way? Recognize something as wrong or immoral, reject it on the spot, then stop thinking about it. Simple, practical, time-saving. It would be easier, but life likes color, not just black-and-white.

I was sitting alone in a park watching some kids do tricky things on their bicycles—handstands on the seat, flips, wheelies. Wyatt and I had just had a meeting with the producer of *Midnight Kills* and told him a few of our ideas. He was so happy to have us both working on his film that I think we could have done anything and he would've accepted it. His only concern was when it would be finished, but we assured him it would be wrapped on time.

The kids spun and leapt with real bravery and grace as well as keen attention to what the other riders were doing. They were their own best audience. A number of other people were watching them perform, but the kids' blasé air said we, their second audience, didn't count.

Watching them do their stuff, I mulled over what I'd been doing and particularly what I'd done about Sasha's tape.

On our flight back to California from New York, I'd read an article on nuclear disarmament. It said one of the greatest problems humankind faces is that even if every country that has bombs were to get rid of them, the *knowledge* of how to build them still exists and someone can always make another. How do you get rid of knowledge?

The moment I learned what Sasha's secret film was about, it wasn't even necessary to see it because something self-serving and dangerous had already risen in me. I *had* to use Phil's idea. It was immoral and the utter betrayal of a friend's trust, but the power of his concept was irresistible: Force an "audience" to cross from their familiar world to another one, well known yet impossible. Then film their every reaction . . . for yet another audience!

After visiting Max in the hospital with Sean and James, I'd explained what I wanted to try. They got very excited, and after an hour in the hospital coffee shop we'd worked out a scene we'd try at our next rehearsal. It wasn't what Phil had done to Sasha, but it was the same geography: the same shock of betrayal, sex through the keyhole, life turned around and inside out until no one knew who held the camera or who was being filmed.

Later, when they tried it, every time through was better. James and Sean had been lovers for a year, but they had big problems. What evolved when they got into the scene was a blistering candor and maliciousness that made you want to look away because you knew too much of this was the real acid in each face.

I filmed it all. When they were completely somewhere between their own real world together and the lives of the people they were portraying, the room crackled with a mixture of truth, love, and hurt that flew crazily through the air like Kansas heat lightning.

When it was over, I asked them not to tell anyone anything about what we were doing, including Wyatt. At home I looked at the tape and knew we'd been mistaken. It wasn't wonderful enough. I called them up and said that. Think about it and we'll start again tomorrow.

We showed Sasha my *Midnight,* and afterward Wyatt told her his idea about including scenes from my films in it. She loved that, and the two of them began screening my work to see what they thought should be used.

It felt as if we were all working on separate projects: Sean and James on their "scene," Wyatt and Sasha editing, me pulling it together and . . . adding.

I kept a video camera with me constantly. When I wasn't with the others, I was filming. The inside of a comic book store, two bums eating pizza on the curb—I followed a garbage truck one morning and filmed the men at a distance. Joggers, beautiful cars, women coming out of restaurants on Canon Drive in Beverly Hills: these bits and pieces were everywhere, shimmers of life like coins found on a sunny street. I wanted them despite having no firm idea of where they'd go in the final work.

It reminded me of my first day at the Budapest flea market, thrilled by what was for sale: old pocket watches, alligator briefcases, Nazi radios, and cigarette tins from Egypt with camels and pyramids painted on the lid. I wanted it all, and it was so cheap I could afford it. What I'd ever *do* with a brass ashtray from a coffee distributor in Trieste was beside the point.

The bicycle gang was doing tandem tricks now. Arms entwined, two of them rolled backward together, handlebars turned exactly in the same direction. One kid got on the shoulders of another and spread his arms like wings. An old man on a bench nearby clapped for them. The sound was small and alone in the bright blue openness. "You guys should be on TV!"

I was sleeping less and less, another old habit from my Hollywood years. The more excited I became about a project, the more it felt like a day was trying to cheat me out of interesting things if I let its night side push me toward sleep. Also, the more drained I was, the more unortho-dox ideas came to me—usually about two-thirty in the morning with the televisions turned low and a pad full of notes in my lap. The agree-able part was I would awake charged and roaring to go the next morn-ing.

Whether that energy would continue was another question. I was over forty. I wore glasses more often, and my once-five-mile-a-day walk had been cut to two. Growing older was all right, growing slower and less spry wasn't.

"Hey, mister! Hey, shoot me with your camera!"

A black boy swung out from the crowd of bike acrobats and rode over to me.

"How come?"

As I said this, a small child came running up to us, screaming and laughing. He went over to the kid on the bike and started hitting him.

"Cut it out, Walter."

Walter was seven or eight, and when he turned for a moment I saw he had the unmistakable face of a mongoloid.

"Take a movie of Walter and me." He hefted the smaller child onto his bike and rode off in a slow wobble. When the other boys saw him coming, they made a big circle around them.

Walter was having a great time, banging his hands down on the handlebars, shouting and whooping like a bird.

The others continued circling but did no more tricks. It was hard to tell whether they were being respectful or only waiting for the right moment to begin their next wheel dance.

"You should only take pictures of us!"

I waved and brought the camera up to film them. When the kids saw that, they broke their circle and began every show-off routine they knew. Half of them landed on their asses, but the ones who stayed up pulled off some moves that defied gravity. They jumped and bounced around like ponies.

"Check this gambado, man." The black kid with Walter still aboard did a jump turn in the air that should have won him a prize.

"What's a gambado?"

"You just saw it, sucker. You catch it on film?"

"Caught it."

"We gotta go now, but we'll be back. Come check us out again, but next time bring a real moviecam, dude, not that little Sony shit!" Leading the pack with hooting Walter, he pedaled off into the sunset.

The old man nearby got up. "They're here almost every day. I come just to see them. Fabulous, huh? They should be on television, those kids!"

At home, Sasha and Wyatt were gone but had left a note on the refrigerator.

> Some papers have to be signed down at Fast Forward. Sasha's finally being called back to work. Look at the cassette we left in

the first machine. I didn't want to tell the guy about it today because you have to see it first and give the big okay. Both of *us* think it is just right and good enough to do the trick.

Before I did that, I went and found a dictionary.

The boy had used the word "gambado." At first I thought it was a bastardized Latino word that just sounded good and tough—"Check this gambado, sucker." But the more I thought about it, the more it seemed real, and until I checked it'd drive me crazy with its light tickle.

Gambado: "The spring of a horse." How'd a ten-year-old kid know a word like that, much less use it in the proper context? I tried to remember what he looked like, then remembered I had him and his gang on film. After Wyatt and Sasha's *Midnight Kills* scenes, I'd have a second look.

I made a sandwich that needed horseradish. There was none. I got angry and seriously contemplated going to the store. How could you eat this sandwich without horseradish?

"Why don't you go watch their film?" I asked my procrastinating self. "Because what if it's bad and you have to tell them?"

One's own art should be added to the list of things friends shouldn't discuss without hanging a DANGER! sign over the door. Religion, politics, our art. Ninety percent of the time it leads to deep silences or oddly twisted feelings.

We're all black holes when it comes to compliments anyway—who can ever get enough? And those we do get feel good for too short a time. Black hole is an appropriate image. But then, when it comes to *our* creations, those delicate children we hatched from our own eggs with no one else's help, watch out!

I took the sandwich and a drink into the television room and turned the machine on.

On my first trip to Europe, years before, I spent some time in Dijon. Near my hotel was a small park that was jammed most of the day because it was the only green in the neighborhood. Besides, it was summer and parks *are* summer—lovers, dog walkers, babies crawling for the first time on the sweet July grass.

I discovered, though, that for some reason, even on the warmest, friendliest nights the place emptied by around ten. The only ones left, till almost midnight, were four women in black. They ranged in age from about thirty to seventy or eighty, one for each decade or so. I guess they were Arabs because they spoke in a loud, throat-clearing, held-*l* tongue that always sounded vaguely like singing or a call to prayer.

If they were dressed in black because they were widows, they were the merriest widows I ever saw. The four of them sat there nightly, telling each other stories. I watched as often as I could because they were irresistible.

Whatever any one of them said, the other three sat with the most attentive expressions and gave the greatest responses I've ever seen from any audience. They gasped, slapped their cheeks, or stuck closed fists in mouths. But in the end their final reactions were usually the same: "No, that's *impossible!*" or wild, side-splitting laughter. Of course I have no idea what they *really* said, but that's how it looked from fifty feet away. Those women and their absolute interest in each other haunted me until I put the memory of them at the beginning of my film *How to Put On Your Hat.*

And that was the scene Wyatt and Sasha chose to begin with: the four women (now in black bathing suits) sitting in a park overlooking Lake Almanor in upstate California (the town Phil later used for the first *Midnight*).

I had a mouthful of food but said around it, "How the hell are they going to follow *that* up?" But, by God, they did.

The cut to the next shot was perfect—Bloodstone's small hand picking up a cut crystal paperweight and bringing it to the camera's eye. The movement is slow and theatrical—Phil wanted us to see the strange child's hand and linger on it before we noticed what it was doing.

Through the prism's different faces we see a bright green object, split into four. The hand moves, and now we see something red split into four. A quick move again, to something black split into four. Since we never know what it is we're actually seeing through the glass, it could just as easily be the four women in the park.

The sandwich tasted great. The drink tasted great. They were doing it! The prism scene dissolves into one from *Sorrow and Son*—a black bedspread being shaken once and then used to cover the dead beekeeper. The woman doesn't see the jar of honey in a corner that's fallen over and oozed its muck onto the floor.

Before it changed, I said, "Bloodstone and the honey!" which was their next scene.

Besides my growing excitement and relish for what my friends had assembled, a parallel dismay had set in when I realized again how much Strayhorn had taken from my work. Not just favorite images—honey, prisms, the grain in oak wood—but also a very specific way of turning the viewer's head in a certain direction so they'll be sure to catch an angle or fall of color that makes everything come together.

I was a fan of Phil's razor-sharp *Esquire* column, but not of his films. I'd liked *Midnight* very much, when I first saw it, and told him so plenty of times. The fact I didn't like it so much now, or like the other ones, didn't make any difference.

On the other hand, my films could do no wrong in his mind. Whenever we got together, he would grill me on how I'd done a specific shot or what had influenced me when I was writing a section of dialogue. He always wanted to know what I was reading and what new ideas I had for movies. The day he showed me his video *The Circus on Fire*, I put my arm around him and hugged him. I'd forgotten his answer in the burst of my enthusiasm but now, thinking hard, I vaguely remembered something like, "Maybe there's hope yet, huh?"

What embarrassed and annoyed me now was not having noticed this "borrowing" when I'd originally seen the films. There's very little of it in *Midnight*, but a hell of a lot of it in the others.

Sure, being copied is great flattery. But not in this case, not with a friend who was so full of his own vision and talent that he didn't need to suck on my straw to get sustenance.

Sasha and Wyatt's piece was still running, but I hadn't been paying attention. I rewound the tape and fixed my mind on business.

When it was finished I knew it wouldn't work. Witty, imaginatively conceived, and sinister in many of the right places, the clip was nevertheless too thought out and smooth, if that's the right word. It was horror with style but no honesty. The work of damned good professionals who knew their business, but clearly thought what they were doing here was silly bullshit and not to be taken seriously.

One of the reasons why *The Finky Linky Show* was such a big success was the famous tongue-in-cheek humor that was so much a part of the personality of both Finky Linky himself and the weekly half hour. Any age could watch because there were jokes on so many different levels. In-jokes, kid jokes, smart-ass jokes, clever jokes . . . the gamut. Wyatt did it like no one else.

But some of that double- and triple-entendre approach came over to their *Midnight Kills* sequences, and in the end it was annoying. If you're going to make a horror film, damn it, go flat out. No winky asides or additions that say, We're all above this, aren't we?

When Wyatt gave me the Umbo book and said he thought we should give *M.K.* "that" feeling, I thought he'd meant the sinister, edgy mood of Europe in the 1920s and 1930s: *Cabaret,* Otto Dix, Bruno Schulz. But the way he intercut my work with Phil's, it appeared what he intended was a contemporary *film noir,* a thinking man's B movie. It had begun so well, too: quiet and tender. The sight of the nailless child hand was enough to set off small alarms inside. You were waiting for more not-so-nice to come. But it didn't. Only fancy cutting and sliding pieces and scenes around. We easily could have used this to end Strayhorn's work, but I knew it could be much better.

There were three other cassettes stacked on top of this television. The first one was of the bicycle kids I'd filmed that afternoon, the gambado boy and retarded Walter. I slid it in and watched them wheel around. Gambado had asked me three times to use the camera. "You should only take pictures of us!" Where had he gotten that word? The question wasn't intriguing since I'd seen the Finky Linky tape. There were more important things to think about.

You know how, when you're nervous sometimes, you pick things up and put them down without really knowing you're doing it? That's what happened to me, only my nervousness manifested itself by sliding tapes in and out of the video machine, watching them for fifteen seconds, then going on to another. It felt stupid but necessary. I was thinking, but I was nervous and wanted my hands and head to be functioning. That worked for a while, but the nervousness grew and I switched on the other two TVs and their respective videos.

The room was a bombed-out mess. Every day Sasha groaned over what had happened to her once-nice TV room, and I kept promising to clean it but hadn't. Books, notes, videotapes, clothes. Small mountains of "I don't need it now but I might any minute, so leave it there." The other great slob I knew was Max Hampson. He used to joke about how he could get away with it because—

"Max!"

Where was *that* tape? I looked and looked, frenzied, hysterical, finally laughing because I wanted to find it so goddam much.

"It's on the fucking TV, asshole!"

One of the three I'd seen up there before; it was even marked with his name. My hands were in such a hurry to get it out of its box that they tried to jiggle and pull it at the same time. I realized I was saying "Oh, yay! Yay! Yay!" while I worked it out and plugged it in.

The dinner party. *Fast forward.* Greetings. *Fast forward.* More. People talking. Eating. Camera on Sasha putting a forkful of brown cake in her mouth. That's it. Question: "What do *you* think is in Poodle Cake?" She shrugs and goes on eating. Cut to Dominic Scanlan. ". . . and Blow Dry!" Everyone laughs. Camera pans to Max, and it takes only a moment to see something's broken in him and he's collapsing.

I don't know why I kept the film in the first place, but there it was. I ran it back and watched again, marking the number on the counter to zero at the point where Max appears and we see the metamorphosis.

How long did I sit there, watching that one- or two-minute sequence, again and again? How many times? When did the quiet, familiar voice inside say, "We want this scene. We need it."

I don't know the answer to those questions, but the more troubling one was why none of those other inner voices protested. We were unanimous. Use Max Hampson's agony to make this picture better? Okay.

What shall I give for my reasons? What would be an impressive excuse? Max was still in the hospital but getting better every day. If Pinsleepe could be trusted, filming his attack might even result in saving him. She'd said not to feel bad because it had been for the project, and if I could pull *that* all together in the end, my sick friends would be healed.

That sounds reasonable and fair, doesn't it? A little utilitarianism never hurt anyone, especially if no one gets hurt in the end.

We spend our lives learning how to rationalize our imperfect behavior, but let me tell you something: It all boils down to the three sizes of guilt.

When it's small, we can slip it into our pocket and not think about it the rest of the day. Didn't do your exercises? Write the letter to your mother? Make the call? Fix the nice soup you planned? Screw it—the day was hard enough and you did your bit.

Medium-size guilt doesn't fit into the pocket and must be carried awkwardly in the hand like an iron barbell or, when it's really bad, a squirming live animal. We know it's there every minute, yet still find ways to lessen or shift our discomfort. Having an affair and aren't so nice to your spouse because you're spending too much energy on this new love? Then buy that old love some obscenely expensive, thoughtful gift and, what time you *do* spend together, be so passionate and concerned that you glow in the dark.

Large-size guilt either crushes you or bends you so far to the ground that, either way, you're immobilized. No shifting this weight. No way of getting out from under it.

Phil had it, I'm sure. Particularly after defying Pinsleepe's advice and making the scene that resulted in the death of Matthew Portland and the others.

I didn't feel that crushing guilt about including the Max scene because I hadn't defied anyone and my intentions were 90 percent honorable. Yes, I wanted to do this work with originality and vision, but hadn't that always been my goal in anything I did? What was new or changed for the worse? It wasn't like finding treasure and, ignoring the friends who'd helped, deciding to keep it all for myself.

Besides, doing a good job had been Pinsleepe's mandate. After what happened to Strayhorn, I was pretty wary of defying her!

I'd thought so much about Pinsleepe. Was she real? Good, bad, an angel? She was powerful magic, that was the only sure thing. The memory of her hands on her swollen stomach and that milky light beginning to emanate from it a moment later was an image I would take to my grave. Then all of her appearing and disappearing, the cryptic adult remarks followed by a childish naïveté that was almost beautiful in its innocence—if that's what it was.

I did conclude that if she were some kind of evil she would have told me specifically how to make this scene, because it was logical she'd want it precisely *so*, to be right. But there'd never been any directions on what to do, which was why I leaned toward believing she was good, or at least . . . neutral.

People have often been surprised by the way I work. Usually when I find the idea I'm looking for, I put everything down and leave the desk. Obviously not on a movie set, but when I was writing poetry or scripts, once I'd found the right metaphor or solution to a problem, I'd get up and leave the room instead of putting the answer down and moving on. Maybe it's superstition—don't ask the gods for more than that—or just self-indulgence, I don't know.

That day too, when I had what I wanted and knew the order, I left the house with an empty head but an excited heart. What would Wyatt and Sasha say when I told them these ideas? Or should I just go ahead and make what I had in mind and show them when it was finished?

It was early evening. The delicious peach light and calm air said, Come, take a stroll and enjoy us. The white stone sidewalk was still radiating the day's warmth, and for a moment it reminded me of the time I'd worked for the Forest Service in Oregon, fighting forest fires. The first thing they'd told us to do was go buy a pair of very thick natural-rubber boots. Forest floors got so hot during a fire, if you didn't have good protection—

"Hey, dude."

I'd been enjoying my dream of hot floors in Oregon and hadn't paid attention to who'd come up in front of me.

4

I t was the bike riders from the park that afternoon—what looked like all of them, including Gambado in the lead with little Walter again sitting crossways on the other's black-and-yellow BMX.

"Hey, hello! Do you guys live around here?"

The kids looked at each other slyly. No, they didn't, but who was going to be the first to volunteer that information?

Gambado. "No, man, we followed you home before, but you didn't even see us!" That brought on a bunch of snickers and nods; either they were good tails or I was completely out of it.

"You followed me and've been waiting here since? What for?"

Gambado had a nice face, friendly and open, but some of the other kids, both black and white, looked sneaky and dishonest. If you made eye contact they either looked away fast or gave you one of those wise-guy "fuck you" smirks kids are so good at.

"I guess we want you to go with us."

"You guess? Go where?"

"Just down a couple of blocks. We want to show you something."

"What?"

He had on a black RUN DMC baseball cap, turned backward. "Aw, man, chill out. We ain't gonna rob you. We got something to show you, okay?"

"I don't think so."

A car drove by slowly. No one watched it.

"Walter'll show you something. Maybe that'll make you want to come. Go ahead, Walter."

The boy with the tragically round, marked face slid off the bike and clumped down the street. Ten feet away, he lifted off the sidewalk and rose into the air. Imagine those Renaissance religious paintings of any of the saints ascending, and that is what it looked like. We could hear Walter ascending through the leaves of the trees until he was a large silhouette against the California sky. A child across the sky.

Gambado put two fingers together and gave a long, shrieking whistle. Like a pet bird, Walter came right back down, slowing as he got closer to earth. A foot from the pavement, he swung up like birds do and landed with the gentlest touch and hitch on his sneakered feet.

"Pinsleepe sent you?"

The kids snickered.

"Shut up, you guys. No, she didn't send us, but sort of. You want to come with us now." It wasn't a question.

"All right."

"Good. It's not far. Come on."

There were nine of them on bikes—ten, including Walter. They rode slowly but kept spurting forward like young dogs on leashes. I walked along behind them, Gambado always right beside me.

"Where are we going?"

"You'll see in a minute."

One of the others, a boy with a skinhead haircut and no shirt on, turned and said, "To the movies, man!"

That set the others off hooting and catcalling, but Gambado got mad and told them to shut up or he'd turn their faces into dog food. More yelling and insults, but none of them said any more to me.

Eleven-year-old boys on bicycles ranking each other out, right before dinnertime. What else is new? "Walter! Come home, dear. Dinner's on the ta-ble!" But Walter had just flown above Third Street.

"Are you supposed to tell me anything else?"

"No, just take you over to the place." He said no more, and we continued on our way.

I was so thrown off by what had been happening that it took me awhile to realize there was no traffic on the street. We were moving along Third, which is always busy and buzzing, but not then. No traffic, no cars, nothin'.

A moment after that realization struck me, one by one the kids began weaving their way out onto the empty street, where they began performing again. Only now the repertoire included bikes floating in the air, riders lifting off them to fly alone, like Walter had done, and other variations.

It was a child's dream, a child's drawing. You see them in crayon colors on the walls of any kindergarten class. Me on my bicycle, flying. Everyone's favorite scene in *E.T.*

I looked at Gambado. He gestured at his friends. "You don't like it? They're doing it for you. You're the guest of honor tonight."

"At what?"

The Ruth Theater was flanked by a take-out Mexican restaurant on one side and June and Sid's Exquisite Catering on the other. In the window of the Mexican restaurant was a wilted, sun-bleached sombrero. For some mysterious reason, in June and Sid's window was a stuffed Pekingese dog. The kids noticed that and crowded around the window talking about it.

The theater interested me more. It was one of those small, pre–World War Two neighborhood theaters that were built when going to the movies was still a major event. Scalloped walls, brass on the doors, and miniature pillars made you feel like someone special on Saturday night, two tickets in hand and your girlfriend close by in her new high heels, walking across the red plush carpet. The place had seen better days, but it was in decent shape and, like so many smaller houses, was now reviving old films. On the billboard it advertised a 1954 film, *New Faces*.

"Go on in."

"This is it? We're really going to the movies?"

He nodded. His friends wheeled their bikes up to the door of the lobby and leaned them against whatever wall was nearest. None of them locked or did anything at all to protect the bicycles. Trusting souls.

"Are we seeing *New Faces?*"

"No, you know everyone there."

We walked through the glass doors together, past a copper stand where the ticket taker usually gave you back your stub. There was no ticket taker, but there were posters up on all the walls: posters of my films, posters of Phil Strayhorn's films.

Walking by *Wonderful*, Gambado pointed to the poster and said he liked that one best.

"What's your name?"

"Gambado's good. Call me that."

Two of the others stood at the doors, holding them open. When we passed, they both bent at the waist and beckoned us in with long sweeps of the arm.

The lights in the theater were already dim, so it was almost impossible to make out anything besides the fact there were others in the audience, seated in different places around the room.

"Where do you like to sit? How about in the middle?"

"Fine."

We walked past a woman sitting in an aisle seat. I looked at her as carefully as I could but she was unfamiliar.

"Here. Yeah, go in here, to the middle."

We sidled our way into the middle of a middle row. I was trying to count the number of heads in there and could make out maybe twenty.

There was music playing, the theme song to *Midnight*.

When we were seated, the music stopped immediately and the curtains parted in front of the movie screen.

The lights came up on a familiar setting: Phil Strayhorn and his dog sitting on the couch in his living room, looking at the camera.

Oddly, what was most disturbing about it, in the midst of all these other disturbances, was seeing Phil large like this. I'd watched him again and again on the video screen and grown accustomed to his face TV size, not a face that covered a wall, a hand as big as the chair I was sitting on.

"Hi, Weber. Here we are, and today you get the whole story." Hearing something off-camera, he turned to it. A moment later, Pinsleepe appeared and sat down beside him on the couch. They smiled at each other. She handed him a dog biscuit, which he gave to Flea. They both watched the Shar-Pei for a few seconds, then looked back at the camera. Phil smiled.

"I lost a bet because of you, Gregston. What do you think of that? Poor old Flea just ate his last dog biscuit." He scratched the dog's head. "Pinsleepe and I thought about making a big production of this, but then I remembered how much you hate Dimitri Tiomkin music and credits that go on forever, so we cut it right to the bone. If you want, after I'm finished telling you this, we have movies of everything and'll be happy to show you things as they actually happened. The last home movie, sort of.

"Okay." He took a deep breath and sat forward. "A long time ago, Venasque told me in his oblique way this would happen. The only thing I could do was prepare for it, so when it *did* come, I'd at least be ready. I did what I could, but as you know yourself, who can ever can be prepared for the miraculous?

"He told me to make the films and see what I'd find there. The only thing I found making *Midnight* was money and fame for the wrong reasons."

One of the kids in a row behind us whistled and screamed out "Bo- *ring!*" Strayhorn smiled and nodded.

"You're right. What do you think of those little shits who brought you here, Weber? Figure out who they are yet?"

Gambado gave the screen a big raspberry. "You were better as Blood-stone, man! Nobody's gonna give you an Oscar!"

"Do me a favor, Weber. Reach over and touch him on the arm or someplace. Anywhere'll do."

I looked at Gambado. His face in the theater dark was close enough to see he was very frightened.

"Should I do what he says?"

The boy licked his lips and tried to smile. "You have to. We're out of it now. Do it, huh? Just do it, man!" The last sentence came out trying to sound tough, but it was a scared boy sounding tough which didn't work. *"Do it!"*

I put my hand out and touched his face.

Remember what you see in the theater when you turn around and look toward the projector while the film is running? Pure white light like a laser flipping up and down energetically, with perhaps some ciga-rette smoke or dust bits hanging lazily in it. That's what Gambado became when I touched him: sheer white movie light for a moment and then gone. Nothing.

"It's never like you expected. Even angels! You'd think they'd have a little class. Not necessarily wings or harps, but at least well-behaved and innocuous. But what do you get? Little shits on racing bikes who don't know when to keep their mouths shut!"

To soothe him, Pinsleepe put her hand around his shoulder and hugged him to her. He paid no attention.

" 'God is subtle, but not cruel.' Do you agree with that now, Weber? On your last, last chance to turn back, God sends out his legions to warn you, only they turn out to be prepubescent rats on orange bicycles! Today's version of the flying monkeys in *Wizard of Oz*.

"And weren't his warnings effective? An actor gets murdered. Blow Dry disappears. Bike flips in the air and you're told a few times to photograph only them? Didn't you recognize all his CAUTION signs? I'm not surprised. Who would?"

Phil stood and, picking up the now-lifeless body of the dog, put it gently in its basket next to the couch. "Things change when you're here. Time, sequence. Different rules.

"Think of it as a moving sidewalk in an airport next to a normal one. On mine you can go twice as fast if you walk while it's moving. Or I can just stand here and be whisked along while people next to me have to walk. Another possibility is to turn around and run as hard as I can *against* the flow of my sidewalk.

"What I'm saying is Flea just died now, but we'll put him back in time so Sasha sees him when she finds me. This is off the subject. I want to talk about you and me, Weber.

"You never realized I stole from you because you were always too busy being original to notice. But I did, and so did a lot of others. You were always so sure of what you did, and you were inevitably right.

"Even leaving town was right! You win an Oscar and you leave town! Do you know how much I hated myself watching you go? Feeling like such a fool staying here to play Bloodstone, while you drank wine in Portofino and then came back to work with *dying* people?

"So at least I could try to change a little, right? Do something artistic and redeem at least a few inches of myself.

"First I wanted to do '*Mr. Fiddlehead*,' but no one was interested. So I made that fucking video which everyone hated. Two for two. What else was left? You tell me. What else could I do besides play a ridiculous monster for the rest of my life?" He was enraged: jerking his head, throwing his hands in the air, shoving them deep in his pockets.

Without being aware of it, I said, "Pinsleepe."

He stopped, turned, and pointed at me. "Exactly. Pinsleepe. There she was in that run-down church, and I knew right off the bat what was up. My old friend come to help.

"She said the only way I was ever going to do it—make a piece of art that'd mean something and last longer than five minutes—was through *Midnight Kills.* I'd come close with the first one, but no banana. What I had to do now was pull together every inner resource and strength and use them all. Give this film a vision like nothing ever done before. *The Cabinet of Dr. Caligari, Freaks, Psycho.* That kind of phantom and illusion.

"But I couldn't do it! None of what I did worked. Not even the fucking Bloodstone monologue that took so long to write!"

"What about Portland? What about the people who died when those cars fell? It *must* have worked!"

On screen the two of them shared a smile. Pinsleepe spoke for the first time. "That's what you were supposed to think, Weber, but that accident at the shopping center had nothing to do with this. Nothing at all.

"I told Phil I'd help him however I could. But if he wasn't successful, he had to agree to do two things: kill the dog and help me get you here to make the scenes."

"Why the dog? Why *me?*"

Strayhorn made a nasty face. I'd seen it before when he was at the end of his rope. "Because she knew you could do it, roommate. Because we all know you're the only real contender around. I was just the lightweight who wanted to try and go a round with you in the ring."

"Why the dog? Why'd you kill Flea?"

"It was waving the white flag: I give up. I was even wrong about you, pal. No offense."

Pinsleepe pursed her lips. "Phil was sure you'd never do this because there's too much good in you. I said art and virtue live on different sides of town and you'd do it because, when you got interested, you wouldn't be able to resist."

"Do what? Make the scenes for the movie? What?" I had an idea but was afraid. How could they know, even them? How could anyone know? It hadn't been done yet. Only words on yellow sheets of paper.

The screen went dark, then grew light again: four women in black bathing suits chatting together.

Despite my growing apprehension, it was fascinating to see, because before leaving the house that evening I'd only made notes on what I wanted to do with the tapes when I could get into the cutting room again. But here it was in front of me on a full movie screen: a perfectly finished version of the two scenes I'd visualized.

Finky Linky's ideas were there, as well as the other parts of my films, Max's attack, even three brief glimpses of Sean and James acting out their own version of "A Quarter Past You."

How beautifully the disparate pieces fit together! How they enhanced each other, once assembled in that particular order. It was as sure and balanced as I'd envisioned—darks and lights playing off each other, humor, pain, surprise. No more than seven minutes in all—or, rather, seven minutes not including the last scene.

When that was about to come on, the picture stopped. Pinsleepe and Strayhorn reappeared.

She spoke. "Do you want to see the last part? We don't have to show it."

"Of course I want to see the last part, damn it! Why did you interrupt? You have to show it all together. It's of a piece, or—" I looked at Strayhorn and saw him mouth the words "You asshole" before the screen went dark.

They showed it again from the beginning, but this time continued to the end.

Only, then, seeing it on a giant movie screen for the first time, did I realize what I had done—what I'd been willing to do—in the name of Art. In the name of Gregston.

If I'd been making a film of this, I might have had the Weber Gregston character stand up at this point and run out of the theater. Or at least shout at the screen, something like *Don't do it!* or *Take it off! I was wrong! I'm sorry!* But that would be kitschy, and we're here to make Great Art, no matter the cost.

In real life, I sat there and watched the last scene I'd chosen to include: the crucial scene. The one that made it all work. The smartest touch.

I watched my good mother look out the window of the airplane that would kill her in the next five minutes. I'd used the entire tape

Strayhorn had given me to reassure me she hadn't died in agony. Mama's last act. I used every second of it.

Coming where it did in the film, it was brilliant.

Sasha's child is due to be born about the same time *Midnight Kills* is due to be released.

Pinsleepe said it is my child from the one night (so recently past) Sasha and I spent together. When I said that was absurd, Strayhorn said to remember his moving sidewalk analogy. The child is their gift to me. I didn't mention that Pinsleepe was no longer pregnant when I saw her for the last time on the movie screen.

So there will be a child, and it will be born when the film is born. Is that supposed to be symbolic? Am I again being told something I must decipher, like the haruspex in Rome? When I think of children now, all I can see is that retarded boy rising off the street and up through the trees: Walter, the mongoloid angel.

When I asked why it was so important that *I* work on Strayhorn's film, he said, "There's no human beauty in evil. You were the only one who could give it that."

Pinsleepe said, "It will make people cry. That's the beginning. Remember 'binary weapons'?"

Strayhorn said, "There's a line from Rilke: 'Works of art are of an infinite loneliness. . . . Only love can grasp and hold and fairly judge them."

"You mean seeing *Midnight Kills* will make people *love* evil?"

"Yes. Because of your art."

At the end of every *Finky Linky Show*, Wyatt always read a fable or myth or something wise from long ago that had a moral or meaning to it way beyond the typical kid's story. It was one of my favorite parts of the show. When we were flying to California, Finky told me he'd recently heard one that he loved. Was it a Sufi tale? I can't remember.

A scorpion and a turtle were best friends. One day the two of them came to the edge of a very wide and deep river they had to cross. The scorpion looked and shook his head. "I can't do it—it's too wide."

The turtle smiled at his friend and said, "Don't worry, just ride on my back. I'll take us both across." So the scorpion got on the turtle's back, and in no time at all they were safely on the other side.

But once there, the scorpion immediately stung the turtle.

Horrified, the turtle looked at the other and asked with his last breath, "How could you do that to me? We were friends and I just saved your life!"

The scorpion nodded and said sadly, "You're right, but what can I do? I'm a scorpion!"

BOOK MARK

The text of this book was set in the
typeface Avanta and Gill Sans Light
by Berryville Graphics, Berryville,
Virginia.

The display was set in Vero Tall
Antiqua and Helvetica Bold
Condensed No. 2
by Maxwell Typographers,
New York, New York.

It was printed on 50 lb. Glatfelter,
an acid-free paper,
and bound by Berryville Graphics,
Berryville, Virginia.

Designed by Claire M. Naylon